A GRISLY HALLOWEEN TREAT

Stan moved forward, peering around Emmalee's shoulder. In the growing darkness, she could just make out a figure behind the short, wire fence containing the corn, face up, upper half immersed in a mud puddle left over from the weekend rain. She moved closer to get a better view. And wished she hadn't. A menacing hook-shaped weapon protruded from Hal Hoffman's chest, a dark stain covering most of his upper body, discoloring his blue and green flannel shirt. His eyes were open. Empty.

For a second, she thought maybe this was the farmer's idea of a bad joke. A staged murder in the corn maze for full Halloween effect. She waited for Hal to jump up, laughing, and pull the rubber prop out of his chest.

But he didn't . . .

Books by Liz Mugavero

KNEADING TO DIE

A BISCUIT, A CASKET

Published by Kensington Publishing Corporation

A Biscuit,
A Casket

Liz Mugavero

KENSINGTON PUBLISHING CORP.
http://www.kensingtonbooks.com

KENSINGTON BOOKS are published by

Kensington Publishing Corp.
119 West 40th Street
New York, NY 10018

All Kensington Titles, Imprints, and Distributed Lines are available at special quantity discounts for bulk purchases for sales promotions, premiums, fund-raising, and educational or institutional use. Special book excerpts or customized printings can also be created to fit specific needs. For details, write or phone the office of the Kensington special sales manager: Kensington Publishing Corp., 119 West 40th Street, New York, NY 10018, attn: Special Sales Department, Phone: 1-800-221-2647.

Kensington and the K logo Reg. U.S. Pat & TM Off.

ISBN-13: 978-0-7582-8480-8
ISBN-10: 0-7582-8480-2
First Kensington Mass Market Edition: April 2014

eISBN-13: 978-0-7582-8481-5
eISBN-10: 0-7582-8481-0
First Kensington Electronic Edition: April 2014

10 9 8 7 6 5 4 3 2 1

Printed in the United States of America

For Kim, for a thousand years

Acknowledgments

Once again, I'm indebted to my agent, John Talbot of the John Talbot Agency, Inc., who made this series possible. It's been a great ride so far. And to my editor, John Scognamiglio, and the rest of the folks at Kensington who do such amazing work from the copy edits to the covers, you guys rock!

I can never thank enough the amazing Sherry Harris, my Wicked Cozy sister and blog mate, first editor, and reality checker, for her support, friendship, and editing prowess. This book is unequivocally better because of your eye for detail—and plot holes. And to the rest of our Wicked Cozy blog mates—Edith Maxwell/Tace Baker, Barbara Ross, Jessie Crockett, and J. A. (Julie) Hennrikus—I am so grateful to be part of such an amazing group of women who are supportive, talented, honest, compassionate, and just all-around wonderful. I love you all.

And to all the other writers and mentors in my life, I wouldn't be here without you: Hallie Ephron, Roberta Isleib, Hank Phillippi Ryan, my Sisters and Brothers in Crime, and my fellow Mystery Writers of America, thank you, thank you. John Valeri—so grateful for that first Seascape Writer's Retreat and the friendship we've sustained. You are awesome.

Robin Chesmer and David Hevner at Graywall Farms in Lebanon, Connecticut, members of the Farmer's Cow, deserve major kudos for opening their farm to me and all my questions and giving me such a great setting for murder and mayhem. Any discrepancies from how the farm really works are all made up to help my story.

Eric Walsh at the Big Biscuit and Cathy Sutton at Happy Tails Doggy Daycare, Inc., thank you for the best launch party ever! And Eric, your recipes keep these books going. Thank you for sharing your expertise.

Huge thanks to all my Prudential friends, especially Kris Wells and Heather Sullivan, who have been wonderful fans of this series already. Your support makes all the difference.

Cynthia and Doug for your unwavering support, love, and encouragement. Without you, I wouldn't be here. And to Kim—none of this would be possible without you. Love you.

To the New Jersey Schnauzer Rescue Network, Inc. for rescuing the best breed of dog ever, and to the Pittie Love Rescue in Massachusetts for helping the real underdogs. Pit bulls deserve better and you're helping to make it happen. Thanks also to Alley Cat Allies, making life better for feral cats every day. And the Gentle Barn in California—your work promotes good in the world.

To all the cyber-rescuers who spend countless hours sharing, pledging, arranging fosters and adoptions, and spreading the word about animals in need—thank you for your efforts. You've all made a difference in the lives of so many animals.

But most of all, thanks to the readers, booksellers, and librarians for their support of the Pawsitively Organic Mysteries. I am so grateful for all the fans and new friends I've made since the series began, and I hope you'll all continue to enjoy.

Chapter 1

The chain saw appeared out of nowhere, its wide arc narrowly missing the top of Stan Connor's head.

The revving sound filled her ears, loud as a swarm of attack bees surrounding her. She caught a flash of the blade, sharp and silver in the moonlight as it swung. She heard a scream—her own? Diving for the grass, Stan clutched her Pyrex containers of bat- and pumpkin-shaped doggie treats for the party tonight, not ready to sacrifice them yet. A fleeting thought ran through her brain—*Does it hurt to be decapitated?*

The buzzing noise ceased, abruptly. Behind her, Brenna McGee, her new assistant, burst out laughing. Stan risked opening her eyes. Brenna was bent over, her long hair covering her face, hand over mouth, laughter rocking her body. The chain saw hung at the side of a figure dressed completely in black, save for the grotesque mask of a face twisted into a scream. A rubber knife protruded from its head. He must have been hiding behind the ginormous election sign staked into the ground, proclaiming TONY FALCO FOR MAYOR. The figure pulled the mask up.

"Thanks for blowing my cover, McGee." The high-pitched voice didn't fit the costume. Stan took a closer look. The boy under the mask couldn't have been more than fifteen. He seemed annoyed that he couldn't actually hack someone up in his role.

Brenna wiped her eyes. "Really, Danny? You couldn't scare a pack of kindergartners." Both their eyes turned to Stan on the ground. Brenna reconsidered. "Well, she's not in kindergarten. And does your mother know you're out here with that thing? Bet she doesn't."

Brenna reached for the containers of treats and Stan's bag of party goods. Stan handed them over. Luckily, everything had survived the fall unscathed. If they hadn't, she might've turned the chain saw on this silly teenager. She'd spent the last two weeks baking the darn things.

The boy hung his head, the chain saw drooping by his leg. "I was just playin' around. Trying to get people amped for the maze. Don't tell my mom, please? She gets, like, mad about stuff like that." Danny shifted from foot to foot. The mask slid halfway down over his face again. "You okay, miss?" he asked Stan, still sprawled in the dirt listening to the exchange.

Stan got to her feet, brushing her jeans off with her free hand. Despite the fact that seconds ago she'd thought she was going to lose her head, she had to hand it to the kid. Stan had been queen of Halloween pranks, once upon a time, and couldn't help but admire a good one. Customers walking through the dairy farm gate not expecting to be scared until they got to the corn maze wouldn't expect a masked man with a chain saw to swoop down on them out here. It was a clever way to catch people off guard.

"You don't have to call me 'miss.' I'm Stan. And yes, I'm fine. I love Halloween—I just wasn't expecting *that* on the way in. With a real chain saw," she added, eyeing the machine dubiously. "You should at least remove the chain first. Aren't the Halloween props supposed to be *in* the corn maze?"

Along with its dairy production, the Happy Cow Dairy Farm had acres of corn, which the Hoffmans had been turning into an end-of-season maze for the last few years. Tonight was opening night. It was Friday, exactly two weeks before Halloween, and folks were arriving in droves, their excitement palpable in the small town air. The superb setting added to the mood—crisp fall air had settled over the town, and the leaves were brilliant with color. Fall in New England.

Some whispered the Hoffmans were doing the corn maze for the money, that things had been tough for dairy farmers, and especially for the Hoffman family, in recent years. Stan was still too new to Frog Ledge to know if that was true or not, but she did like corn mazes. If the doggie birthday party she was running ended at a decent hour, she'd like to take a trip through it.

"Danny was never good at following directions." Brenna winked at him. "I used to babysit him," she explained to Stan.

Danny rolled his eyes. "Like, a million years ago. So you think the chain saw would be cool *in* the maze?" His eyes brightened again at the thought.

"You probably shouldn't have said that," Brenna said to Stan.

"I guess not. No," Stan said to Danny. "I think the chain saw might be a bit much for most people. Not to mention a liability."

"So you gonna tell Mom?" He jumped from foot to foot, teenage adrenaline raging.

"Just go put it away before you actually slice someone up by mistake. The last thing your parents need is someone losing a limb on their property." Brenna shook her head. "We'll go find your mother. We have to set up for the doggie party."

"She's in the house." Danny pointed. "And thanks for not telling her!" He took off running toward the cow enclosures, the weight of the chain saw dragging one side of him down, giving him a monsterlike moonlit shadow.

Stan looked at Brenna, who shrugged. "The Hoffmans have always been a little crazy. Emmalee's sweet, though. It's Hal and the kids you have to worry about. They're all a little nuts. Come on, we should get set up. The maze opens soon. Wait'll you see it. It's getting way better every year."

From her house two doors away, Stan had watched the transformation from neighborhood farm to Halloween wonderland with the same excitement she'd had as a kid heading to a scary haunted house. The Happy Cow Dairy Farm's innocent-by-day atmosphere had become a Halloween junkie's dream. Illuminated figures lit up the yard every few feet, from witches to ghosts to scary scarecrows to arched-back black cats. Even the roof of the barn where the dairy cows stayed had been draped with glittering cobwebs and enormous spiders. Off to the right, the Hoffmans' farmhouse was strung with purple and orange lights, more cobwebs, and evil-looking pumpkin faces flashing eerily in the dusk. A family of skeletons sat on the porch, clustered around a table. Their bony mouths lit up with green lights every few seconds. Other decorations hung from the roof or swung from trees, ghostly or witchy figures dancing a macabre dance in the moonlight.

Stan loved Halloween. In a family of people who were Christmas types, she'd always been the odd one who adored getting scared senseless every October. While she'd first been skeptical about her dairy farm neighbor taking on a ghoulish persona, she wasn't one to turn up her nose at any type of Halloween festivities, as long as they were reasonably well done. And it looked like the Hoffmans were pretty good at this after all. Aside from the ad hoc chain saw.

"You're gonna go through the maze later, right?" Brenna clearly itched to partake in the festivities. "Did you see the pictures of the design? It's a witch on a broom. Pretty cool, right?"

"I did see it. They did a nice job. And I'd love to check it out. We'll have to see how the party goes first." Stan checked her watch as they made their way to the farmhouse. "Is this really the town's first doggie costume party?"

Brenna turned back to Stan and arched an eyebrow. Before she could respond, a ghost popped up off the grass and screamed at her. She and Stan both jumped.

"Oh, cool! I haven't seen those in years." Stan stopped to admire the ghost, which immediately dropped to the ground in preparation for the next unsuspecting soul who stepped on the booby trap.

"They're going all out this year. Anyway, you think people really had doggie parties around here before?" Brenna's tone indicated Stan would be a fool if she replied affirmatively.

"Why this year?"

"Because every dog around here loves your treats, and Emmalee has a fenced-in area that's perfect for a doggie party. It's the natural next step." Brenna waved in the general direction of the house. "Benny is psyched, I'm sure."

Benny was the fox terrier guest of honor. His parents, Nancy and Jim, had contacted Stan a few weeks ago, doing serious due diligence on a prospective birthday/costume party. Emmalee had offered her fenced-in patio area for a nominal fee, and they had asked Stan to cater.

Stan was thrilled to oblige. Her new business, Pawsitively Organic Gourmet Pet Food, serving homemade organic pet food and treats to Frog Ledge's four-legged friends, was just getting off the ground. A party with the neighborhood dogs provided a great way to get exposure and it gave her a chance to get Brenna involved. Aside from working nights and weekends at her brother Jake's Irish pub in town, Brenna studied political science by day at a nearby college and harbored a secret interest in animal nutrition. She was all about baking treats and had begged Stan to let her be part of the business.

"Plus, I think it really is true—that Em needs cash." Brenna lowered her voice as they neared the Hoffmans' big, weary-looking farmhouse. "Hal's at the bar almost every night. Jake had to shut him off a couple of times lately, and I think he just goes somewhere else after that. He's really giving Em a run for her money."

"That's too bad." Stan had never met Hal. She'd seen him around town here and there, a hulk of a man who looked like he'd spent the majority of his life outside lifting heavy things. He usually looked either unhappy or deep in thought. She wasn't sure which. Emmalee was definitely more outgoing. Stan knew she worked at the farm pretty much nonstop. She also sold their goods to local farmers' markets, did home deliveries of milk around town, and opened the farm for tours to anyone from schools to the general public. Now she was renting her yard out, too. If the stories were true, Stan felt sorry for her.

She followed Brenna up the porch steps. The old Lab that always hung out on the porch didn't bother to get up, but barked halfheartedly and wagged his tail.

"Well, hello!" Stan petted the dog. "Are you coming to the party?"

The dog licked her hand. Stan took that as a yes.

A minute later, Emmalee yanked the door open. Describing her appearance as frazzled would be putting it mildly. Her brown hair seemed even more shot through with gray than when Stan saw her just last week at the farmers' market. The long hours of physical labor the farm demanded had caused Emmalee to lose weight, but instead of looking fit and muscular she just looked thin and tired. Her jeans and flannel shirt hung off her. The sound of a crying child wafted out at them from another room. The dog finally rose, tail wagging, and ambled over to sniff at the treats in Stan's bag.

"Hi, ladies. Come on in." Despite whatever was going on, Emmalee managed a smile. "I asked Danny to set up some tables for you out back for the party, and I think he actually did it. Nancy and Benny are out there. Jim went to get some pooper scooper bags."

"Ah. Can't run out of those." Stan smiled. "How are you, Emmalee?"

Emmalee shrugged. Behind her the shrieking child got louder. "Doing fine, doing fine. Have you seen Danny, by the way? He told me he'd do tickets for the maze, and it's darn near opening time."

Stan and Brenna glanced at each other. Brenna cleared her throat. "He, uh, went to the barn for a minute. He said he'd be right back. Do you need help with the little one?"

Emmalee glanced behind her toward the sound of the child, fatigue slipping into her eyes. "I suppose so. Hal was supposed to get him all dressed up to scare people in the maze. All the actors should be in their places by now. We have some scary things in there this year. I think it'll be a big hit. But Hal hasn't come home yet." She sighed. "So yes, if you want to entertain Joseph for a while, I'd sure appreciate it."

"I'll do that and meet you outside," Brenna told Stan.

"Come on, I'll take you out." Emmalee led Stan out back. Inside, the child finally stopped crying. Emmalee looked up and crossed herself.

Stan could see the lights from the corn maze ahead. She wondered if Danny had put the chain saw away before manning the ticket booth.

"Benny is dressed up like a bumblebee. He's none too happy about it either," Emmalee confided. "But the other dog owners promised they'd dress up their dogs, too. I have to confess, I didn't give Samson here a costume." She looked down at her dog, who gazed back up at her and wagged.

"I'm sure Samson's not too disappointed," Stan said. "I'll make sure Benny gets special treatment as the host and birthday boy."

Emmalee unlatched the gate and they stepped into the yard, Samson close on Stan's heels, nose pressed to the goodie bag. Benny, a chunky black and white terrier-type dog crammed into a hideous black and yellow striped ensemble, lumbered over to them, his antenna headpiece sliding forward to almost cover his eyes.

"Benny! Your antennas!" Benny's owner, Nancy, equally crammed into her jeans and knitted pumpkin sweater, chased him and stooped to right his headpiece. "He's having trouble keeping it on," she said, standing up and throwing her arms around Stan. "Benny is so excited! By the way, I forgot to ask you when we spoke last week. Is your name really Stan?"

Stan smiled and extracted herself from the enthusiastic woman's grip. It was a question she'd gotten regularly since adopting her nickname. "It's Kristan, but I didn't want the same nickname as everyone else. I'm so glad Benny's excited. I'll set up the treats and prizes I brought for the games. You can pick out Benny's first, since he's the host."

Nancy beamed. "Wonderful. Let's do it. Before Nyla gets here." She wrinkled her nose.

"Nyla?" Stan asked.

"The poodle from down the road. She competes with Benny for everything." Nancy rolled her eyes. "I heard she's dressing up like a mermaid."

A bark sounded from the front, followed by a ringing doorbell. "I'll go let the guests in," Emmalee said. "Stan, set up however you want." She hurried back inside.

"Okay, so here's what we have, Benny. You want to see?" Stan set her bag on the table and began unloading. "These are some new chews that I picked up. All natural, from a local farm. My dogs love them." She held one out for inspection. Benny sniffed, then snatched it and dashed under the table. Samson followed him, tail wagging.

"Ben-Ben! Manners!" Nancy sighed. "You have dogs? You should have brought them! What kind?"

"I have a schnoodle named Scruffy and a pit bull named Henry. Both rescue dogs. My friend Nikki runs a transport service to help rescue dogs, mostly from down south. I have both of them because of her."

"A pit bull?" Nancy sounded dubious. "Aren't they terribly scary?"

"Oh my goodness, Henry is a complete love," Stan said. "He was rescued in that local puppy mill sting a few months ago. Remember?" The perpetrators, a woman who ran a small vegetable farm with her son, had been selling the dogs as puppies to the local dogfighting trade.

"Really? I've never actually met one in person," Nancy admitted. "But everything you hear is terrible."

"Every dog is different. And it's not the dog, it's the owner," Stan said, trying to keep her voice friendly. Stan adored Henry. He was everything the pit bull opponents said the breed could never be—friendly, gentle, and loyal. She'd heard Nikki's stories about breed discrimination for years as Nikki navigated the rescue world, but since adopting Henry she'd seen it firsthand. And the more she faced people's prejudice about her dog, and pit bulls in general, the more adamant she became about making sure the world—or at least her little town of Frog Ledge—knew the truth.

Nancy nodded, but Stan could tell she had gotten bored with the topic. She'd turned her attention to Benny, chewing on his snack and growling at Samson at the same time. "What kind of chew? He likes it."

Stan hesitated. Some people got freaked out when she told them it was a cow trachea. It was the best treat for a dog. Rawhide was junk in comparison. Before she could answer Nancy, she heard shouts from out in the corn maze. Both women turned in that direction. Benny continued to eat his chew toy. Samson headed to the fence, his tail on alert, looking concerned. Emmalee returned with a man holding a boxer on a leash, the dog wearing a pirate hat. They both paused when they heard the shouting, now joined by screams.

"What's all that ruckus about?" Emmalee asked, peering over the fence in the distance. She shook her head. "If that boy is up to something again—"

"Mrs. Hoffman!" A girl dressed as a sexy vampire with a stake in her heart ran up to the fence, terror blatant in her black-rimmed eyes. She spit her fangs into her hand and cried, "You've gotta come right now. To the maze. Something's happened to Mr. Hoffman. Something . . . bad."

Chapter 2

Emmalee bolted out of the gate and raced to the corn maze behind the vampire, Stan on her heels. Stan hoped Em knew her way around the maze, otherwise they'd be running through it like beheaded chickens. She'd been lost in a corn maze once and it hadn't been pretty. Then again, she was quite directionally impaired.

Yellow, coarse cornstalks slapped at her as she hurried after Em, heart pounding, wondering what in the world was happening and wishing she had sneakers on instead of her glittery gold flats. Then again, she had planned on hosting a bunch of dogs on the patio, not running willy-nilly through a corn maze. The vampire led them through a series of twists and turns, slowing when they came into a straightaway.

Stan could already see a crowd of costumed people gathered up ahead. Heading away from the scene was a short, skinny girl dressed like an evil nymph clutching the hand of a boy with a fake ax through his head. They were both crying as they fled, which sent a stab of dread through Stan's belly. She'd been hoping to find Hal with a broken bone or something, after tripping and falling over one of the cornstalks. But why would people be fleeing from the scene crying? Stan thought of Danny Hoffman with his chain saw and hoped he hadn't been part of an accident.

They finally reached the crowd at what appeared to be the top of the witch's pointy hat within the maze design. They were at the end of the field. Emmalee elbowed her way through the crowd of kids. A girl wearing the bottom half of a werewolf costume sobbed. A boy with Dracula fangs had his arm around her shoulder. Stan could see his fingers, white with tension, digging into her arm.

Then Stan heard another noise—a wailing sound, starting out low in volume, then reaching a disturbing crescendo. Emmalee had reached the front of the crowd, and whatever she saw was not good.

Stan moved forward to stand behind her, peering around Emmalee's shoulder. In the growing darkness, she could just make out a figure behind the short, wire fence containing the corn, face up, upper half immersed in a mud puddle left over from the weekend rain. She moved closer to get a better view.

And wished she hadn't. A menacing hook-shaped weapon protruded from Hal Hoffman's chest, a dark stain covering most of his upper body, discoloring his blue and green flannel shirt. His eyes were open. Empty.

For a second, she thought maybe this was the farmer's idea of a bad joke. A staged murder in the corn maze for full Halloween effect. She waited for Hal to jump up, laughing, and pull the rubber prop out of his chest. Chide them all for falling for it.

But he didn't.

Stan felt the contents of her stomach shift and had to turn away. She wondered how long it would take to erase the image of all that blood from her mind.

Emmalee snatched a flashlight from someone and pressed

up against the green wire fence, shining the light square on the figure. Her screams grew louder, momentarily silencing the other sounds of the young kids who had first witnessed this scene. She moved forward, one hand on the low fence, ready to vault it.

Stan reached for her hand in the darkness, partly for support and partly to hold her back. "No," she said quietly.

"But we have to help him," Emmalee protested, her voice high, childlike. She yanked her hand away from Stan, but pounding feet and shouting froze her in her tracks as her son, the chain-saw–wielding Danny, crashed through the corn leaving broken stalks and scattered cobwebs in his wake.

"Where's my dad?" the boy demanded, his voice dangerously shaky.

"Danny—" Stan stepped to the side, blocking his way. He shoved at her until his mother, finally realizing he was there, grabbed him and hugged him tight, forcing herself into some kind of composure. Her head barely grazed his chin.

"Danny, you can't be here." She locked desperate eyes with Stan over her son's shoulder. "We need to get help."

"We'll get help. Did anyone call nine-one-one?" Stan called out, focusing on the vampire girl standing off to the side.

The girl shook her head, eyes wide as saucers as she watched Stan, clearly hoping for direction. Stan pulled her phone out of her back pocket. Noticed her hand was shaking. *Great. Another call to Trooper Pasquale about a dead body.*

Because Hal Hoffman was clearly beyond help.

Chapter 3

Stan wasn't sure how she ended up in charge, but someone had to do it. Emmalee wasn't up to the task. After placing the 911 call, Stan took Em's arm. "We have to go out front and wait for the police." She led Emmalee out of the maze. A large group of teenagers, who'd come to work in the maze, huddled on the grass talking in hushed whispers. Those who had brought their dogs to celebrate with Benny had also gathered in a group. The dogs seemed as worried as their owners. Some were howling. Others were sitting on alert. Dogs could always tell when something was wrong.

Stan could hear the hushed whispers in the crowd. "What happened?" "Was he murdered?" "Who would do such a thing?"

The blinking Halloween lights seemed to taunt them. Someone had shut off the spooky sounds playing in the ticket booth, and now the night was too quiet, save for the random evil laughter from one of the props either caught in the night breeze or urged into action by someone moving too close. The roll of stickers proclaiming "I survived the maze" fluttered in the breeze, a sinister joke.

Stan stood to the side, clutching her cell phone. She never thought she'd be eager for Trooper Pasquale to show up anywhere, but she couldn't wait for her to arrive and take over. Stan's brain, in an effort to block out the image of death, played Blue Oyster Cult's "Don't Fear the Reaper" in a constant loop in her head. She pressed her fingers to her temples, willing it to stop. Totally inappropriate.

She saw movement over by the cow barn and turned to get a better view. One of the farmworkers. She hadn't realized anyone was still on the property doing dairy farm duties, but it made sense. She didn't know much about dairy farms, but figured someone needed to be on duty most of the time. The man—boy, really—was short with Latino features. He stood next to the cow enclosure, eyes glued to the action. His eyes met Stan's across the field, then he turned and disappeared around the side of the building.

Frantic barking pulled her attention away. A Weimaraner galloped toward her, throaty bark heralding his arrival, a man holding a dangling leash close behind. Jake McGee and his sidekick, Duncan. Despite the gravity of the situation, Stan felt her stomach do that familiar flip thing it did whenever Jake was anywhere in the vicinity. The thing she always tried to ignore. As soon as Duncan saw her, his gallop turned into a full-on race and he headed straight for her. Stan bent down to greet him, bracing herself with one hand on the ground so he wouldn't knock her over. He almost did anyway, covering her face with kisses.

Jake caught up to them, Duncan's leash dangling from his fingers. If it had been a regular day, Stan would've lectured him about always having the dog off leash. She also would've asked where Duncan's costume was, since he wasn't wearing one and all Benny's friends—well, their parents—had promised costumes. But she couldn't say a word.

Jake had already picked up on the vibe. "Late to the party and miss all the action. What's going on?" His words were light but his eyes were serious, searching her face. Even he could feel that something was very wrong. Stan could see him assessing the scene much like his sister, Frog Ledge's resident state trooper Jessie Pasquale, would do when she arrived.

She shook her head, feeling the tears finally well up. Of course she'd have to lose it when he arrived. "Hal," she said, then cleared her throat, trying to hold it together and keep her voice from shaking. "In the corn maze. He's . . . he's . . . been killed."

"Killed?" he repeated, his voice sharp. He knelt next to her. "Stan. Talk to me. What happened? Where's Emmalee?"

She pointed to where Emmalee stood, away from the crowd, her grip still tight on Danny. The boy hadn't stopped crying since he'd realized his dad was the person on the ground in the maze. His face was buried in his mother's chest. Stan hoped he hadn't actually ventured in there and seen the body. As it was, it would be a long, hard road to get over this. Thank goodness Brenna was still inside with the little one, and had the sense to stay there after someone had gone in and alerted her to what had happened.

A burst of sirens drowned out her answer as the EMTs roared to a stop out front, followed by a state police car. Barely ten minutes since she'd placed the call. Stan watched Trooper Pasquale climb out of the car, crisp and professional in her uniform. She recognized Trooper Lou Sturgis, Pasquale's sidekick, lurching out of the passenger side, his short, stocky body hampering his attempts to appear cool and in control. She wondered if Pasquale and Sturgis had been on duty, or simply heard the call and volunteered to take it.

Jake, too, noticed his sister. Stan heard his sigh, barely audible over the murmur of the crowd.

Pasquale walked over, one hand on her weapon. Stan watched her gaze sweep the crowd gathered in the dusky night, taking in the odd mix of people costumes and animal costumes, the Halloween decorations an ironic backdrop for the horrifying scene. The crowd anxiously watched her, too. Pasquale's eyes landed directly on Stan and Jake, held just an iota too long, then continued her assessment.

"I better go talk to her," Stan murmured, and stepped away from Jake. Duncan followed her anxiously as she moved to where Pasquale had stopped a few feet away.

"Trooper."

Pasquale raised an eyebrow. "Ms. Connor. What's going on? You called in a possible deceased?"

Stan nodded. "It's Hal Hoffman. Some of the kids found him. In the corn maze. Do you want me to take you there?"

"As soon as I talk to Mrs. Hoffman." Pasquale motioned to Emmalee.

Emmalee handed her son off to a woman standing next to her wearing a cowboy hat, and walked over.

Pasquale's gaze was like an X-ray machine. "What happened, Emmalee?"

"I . . . . don't know," Emmalee said softly, then cleared her throat and spoke louder. Trying to be strong for her son. "They came shouting for us that something had happened to Hal." Her voice broke. "We all went to see. . . ."

"Who's all?" Pasquale interrupted. Stan saw images of ruined crime scenes running through Pasquale's head.

"A lot of us. All our actors and actresses were in the maze—I'm not sure how many. Can you please go help him?"

Her face crumpled. She gave up the guise of self-control and wept again. Jake reached over and took her hand. She squeezed it gratefully.

"I'm going. Please stay right here. Lou. I need you to round everyone up and keep them here. Start asking for witnesses. To anything." She motioned to the EMTs, then nodded behind her. "Were *all* these people on the premises?"

"Yes. Well, most of them. People have been coming and going all night," Stan said.

"Great," Pasquale muttered. She motioned to the EMTs, then nodded to Stan. "Let's go."

For the second time, Stan found herself traipsing through the corn maze, although this time it was easier to get where she needed to go. The stalks had been trampled in certain spots where the wire fencing had been dislodged by the earlier rush, leaving the proverbial trail of bread crumbs to lead her back. Pasquale moved cautiously, obviously concerned with someone still hiding in the stalks. One hand rested on her gun, the other swept each side of corn with her Maglite as they moved.

The site where Hal's body rested had been stripped of corn. The gaping hole in the maze where people—Emmalee, probably—had ripped at the stalks and yanked the plastic fence away allowed a clear view of Hal's silhouette as Pasquale shined her light ahead. Stan hung back while Pasquale stepped over the short fence, taking care not to further trample the ground that so many people had covered earlier. The EMTs waited, too, watching her for the signal that they could take over. Pasquale walked around Hal, observing from different angles, even standing in the muddy puddle to get a look at him. Finally she snapped on gloves, bent down, and stared at the wound and the weapon, shielding the body from view.

Not that Stan was looking. Heck, she'd seen enough already. She turned away and concentrated on the stillness where they stood, in the midst of the corn. Thought of that old horror movie, *Children of the Corn,* and shivered. She remembered how much that movie had freaked her out as a kid. Could someone be hiding in the corn right now? Someone who had evaded Pasquale's bright light? Hal's killer? A rustle in the stalks made her jump. She whirled, saw nothing. The leaves settled back into place. Must've been the breeze.

Pasquale walked over and said something to the EMTs. They nodded, stayed where they were. Pasquale took out her radio and spoke briefly into it, then she walked over to Stan.

"Where were you when you heard the girl calling for help?"

"I was on the patio. Getting ready for the doggie birthday party."

Pasquale didn't comment on that. "Walk me through what happened."

"One of the kids working in the maze came up to the fence, screaming for Emmalee. We followed her. The crowd was already here." She hesitated. "Has . . . has he been dead long?"

Pasquale didn't answer. Instead she said, "You don't have much luck, do you?"

"I'm sorry?"

"With this." She waved a hand behind her. "What are the odds? Twice since moving here?"

Stan sighed. She would never live down her first-week-in-town experience of encountering a real dead body. And she'd known that placing another similar call to the police would not be a feather in her cap. But what was she supposed to do? No one else had been thinking straight. She hoped Pasquale wasn't insinuating she had been involved. Instead of answering her question, she said, "Who would kill the local dairy farmer?"

Pasquale watched her with those intense green eyes, long enough to make Stan antsy. The trooper looked more like an Irish model than a cop, with her gleaming red hair and flawless white skin. She never wore makeup that Stan had seen, and her long hair was usually pulled back in a ponytail or a braid. She was one of those people who didn't need to put in a lot of effort. Which probably didn't endear her to a lot of women. "That's what we're going to find out," she said finally. "Why don't you go back out front. I'll be there as soon as the crime scene folks show up."

Stan didn't need to be told twice. She beat it back to the exit and searched the crowd for Jake. He was on the edge of the group, standing near Tony Falco's election sign, where Stan had almost lost her head to Danny's chain saw. The prank seemed like hours ago. Duncan sat quietly at his feet, seemingly understanding the somber situation. He wasn't up to his usual hijinks, which disturbed Stan even more.

Other familiar faces wandered in and out of her vision. Abbie Patterson, the woman who owned the general store in the center of town. Her salt-and-pepper hair looked frizzier than usual tonight, standing in a halo around her head as she bent to speak to another woman Stan didn't recognize. Sadie Brown, a local goat farmer, hovered near Em and Danny. Don Miller, a town councilman and karate instructor, stood off to the side, his arm around a young boy, probably his son. Not what they had expected during a night out at the corn maze.

She walked past all of them, over to Jake and Duncan. A new police car drove up, silently, lights flashing. They cast strobes across Jake's face. His eyes were glued to her as she approached, which unnerved her even more.

"You okay?" he asked as she came up beside him.

Stan shrugged. "I have no idea." She watched two male cops spill out of the car and approach Trooper Lou, who pointed in the direction Jessie had gone. "I never met him, but . . . it's horrible. It looked horrible. I don't even know what that thing was that he got stabbed with." She shivered. "It was shaped like a hook. With a wooden handle."

"Stabbed?" Jake asked, his voice grim.

She dropped her voice and checked to make sure no one was listening. "I saw it. It was still"—she forced a breath into her lungs—"in his chest."

"Jesus." Jake ran his hand through his hair. "Please tell me Danny didn't see."

"I don't think he did. I tried to get everyone out of there as fast as I could. And stop Emmalee from jumping over the fence and touching him." She shook her head, swallowing back tears for a man she didn't know. Jake slipped an arm around her shoulder. She let him. They stayed like that for what seemed like hours, until Trooper Pasquale returned, her face grim and her attitude no-nonsense.

"Folks!" she called, clapping her hands once to get attention. "I need everyone who was on the farm today to answer a few questions. We're going to move this along as fast as we can. But this is officially a crime scene, and I need everyone to cooperate."

Despite their desire to help, most of the corn maze guests hadn't seen anything out of the ordinary upon entering the Happy Cow premises, much to Pasquale's apparent frustration. Some of them didn't know Hal. Others were locals who knew the family well. Stan heard bits and pieces of witness conversations from her spot near the ticket booth with Jake and Duncan. A couple of the locals had seen Hal in his normal rounds earlier that day—picking up a part from the tractor supplier, dropping off four gallons of milk at the local day care. Abbie from the general store confided that Hal had come in to buy coffee and a pack of Marlboro Lights early that morning, despite his promises to Em that he had quit smoking. Myrna Dobbins and her dog Phineas had been out for their morning walk around seven a.m. when they'd seen Hal drive by, alone in his beat-up farm truck.

But the sighting that had generated the most interest on Pasquale's part was Kathryn McKitchum's. Kathryn ran a local restaurant on the outskirts of town called Crystal's Country Kitchen. She appeared to be in her early fifties, with reddish hair frozen high above her head with what seemed to be a large amount of hairspray. Her high-pitched, nervous voice pierced the still night air, and Stan couldn't help but overhear.

"There was two customers this mornin'," she said. "Slow day, but typical for Fridays. Saturday's better for breakfast crowds, but Sunday's always the best. Anyway, I see Hal pull up and park. But he don't get out of the car, just sat there. Didn't think nothing of it, but then a Ford Explorer drives up. Guy with a big beard's driving it. Hal gets out of his truck and goes over to the driver's window."

Stan glanced at Jake, who listened just as intently. She raised her eyebrow. He shrugged as if to say, *I don't know who she's talking about.*

"Could you hear what they were saying?" Pasquale asked.

Kathryn shook her head. "No, ma'am. It's gettin' chilly this time of year, so I had the screens off the door. Besides, they were a ways away. But Hal didn't look happy. I did hear some yelling when someone opened the door, but I had to go back in the kitchen and oversee Mr. Hallihan's eggs. He gets cranky if the yolks are overcooked."

Stan could see Pasquale tense with impatience at the long-winded story, but she kept her voice even. "Then what?"

Kathryn shrugged. "Then nothing. Next time I looked out, they were both gone."

Pasquale motioned to Kathryn to come with her, and they walked over to Em. The three of them moved into a circle and Stan couldn't hear anymore.

Who would fight with Hal in a public place? She turned to Jake, but he'd moved away to talk quietly to Danny Hoffman, who had insisted on staying outside with his mother even when Em's sister had arrived and tried to usher him inside. Stan couldn't tell if the boy was responding to Jake or not—his face was sullen and he stared straight ahead, but every now and then he swiped angrily at his eyes with the sleeve of his sweatshirt.

Stan scanned the yard to see who was left. The crowd started to thin as Trooper Lou and the other two cops released people. The poor guys had their work cut out for them, taking down names and trying to make sure any potential witnesses hadn't left the premises before they did so. Stan would hate to see what Pasquale would do if they screwed something up.

"I'm going to send a car over there right now to question him." Pasquale's voice floated by as she walked away from

Em and Kathryn. Stan inched closer to hear what she said when she pulled out her radio. Something about dispatching officers for questioning. She caught the name "Fink" and the town Woods Hole.

Abruptly, Pasquale turned, her eyes landing on Stan. Stan averted her eyes, pretending she hadn't been listening.

"Lou," Pasquale said, pocketing her radio, "I'm taking these folks inside."

Maybe now was a good time to leave. Stan tried to catch Jake's attention, but didn't succeed. Before she could decide, Pasquale reached over and laid a hand on her shoulder. "You're joining us, right, Ms. Connor?"

Stan bit back a sigh. "I'd be happy to."

Chapter 4

Stan didn't think she'd ever been so tired—or chilled—in her life. Even though the troopers had moved operations into Emmalee's living room, warmth eluded her. She had been outside for a long time, since seven when she'd arrived with Brenna, and it was now nearly two in the morning. Still, she was sure the chill of the fall night wasn't the only culprit. Just the thought of Hal Hoffman's lifeless body, weapon still protruding from his chest, lying half submerged in a puddle was enough to make her shiver despite the mug of hot apple cider she held. The sweet liquid, prepared to serve to people coming out of the maze, tasted slightly burned after being forgotten in the Crock-Pot for too long.

Hal's body had finally been removed. Pasquale had moved them inside so that job could be done without the family watching. Stan had seen the slow, somber ambulance lights as the vehicle pulled away from the farm. She wondered, randomly, how the cows were handling all the excitement, or if they'd even noticed.

There were only a few people left at this point. Pasquale and Emmalee had disappeared into the study to talk. Brenna sat on the cozy armchair, her legs curled up under her. She played with her hair, viciously twirling a lock tight around her finger, letting it go, twirling it again. She'd stayed inside with the youngest Hoffman boy after the news had reached her, trying to shield him for as long as possible against his family's grief. Emmalee's sister, Francine, sat on the love seat. Clearly a nervous Nellie, she hadn't stopped fidgeting the entire time. Her leg jiggled nonstop and she picked at her fingernail until Stan wanted to get up and rip the fingernail out. From her seat on the floor with Jake beside her, Stan watched Francine until she thought she would scream. She tried to concentrate on Duncan, sprawled across their feet. Despite not actually being on the farm when Hal's body was found, Jake had remained with them after everyone else had dispersed. Em had seemed comforted by his presence, and he'd been a godsend for Danny. The boy had been trying to be strong for his mom but deal with his own teenage grief at the same time. Watching Jake with him, just offering support, had melted Stan's heart. Not that she'd ever admit it.

Emmalee and Hal's oldest son, Tyler, who had returned from college a few towns away, sat on the couch. A soft-spoken, gentle boy, he'd finally gotten his little brother, Joseph, to sleep. Danny had resisted going to bed, but he was curled up on the other side of the couch now, dozing restlessly. Samson had curled up near him, his paws on his young master's leg. There was still one Hoffman son who had not been told. Ten-year-old Robert was at a sleepover at a friend's. Neither Emmalee nor Tyler had the heart, or the strength, to go get him right now. They'd made the decision together with no words, a moment Stan had witnessed and been touched by. In just a matter of minutes, the student had realized and accepted his new role as man of the house.

She wondered what that would mean to his studies and the life he'd just started to get used to away from home.

Tyler jiggled his knee, emitting sighs of frustration every few minutes. He clenched his hands into fists and slammed them into his knees. "What are they doing in there?" he burst out. "Can I go in and get them? I don't want her bothering my mom."

Trooper Pasquale and Emmalee had been locked in Emmalee's study for the past hour and a half. Stan understood the boy's frustration. Having been on the receiving end of a Pasquale interrogation in the past, she knew what Em must be feeling, listening to the relentless questions and trying to formulate coherent answers that would satisfy her.

"I wouldn't do that, Tyler," Stan said. "Trooper Pasquale is just trying to understand what happened here tonight."

"My father's dead," Tyler said, his voice flat. "And she needs to find out how it happened, not stress my mother out."

As if Pasquale had heard, the office door opened with a snap. All eyes in the room followed it. Emmalee emerged first, clearly doing her best to hold it together, but she looked exhausted and unfocused. Trooper Pasquale followed, her face still grim but showing no signs of fatigue. Instead, her perfect skin glowed with the excitement of the chase in front of her. She observed the people still in the room.

Tyler ignored her and jumped up to put an arm around his mother. "Are you okay, Mom?" he asked.

Emmalee focused on him and smiled wanly. "Fine, honey. Why don't you and Danny go up to bed? It's so late." Em raised her wrist to check her watch but there was nothing there. Her voice trailed off as she glanced around the room, maybe looking for a clock, or just something steady to focus on. Brenna got up and hugged her. When Em pulled away, she had tears in her eyes.

"You're all so sweet to stay," Em said, motioning to Jake and Stan, too.

"Of course we stayed," Brenna said. "I can stay over if you want."

"I would love that," Em said.

Stan envied the younger girl's ease with the family, an ease that came from knowing them forever, growing up together, having a bond within the community. It was something she'd never thought much about until she moved here. Maybe she'd become close enough to people in Frog Ledge that these gestures would seem like second nature to her, too.

Tyler ignored his mother's suggestion to go to bed, instead directing his next question to Pasquale. "So what's next? How do you find out who killed my father?"

Pasquale met his gaze head on, unblinking. "We investigate. We talk to everyone we can think of, just like we've been doing tonight. We find out what your dad did today, before this happened. It might take some time, but we'll find who did this."

Tyler processed Pasquale's response, then nodded. "So do you need us to help?"

"I absolutely will need you to help," Pasquale said. "But not tonight. You and your brother should go get some rest, and let your mother get some rest. I'll come back tomorrow and we can talk. Okay?"

Tyler looked at his mother. She nodded.

"Okay," he said. "I'll be here."

Emmalee went over to Tyler, her eyes brimming with tears, and wrapped him in her arms. They stood that way for a long time, while Danny slept on the couch next to them. "Go upstairs," she told him, finally.

Tyler kissed her on the cheek and obliged. Stan could hear his shoes, heavy on the creaking staircase, as he disappeared from sight.

A fluffy calico cat wandered in from the same room Pasquale and Em had vacated. As did most animals, she made a beeline for Stan, her erect tail reminding her of Nutty, her own Maine coon cat. She missed him, and her two recently adopted dogs. Wanted to go home. She stroked the cat's back and checked her tag. Petunia. She remembered the homemade treats she'd brought for Benny and his friends in her bag. She pulled one out, trying to be as inconspicuous as possible, and fed it to the cat. Duncan perked up, and she tossed him one, too. Samson hadn't woken.

Em looked at Pasquale. "Need anything else?"

Pasquale started to answer, but Stan cut in. "Sorry to interrupt. Did anyone talk to the guy working tonight?"

"What guy working?" Pasquale asked.

"You mean Enrico?" Em asked. "The milker," she explained to Pasquale. "We have someone on all night."

Pasquale looked at Stan. "Did you see him doing anything?"

"I saw him in the barn, so I just wondered," Stan said. "He was watching all the action."

"I'll get Lou to talk to him, if he hasn't already," she said.

"That might be tough," Em admitted. "He doesn't speak much English. He's legal, though. All the papers are on file."

"What time does his shift start?" Pasquale ignored her explanation about the worker's immigration status.

"He came on today around four. They work twelve-hour shifts."

"Okay. I'll need to talk to everyone on staff as well. First thing in the morning, unless they're here now. We talked about that, Em."

"And I told you the boys would be difficult."

"We can bring a translator." The two women stared at each other for a few seconds, leaving Stan to wonder what had occurred in the other room.

Em dropped her gaze first and nodded, weary. "Fine."

Pasquale nodded. "I'll talk to you tomorrow. Get some rest." With one last glance at Jake and Brenna, she walked out, shutting the door firmly behind her. Stan watched her flashlight bounce across the grass as she collected Lou. They strode toward the cow enclosures. Em watched them go.

Stan's heart ached for the family. It was time to leave. Beside her, Jake shifted, signaling he was ready to get up.

"Leaving?" Brenna asked. She looked more like Jake than their older sister. She had the same dark blond hair he did, the same easy smile. Her eyes were a light hazel instead of his multicolored, green-tinted eyes and she had a smattering of freckles across her cheeks and nose. She laughed like he did, too, often and loudly, although there was no mirth tonight. Pasquale, however, oozed cop all the time. If she had even a quarter of the personality her brother and sister had, Stan had never seen a glimpse of it.

They bid Emmalee good night. Stan looked back at her as they walked out the door. She looked slightly bewildered, as if she had no idea how she'd come to be standing in this room, in this situation, with such a long road ahead.

Outside, Jake motioned to his truck. "Come on, I'll drop you off."

"I live two houses down," Stan protested.

"It's two in the morning. Probably closer to three by now. Humor me."

So she did. She really didn't want to walk anyway after tonight's events, but didn't want to look like a baby. The short ride was quiet. Even Duncan remained subdued. When Jake pulled into her driveway, the sight of her house made her feel better instantly. The mint-green Victorian with the white wraparound porch had seduced her from the moment she saw it on a drive through town with her best friend, Nikki. Newly unemployed, she had been miserable. And then she saw the FOR SALE sign, and everything changed. Now it was home. She heard barking when she opened the truck door. Henry the pit bull's deep, strong bark coupled with Scruffy the schnoodle's sweet-sounding *woo woo woos*.

"Oh, my God, the dogs haven't been outside in hours," she said. "I'm a terrible parent."

"No you're not. You're a good friend. Come on, I'll take them out for you."

"They can go out in the back. It's fenced," Stan said, then stopped when Jake gave her that look. The one that said, *Shut up and let me help.* "Okay, come on in."

They went inside, Duncan jumping up and down with the excitement of seeing his friends. They finally made it into the hallway amid a flurry of barking, wagging, jumping, and licking. Through the mayhem, Nutty watched with disdain from his perch on the front windowsill.

"I know, they're crazy," Stan said, bending down to kiss Nutty's head. "And you're probably hungry."

Nutty arched his back and purred in response, fanning his brilliant tail, then jumped down and trotted into the kitchen to wait for a snack. Jake took the dogs out back, allowing Stan a few moments of quiet with her cat. She heated up a small bowl of his chicken, rice, and broccoli mixture and added two homemade blueberry cinnamon treats as garnish. Nutty waited in his usual spot on the counter. When Stan placed it in front of him, he attacked it, flecks of food flying.

"Well, I guess you really were hungry." She filled a fresh bowl of water and replaced the old bowl in the corner of the kitchen. Jake and the dogs came in a minute later.

"All set," he said, as the three of them bounded over to her and plopped on the floor, waiting for their food.

"Thank you," she said. His eyes met hers over the dogs' heads, and she quickly looked away. "So I guess I'm feeding everyone dinner, huh, guys?"

They all wagged expectantly. Duncan looked proud of himself for blending in with the group so well.

"Good thing I'm prepared." She pulled some bowls out of the fridge, and moments later all three dogs were eating contentedly. Nutty, who had already finished his, jumped down and nosed around to see whose plate he could bum something off of. The dogs, even Duncan, understood that he was in charge, and grudgingly let him select a plate to nibble from. He chose Henry's.

"Thanks for feeding Dunc," Jake said.

"No problem. Thanks for coming in. Want anything?"

"No. Thanks. It's pretty late."

She turned to the sink and began rinsing off dishes. "I can't believe Hal's been killed. Who would do such a thing? To someone with four children? I feel so bad for them."

She looked at Jake. "Was he really the type of guy someone could stab like that? In his own yard?"

"That's a good question," Jake said. "Hal was a unique guy. You either loved or you hated him. And plenty of people hated him."

Chapter 5

Stan woke mere hours later to a giant face inches from her own, eyes boring into her like they were trying to suck out her brain. This was followed by a paw hovering over her nose. She rolled away and came face to face with two more sets of eyes—one glaring, the other innocently blinking.

Ugh. Saturday morning already. She was exhausted. And a glance at her Zen alarm clock next to the bed told her she had good reason to be. It was only seven. She hadn't gone to bed until nearly four.

"What, are you all ganging up on me?" She pushed herself up on one elbow and surveyed her audience. Henry had now put both front paws on the bed and pushed his head closer, trying to nuzzle her arm. Nutty, owner of the glaring eyes, stayed where he was, conveying his displeasure at having to wait for breakfast. Scruffy snorted and rolled over on her back, kicking her pretty little paws up in a plea. How quickly they forgot they had eaten less than four hours ago.

"Okay, I get it, I get it. You're hungry. And you two have to go out," Stan said to the dogs. Scruffy *woo-wooed* in agreement. Henry sat back down and howled.

Stan looked at Nutty. He returned her stare. His gaze

seemed reproachful, his flicking tail saying, *Why did you have to bring these dogs here? They're so loud. And now I'll have to wait for my breakfast.*

Reaching over, Stan stroked him, all the way to the tip of his tail. "Ah, come on," she said. "You know you love them. Well, at least Scruffy. Henry's growing on you."

Nutty turned his head and jumped onto his window bed. Crossed his paws and put his head on them.

"You can deny it all you want, but it's true." Stan tossed the covers off and swung her legs over the side of the bed. With one hand she scratched Scruffy's belly; with the other, she rubbed Henry's head. She understood Nutty's position, even though a lot was bravado. But so far, Henry had been nothing but deferential to his feline counterpart. Stan figured Nutty would keep the game going until Henry unequivocally got the message: Nutty was in charge. The posturing had to last in case Henry was slow.

It had been just the two of them, Stan and Nutty, when they'd moved to Frog Ledge in June. Nutty had wandered into Stan's life a few years back as an injured stray cat when she lived in her condo in West Hartford. He had parked himself on the lawn until she went out to investigate. A visit to the vet revealed Nutty had possibly been hit by a car, so Stan had taken him in and nursed him back to health. He also suffered from irritable bowel disease, which had triggered Stan's interest in baking homemade treats and preparing food for him. They'd decided they liked each other, his homemade diet improved his health, and they had gone on to live happily ever after, so far.

Now, a mere four months after moving to Frog Ledge, their family had doubled with Scruffy first, then Henry. Scruffy was a southern transport who stole Stan's heart. Henry had claimed Stan after he tasted her homemade treats when they'd met at the pound. The brown pit bull with the white spot on his face was a muffin. Stan had subsequently learned the depth of his loyalty during a hairy situation. After that, she couldn't leave him languishing there, homeless.

"Let's go, then." She stepped into her furry pink slippers and pulled a sweatshirt over her pajamas. It was chilly today. She herded the dogs out the back door and headed into the kitchen to make coffee.

Stan loaded organic beans from Izzy Sweet's Sweets, the local coffee and chocolate shop, into her grinder. She filled up the water, popped a filter in, and waited, mug in hand, for her drug of choice to brew. She should have whipped up a smoothie first and gone out for a run, but she wanted coffee. Now. It had been a late night. And not a good one, at that.

"Did you hear what happened, Nutter?" she asked her cat when he strolled into the kitchen.

Nutty stared at her, eyes unblinking. Stan figured that meant no.

"There's been a murder on the block." She waited for the appropriate shock. Nutty's expression didn't change. "That's a little coldhearted," she remarked. "Just because you didn't know the guy doesn't mean you can't feel a little badly."

Nutty rubbed on the table leg and meowed. Clearly, he was only interested in breakfast, not the untimely death of Hal Hoffman. "You'll have to wait a few minutes until the dogs come in," she told him. "The kitchen's only doing one shift today."

Nutty meowed at her again. A challenge. Who said animals didn't talk back?

The coffee was taking much too long to brew. She went into the sunroom while she waited to watch the dogs. Henry ambled along as Scruffy bounced around him, trying to get him to play tug of war.

The coffeepot finally beeped and she poured a large cup of the thick, black liquid. The coffee was a welcome jolt to her exhausted system, and she sighed happily with her first sip. Leaving the dogs to play a few minutes longer, she went to the front door to see if newspaperman Cyril Pierce had been on the job.

He certainly had. The *Frog Ledge Holler* sat on her front porch, a perfect throw from whomever Cyril, its esteemed editor, used these days—likely a local elementary schoolkid with a dependable bike and a desire to make a few bucks a week hurling papers at houses. She picked up the plastic-wrapped, skimpy local newspaper and went back inside.

Front page, above the fold: LOCAL DAIRY FARMER FOUND DEAD IN CORN MAZE.

Stan skimmed the story, which detailed how Harold "Hal" Hoffman's body had been discovered by an employee working in the corn maze last night. No further information until the autopsy was conducted. The photo of Hal was full color, clear and bright. She'd only ever seen him in jeans and a flannel shirt, a hat pulled low over his face, as he went about his business around town. But this photo, with no hat and the hint of a dress shirt apparent, showed how attractive he had been. Stan hadn't realized. The years of farming and harsh New England weather had rested a lot better on him than they had on his wife. Then again, if the gossip mill was to be believed, she did a heck of a lot more of the farming than Hal had.

A chorus of barks and *woo-woos* from out back caught her attention. Stan dropped the paper and hurried to the sun-room door to see her dogs at the fence. She stepped out to see what they were looking at. Beyond the yard of her next-door neighbor, Amara Leonard, the Hoffmans' dairy cows were clearly visible as they started their morning stroll to the grassy field at the back of their property. Scruffy loved cows and always tried to get their attention. Henry just followed her lead.

"Let's go, guys. Breakfast!" Stan called. The dogs came charging to the door. "You can't go play with the cows today," Stan told Scruffy, ruffling her ears, which looked like pigtails. "Although I'll probably have to go visit them. See how Em's doing. It's probably the neighborly thing to do, right?"

The dogs stared at her as if to say, *Don't ask us about neighborly etiquette.*

Stan sighed. "Come on, then." They raced to their breakfast spots, meeting up with Nutty, who had already assumed his position on the counter. Stan headed to the fridge, but heard her iPhone ring. Where had she put the stupid thing? She stood still and listened. Traced the sound to her coat pocket, which still hung on the back of the chair where she'd draped it after she'd gotten home this morning. As she pulled the phone from the pocket, she swore she could still smell the crisp, fall, farm air clinging to her coat. It gave her the creeps thinking of that trench of mud behind the corn maze.

Shaking it off, she glanced at the readout. Jake. "Hey," she said. "What are you doing up so early?" He'd probably gone to bed later than her if he'd closed the bar.

"How are you holding up?" Jake asked.

"I'm fine. I'm going to stop by Em's this morning." She went to the fridge and pulled the dogs' and cat's food out. They were all still glued to their spots, watching her every move. "I feel so bad for her. What a nightmare."

"I know. But she's a tough lady. She'll get through it."

"I'm sure she will," Stan said.

Silence on Jake's end of the phone. And no jokes. Odd. Stan popped the bowls of the animals' chicken, rice, and cranberry dish into the microwave and reheated.

"Will you be at the bar today?" he finally asked. Saturdays were usually when she and Brenna got together to discuss the upcoming week's orders.

"Yes. I'll be over sometime midafternoon. Will you, uh, be around?"

"I will," he said. "Big night tonight. The step dancers are coming in."

Jake's place was well known for the live Irish acts who came from all over the country to perform. Tonight, a national Irish step-dancing troupe would pack the place to the hilt.

"I thought about canceling after last night, but the group had already traveled all the way here. And I think Hal, of all people, would've wanted the show to go on. He loved Irish music. You gonna stay to see them?" he asked.

Stan thought about it. She probably would. She didn't get out much these days, and it seemed like a fun way to spend the night. Being in the house alone, thinking about what had happened two doors down, wasn't all that appealing. And she'd get to see Jake, a little voice reminded her. She stuffed a gag in the little voice's mouth.

"I think so," she answered carefully, spooning the food into three bowls. "But we can talk about it later."

"Okay then," Jake said. "I'll see you in a bit. Dunc says bring treats."

"Duncan knows that's a given," Stan said.

She hung up and fed her animals, watching them lick their plates clean. An evening with Jake, even though he would be working, was tempting. She had to figure out if she was ready to give in.

"Someone killed the farmer? With a hook? Like a pirate hook?" Nikki Manning's incredulous voice resonated over the phone, making Stan want to laugh, which she didn't think was appropriate. Instead, she took a long swig of coffee before answering.

"Someone killed the farmer. With a hooklike thing. I don't know what you call the hook, but it looked horrible. Short, curved, wooden handle. Kind of like a miniversion of the Grim Reaper's sword thingy." Despite herself, she shuddered. "And only two houses down from me, might I add." In addition to talking everything through with Nutty, Stan needed her best friend's take on the recent events. Nutty hadn't had much to say about the incident.

"Sword thingy? It's a scythe. Well, the Grim Reaper's tool is a scythe. I think the smaller one is a sickle. Hold on, I'll send you a picture."

Stan frowned. "How do you know so much about scythes and sickles?"

Nikki laughed. "Don't worry, I didn't do it. Rhode Island has farming types, too, remember? My dad had lots of those tools around here. He did a lot of work outside, grew some stuff. Here it comes."

Seconds later Stan felt her phone vibrate in her hand as a text came over. She pulled it away to look at it. Nikki had sent her a picture of what looked remarkably like what had killed Hal. "A sickle," Stan read. "Yep, that's it. Who would've known? And who would've been carrying this around with no one noticing?"

"Wikipedia says it's used to cut corn," Nikki said.

"Makes sense. There's a corn maze there. That's where they found the body."

"Maybe the farmer was using it and someone turned it on him. That's hardcore."

Stan could hear Nikki chewing on the other end of the line, probably her usual granola and fruit combo. Then she piped up again, presumably after swallowing. "But maybe he deserved it. Dairy farms aren't nice places in general. Please tell me this isn't a factory farm."

Stan should've expected that. There was no greater animal advocate than Nikki Manning. She'd started her animal transport business on a shoestring when they were in college and over the years built up her reputation, community support, and a network that extended from Maine to Georgia. The rescued dogs—and sometimes cats—were brought safely to her home in Rhode Island, or to other shelters that helped get them adopted. Although her transport mainly helped dogs on death row in southern states, she advocated nonstop for everything four legged and was quite outspoken about it. She was a staunch vegan who preferred the company of animals to most people. She was also Stan's oldest friend, which in Nikki's mind gave her certain liberties. Like lecturing her.

"It's not a factory farm. I know what factory farms are, Nik. Give me some credit." Stan rose and went to her coffee bar, topped off her cup. It was Izzy's special bold blend, something Colombian and delightful. "This is a local farm. The cows walk around. It's a huge piece of land. They even have a spot down the hill in back with all these little ponds."

Nikki grunted. Stan could picture her in her usual outfit of jeans and cowboy boots, sitting at her messy kitchen table surrounded by cans of dog food, paperwork, and a few cats. "Don't believe everything you hear. They still have a crappy life."

"The farmers or the cows? Kidding," she said when Nikki started to protest. "I get it. Can we go back to the dead farmer for a second?" Stan got up and walked around her bright kitchen. The tangerine-colored walls put a smile on her face even on the gloomiest of days. She'd decorated with yellow and red accents and all red appliances, and hung wind chimes over the sink in front of the window and in all four corners of the skylight. They sparkled when the sun shone on them and cast extra light around the room. She'd wanted a room that made her feel good. Since she started baking for a living, she was glad she'd made the kitchen so Zen with all the time she spent there these days. She straightened the stack of mail she'd been neglecting while she planned Benny's party over the last week, promising to get to it today. She pulled the blinds up on the window to let the hazy sun in. Better than nothing.

Nikki dropped something with a clang that resonated through Stan's eardrum. "Sure we can. So who did it? Maybe an animal activist." Her tone grew thoughtful. "That would be pretty cool, actually."

"Nik! It wouldn't. That would give animal activists a bad name." She waited until Nikki grumbled an assent. "I have no idea who did it." Well, that wasn't true. She remembered the Ford Explorer, the man named Fink—if the name was any indication, maybe they already had their man—and Pasquale sending someone out to question him. She wondered what had happened with that. She told Nikki about it. "I haven't heard if anything came from it yet."

"Stan . . . You're not getting involved in this, are you?" Nikki asked.

"Involved? No. Why would you think that?"

"Because I know you? Look, after what happened last time . . . maybe you should just go about your business. Read about it in the newspaper."

"You're silly." Stan laughed. "I'm not planning on getting involved. I have enough going on. New business, new life, remember?"

"I hope so," Nikki said. "Dead farmers don't seem like a good hobby to take up."

After Stan hung up, she checked her watch. Only nine. Plenty of time to make a stop before heading to Em's. She needed to know if there had been any developments overnight in Hal's murder. Since the pub wasn't open yet, the next best place for information was Izzy's coffee shop. She hurried upstairs to get dressed.

Chapter 6

"Dead. I can't believe it. How could this happen?" Izzy Sweet's hand shook as she poured coffee into a to-go cup for Stan. The tremors caused the hot black liquid to splash on the counter. Izzy muttered a curse and swiped at the spill with a cloth. "Do you know how he died? I've heard it was horrible—that he was stabbed with an awful weapon." She turned away, but Stan could've sworn Izzy's eyes had filled with tears.

Izzy Sweet's Sweets buzzed with the news of the murder this morning, the chatter mixing with the jazz music playing softly through the speakers. Copies of the *Frog Ledge Holler,* many folded to Hal's picture, littered the café tables next to pastries and lattes. The undercurrent seemed less fearful than Stan would've expected, considering there was a murderer on the loose. Instead, people seemed to want to talk about it, sharing and comparing what they knew with the lean details in the newspaper. Human nature, she supposed. *At least we're all alive to talk about it.*

Then again, there weren't many true locals on hand in

the café. Much of Izzy's business rested with the local college crowd and their parents. There were two large universities within twenty miles of the sweet shop, and word had gotten out that Izzy's coffee was to die for. And, it made the tourists feel good to buy local. Unfortunately, Frog Ledge's old guard didn't have the same loyalty—they'd been opposed to the shop, which they called "fancy, highfalutin, and overpriced." They would've much rather seen the greasy spoon diner that had been there previously be resurrected.

Not Stan. Coffee shops were as normal to her as breathing. Especially on a day like today. And this shop was so colorful, it was hard not to be cheery just setting foot inside it. Various shades of greens and purples collided on the walls, decorated with framed photos of coffee shops from around the world. Coco Chanel held an esteemed place on the back wall. Coco was one of Izzy's idols. "Class," Izzy would say, hand on hip, admiring the artwork. "Pure class. And so put together."

Izzy didn't look so put together this morning. Her hair, woven into dozens of tiny braids, looked perfect as usual, and her smooth caramel skin still gleamed with hardly any makeup. But her eyes told a different story. She was shaken.

Stan breathed in the scent of rich coffee and lemony pastry. "It smells so good in here," she said, hoping to take Izzy's mind off the murder. "What did you bake this morning?"

"Thanks," Izzy said. "Lemon pound cake with cream cheese frosting. Are they sure it wasn't a farming accident? I've read about dairy farms—how they can be really dangerous."

Stan fitted a cover onto her cup and took a grateful swig,

not even caring when she burned her tongue. She'd had plenty already today, but she still felt foggy and slightly headachy. The sure signs of no sleep. "There were a lot of people there last night, Iz. Including me. And I saw"—she lowered her voice and glanced around to make sure no one was paying attention—"the body. What they're saying is true, as horrible as it is."

Izzy's hand went to her mouth as if to hold back her horror, fresh tears blooming in her chocolate eyes. "I can't believe it. I just can't. Was it . . . painful?"

Her reaction was oddly out of character. Izzy was normally the epitome of cool, calm, and collected, even when everything around her was in a state of upheaval. It was one of the reasons Stan had taken to her so quickly after moving to Frog Ledge—that, and her dogs, Baxter the boxer and Elvira the poodle. Her tears were unsettling. "I didn't realize you were friendly with the Hoffmans. Did you know them well?"

Izzy abruptly turned and began cleaning her espresso machine. "I get all my milk and cream from the farm. Hal gives—gave—a special discount for local businesses."

"But did you know him personally?"

"Of course I did. We were pretty much neighbors. He came in for coffee a lot. One of the few locals who did." Izzy tossed her rag into the sink.

"I'm sad for his family. That poor woman, with four sons." Stan wanted to ask if she knew Emmalee, too, but a young college-aged woman approached the counter. Stan stepped to the side.

Izzy pasted a smile on and took the woman's order for an egg-white wrap with spinach and a nonfat latte.

"Can I get you something to eat?" Izzy asked Stan when

the woman moved down the counter to wait for her food. "You must be hungry. I'm sure you didn't eat anything after last night."

"Oh, I'm not really hungry." Even as she said the words, Stan's stomach growled. She recalled she hadn't eaten dinner last night. She'd been so worried about not having enough treats for the party that she'd baked extra and run out of time to cook for herself. And after all the excitement, eating hadn't even crossed her mind.

"Here. I have quiche." Izzy spun to the case behind her and sliced a generous piece. Stan could see greens and reds mixed with the egg-colored delight.

"What's in it?"

"Red pepper, spinach, garlic, and onion." Izzy put the plate in the microwave and hit the buttons. "You should eat."

"I won't argue. I'm stopping by the farm when I leave here. I'm sure I'll need strength for that." Stan sighed just thinking about it. "Do you know Emmalee, Hal's wife?"

"Not really."

"I thought she did most of the deliveries," Stan pressed. "She never came in here?"

"Maybe once or twice. Why?" Izzy sounded annoyed.

Stan shrugged, wondering why her friend was getting defensive. "Just wondering. Does she have people to help her with the farm? I mean, what's she gonna do?"

"No idea. Maybe the co-op farmers will help." Izzy pulled the plate out of the microwave and set it in front of Stan. "Careful, it's hot."

Stan picked up her fork and sliced off a steaming piece of quiche. "What do you mean, co-op farmers? This smells amazing," she said. Took a bite, nodded. "It *is* amazing."

Izzy inclined her head in agreement at the assessment

of her cooking. "The Happy Cow products aren't just from the Hoffman farm. There are four other farms that sell their products under that name."

"Really? How does that work?"

"The farmers are the board. They vote on the major decisions, and all the products from each farm are labeled Happy Cow. But Hal ran the whole show." Her eyes welled up again and she busied herself straightening the goodies in her pastry case.

There had to be something more to Izzy's story about Hal supplying her with milk and cream for a discount. Izzy didn't get teary eyed often. Stan would've loved to continue the conversation, but a bell over the door jingled and a group of girls came in laughing and talking loudly. Izzy sighed, but stood up and put her hostess face on.

Stan scooped up the last bites of quiche and deposited her plate. "Gotta go do this visit. Let's take the dogs out later."

Scruffy and Henry loved Izzy's dogs. Baxter and Elvira had also recently welcomed an addition to the family—Junior, an elderly yellow Lab who found himself homeless through an unfortunate recent chain of events. The three dogs had bonded quickly, and Junior had taken on a father figure role to the two younger dogs. He kept them in line.

"Call me," Izzy said, and turned to the giggling girls, who would likely be good for a sale of high-calorie drinks and pastries.

Stan waved and hurried out of the store, feeling stuffed. She didn't have the ability to ignore the goods at Izzy's. If she got out of the visit with Em quickly and hadn't dropped from exhaustion, she could do a real run on the town green before she had to get baking. She had a number of treat orders to fill.

Even though she'd only been in town a few months—and moved here with no intention of starting a business, let alone a pet food business—she already had steady customers, mostly for her fresh baked, organic-ingredient-only treats. But people had heard about the "human" meals she made for the animals and were starting to request them. Char and Ray Mackey, who owned the local bed and breakfast, had been her first customers for meals. Their dog Savannah, who had suffered from allergies and stomach problems, had responded so positively they'd immediately asked Stan to provide her meals. Which meant a lot of research, because she didn't yet feel confident in her ability to gauge the right nutrients to add to a well-balanced dog meal. It was one thing to cook for her own cat, but quite another to be responsible for another animal. And as Char increased the amount of food she wanted, the more worried Stan became.

But it was a good problem to have. Then she'd been asked to do Benny's doggie party, which she considered a real coup. Her business was gaining momentum.

It was unfortunate the birthday party had been last night's second casualty, but his parents had promised to reschedule since Benny had been looking so forward to the event. Although he had gotten to take home all the extra cow tracheas. She wondered when Em would let them reschedule the party. Figured today wouldn't be the best time to ask.

Chapter 7

The Frog Ledge Town Green beckoned as Stan walked to Em's. It was her favorite place in town next to her own house, and she was lucky enough to live right across from the south end. The green—or the mile-long "center of the universe," as Stan thought of it—served as the town's unofficial meeting place, where farmers' markets, parties, music, Revolutionary War reenactments, and many other events occurred. It was also the official billboard for anything going on in town, because inevitably, everyone had to pass the green at least once a day to get anywhere in Frog Ledge. So it was common to see all kinds of signs, official and handmade, clustered at one end. A stone dust path surrounded the grass, and walkers and runners could be found just about any time of the day or night.

The trees still had some colored leaves clinging to the branches, although the reds and oranges and yellows so powerful just a week ago had already faded. Stan loved to run in the fall air, and this morning was still fairly warm, teetering in the low fifties. There was hardly anyone on the trail.

She turned into Em's driveway. The dairy farm was busy. Cars were parked haphazardly all over the driveway and the lawn, and a couple spilled over onto the sidewalk in front of the house. Stan hesitated a minute. Em seemed to have more than enough support. Maybe she should just go about her business. After all, this didn't really involve her.

But questions lured Stan back. Who had stabbed the farmer and left him in his own corn maze to die? Was it a random killing, or had it been someone Hal knew? As much as Stan didn't want to think random murderers had been walking the streets of Frog Ledge and happened upon Hal in his corn maze, it was more disturbing thinking of who in town would've murdered him. Someone he trusted? Had he walked right into an attack?

Stop. You're not on the police force. They'll figure it out.

She half turned, about to sprint across the street to the green and forget the whole thing, when she heard a voice. "Yoo-hoo! Stan!"

Turning, she spotted Char Mackey teetering up the street on boots with impossibly high platform heels. She clung to a foil-wrapped casserole dish, and her ever-present luggage-sized purse hung off the arm she tried to wave with. Stan figured the emergency bottle of vodka that usually lived in her purse made the trip more laborious than it should have been.

"Hey, Char." Stan waved back. *There goes my escape.* She waited for Char to catch up to her.

Breathing hard, Char finally did. Known and loved around town for her flamboyant outfits, overly outgoing nature, and love for all things gossip, she didn't disappoint today, even while paying a visit to a friend who was in mourning. Her fisherman-yellow coat gaped open, displaying black pants stretched thin over her bulk, and a neon red blazer that clashed with her loud red hair. Chunky jewelry and her traditional, glittery gold eye shadow completed the outfit.

"Phew. That's a long walk when you're carrying all this stuff." Char leaned over and air-kissed Stan. "I'd hug you, honey, but I'd dump the food all over you."

"That's okay." Stan took the dish. "Let me help."

"Well, thank you, honey. So nice of y'all to come see Emmy. She's gonna need us all now, that's for sure." Char glanced at the house, her lips pulled together, the only outward sign of her distress. "That poor woman," she murmured, more to herself than to Stan. "Like she hadn't been through enough with that man." Shaking her head, she sighed and turned back. "Shall we go in?"

"Sure. I can't stay long," Stan said.

"No, no, me either. We have a houseful. People coming down to get their Halloween tricks and treats in early this year, before they head up to Salem for the real thing."

Nearby Salem, Massachusetts, was New England's premiere Halloween destination. The entire month of October was like one big costume party. This year, it seemed people were streaming through Connecticut and dropping some tourist dollars in their region on the way, which was great for the local economy. And for Char's bed and breakfast, Alpaca Haven, the only establishment of its kind in town. It attracted customers left and right with a reputation for cozy rooms, delicious food, and excellent service. Being able to pet the cute alpacas on the premises didn't hurt either.

Char led the way to Em's door and rang the bell. Stan suddenly felt stupid. She hadn't even brought anything. It would occur to her to cook food for animals before people. Char sensed her anxiety. "Don't worry about it, honey," she said. "I don't think Em's gonna run out of food anytime soon. It's nice that you came."

Em's sister, Francine, answered the door. She looked even more anxious than she had the previous night. Stan doubted her presence was giving Em any peace at all. "Oh, hello," Francine said. "How sweet of you to come see Emmy. She needs her friends right now."

"Yes, we thought so. We've brought shrimp Creole." Char's New Orleans origins made her especially popular in the area. She made the best food and the strongest drinks, and having fun was a core part of her personality.

Francine brightened and stepped back. "Come in, come in. We've had lots of tuna casseroles, but no shrimp Creole. How generous. Em!" She hollered. "She's taking care of the boys right now," she confided in a low voice. "They're having such a hard time." Her face fell again just thinking about it, and she began picking at her fingernail again. Stan resisted the urge to grab her hands to stop her. "My poor nephews. And we finally told Robert. He was . . . he loved his daddy. This is just going to be so hard for those boys."

"I know. I'm so sorry," Char said. "I can't even imagine what they're going through."

Emmalee Hoffman appeared in the kitchen doorway. If possible, she looked even more exhausted than she had the night before—and then she'd reminded Stan of the walking dead, no Halloween pun intended. When she saw Stan and Char, she attempted to smile.

"Hi, guys," she said, and her voice broke.

Char stepped past Francine, dropping her enormous purse with a thunk on the table. She enveloped Em, who was not a tall woman, in her bulk. Emmalee's face vanished into Char's bosom as Char squeezed. "You'll be okay, honey," she crooned. "It's just going to take some time."

When Char finally let her go, Em stepped back, wiping her cheeks with the back of her hand. "I know," she said. "I know. It's just . . ." her voice trailed off. She glanced at her sister. Francine took the cue easily. "I'll go sit with the boys," she said, and slipped upstairs.

"Thank God," Em said, motioning to the table. "Please, sit."

Stan looked around for a seat. The kitchen table was crammed with casserole dishes, pies, bottles of wine, Crock-Pots. The chairs had coats and stacks of papers piled on them. But despite the many cars outside, no one else seemed to be in the house. It was quiet as a tomb. She stashed her jacket on the chair with the highest pile and perched on the edge of another.

"Everyone's outside on the farm," Em said, anticipating the question. "My brothers all came, and Hal's sister. She went out to get groceries. Some of our sister farms sent workers to help out. People have been lovely." She collected papers off one chair and motioned to Char, her movements slow and stiff. "Here, sit."

Char narrowed her eyes. "Have you eaten?"

Em shook her head.

"Well, let's change that right now." Char set to work clearing space on the counter, pulling eggs and veggies out of the fridge. "I'll whip up some omelets. What do y'all like in them?"

More eggs. Stan hoped Char wouldn't force her to eat. Her friend was known to be overly generous with food.

"I'm really not hungry," Em began, but Char hushed her.

"Of course you are. And the boys are, too. Peppers and onions, right? Tomatoes, too?" At Em's resigned nod, Char got to work. "So what have you found out?"

"I haven't found out anything aside from what I knew last night." Emmalee sank down into her own chair, right on top of someone's coat, and stared at her hands in her lap like she'd never seen them before. "Someone murdered Hal." She looked at Char. "Who would have wanted to murder Hal? I know he was a son of a bitch sometimes, but he had a family. A business that supported the local economy. Why?"

Char shook her head slowly. "I don't know, Emmy." She heated some oil in a pan and began chopping peppers and onions. "Do you think it was random?"

Em lifted her shoulders helplessly. "It had to be. I know he . . . could make people angry, but that angry?"

Stan thought of Hal Hoffman's body again. The protruding sickle under the glow of the flashlight. She shivered. "Where do you think the murderer got the . . . weapon? Would Hal have had it on him? Like, to cut corn?" she asked, thinking of her conversation with Nikki.

All eyes in the room fell on her. She turned red. "I'm sorry. I didn't mean to bring it up—"

But Em shook her head. "No, Stan, that's a good question. I didn't even think of it. I know my father-in-law had a collection of those old tools, but I haven't seen them in a long time. I think Hal kept them somewhere in one of the barns."

Stan thought about that. A family heirloom as the weapon. Was that symbolic, or coincidental? "Was he having trouble with anyone?" she asked. "Kathryn McKitchum said she saw him arguing with the man in the Explorer outside her restaurant. The man named Fink. Did the police get anywhere with that?"

Em hesitated. "Hal had trouble with everyone," she said finally, dropping her voice an octave. "Heck, he had trouble with me. He was difficult, stubborn, and he hated manual labor. He was more interested in his drinking buddies and his get-rich-quick ventures than he was in running this place. But he was smart as hell, too. And handsome. Even charming, when he wanted to be. But there were days when I wanted to kick his behind from here into next week. Asher Fink is one of our co-op partners. Matter of fact, he's here today helping. One of the first to show up. He and Hal argued more than they agreed, that's for sure. But it was never serious. And Asher stabbing him? I couldn't picture it. He can't even slaughter his own beef cows."

Before Stan could digest that lovely visual, they were interrupted by the back door opening. A parade of people filed in. Stan could smell fall air and cow manure wafting around them. The leader, a giant of a man with a cowboy hat and a beard reminding Stan of ZZ Top, took his hat off and nodded at the three of them, his gaze settling on Em. Stan remembered Kathryn McKitchum's description of the man with his "big beard" arguing with Hal. Asher Fink—it had to be. Char turned from the stove, where the first omelet was sizzling away in the cast iron pan.

"Mrs. Hoffman, the morning chores are done," the bearded man intoned in a voice more suited for a Sunday sermon than a farm.

Stan watched him through narrowed eyes. Was this all an act? Was coming over here this morning just to throw the authorities off his track and look like a concerned friend? Maybe Em had no idea what he and Hal argued about. Maybe it had been serious. Serious enough to kill over.

Em didn't seem to think so. "Thank you, Asher. And thank you for coming personally. And all of you, for coming to help," she said, raising her voice to include the men in line behind Asher.

"We're honored to help, Mrs. H," a younger man said. "Mr. H was, like, a super cool guy." He fell silent and shuffled his feet, looking at the floor.

"Thank you, Lee," Em said. "He would be grateful to all of you."

Asher cleared his throat. "A crew'll be back tonight. You gotcher regulars out there now, keeping things going." With one last nod, he ushered the line of men back outside. ZZ Top's "Legs" ricocheted through her brain. She sighed. Her brain could be so predictable.

"That's awful sweet of them," Char remarked after they filed back out the door. "That's the man they questioned?"

"It is," Em said.

"Huh." Char slid the omelet on a plate and placed it in front of Em, hovering until Em picked up her fork and took a bite. "I guess they decided he couldn't have done it."

"Of course he didn't," Em said. She lapsed into silence again.

Char shrugged, unfazed, and kept whisking.

Stan shifted uncomfortably. She needed to make her exit. She tried to catch Char's eye to give her a heads-up, but Char was again intent on her eggs. And then the doorbell rang.

"I'll get it," Stan offered, for something to do. She hurried to the front door and pulled it open.

Two women stood on the porch, each carrying a casserole dish. One wore heels that made Char's look like flats. She had unruly frosted blond curls that had been left loose to find their own way. She wore tight jeans and was nearly slim enough to do so. She smiled at Stan, revealing small, straight teeth. Her lips were coral.

"Hello. I'm Leigh-Anne Sutton."

"And I'm Mary," the other woman broke in. "Mary Michelli. Pleased to meet you." Mary was not in the same style league as Leigh-Anne Sutton, Stan noted. She wore sweats and sneakers and her hair was pulled back in a severe ponytail. No lipstick. No makeup at all, in fact. Much more farmerish.

"We're part of the Happy Cow co-op." Mary shook her head, looked at Leigh-Anne. "We could hardly believe it when we heard the news."

Leigh-Anne nodded in agreement. "We're just devastated," she said. "How is Em? Are you a friend?"

"Oh, sorry, yes." Stan reached out her hand to shake theirs. "Stan Connor. Em's neighbor. Please, come in." She led them to the kitchen.

Em's eyes didn't brighten when she saw her visitors. In fact, Stan could swear she heard her sigh. "Leigh-Anne. Mary." She rose for the obligatory hug, taking the casserole dishes and depositing them on the counter. She didn't even try to fit them in the fridge. "You've met Stan. This is Char."

"Pleased to meet y'all," Char said, waving her whisk. Egg yolk splattered on the floor.

Mary had pulled Em back into a suffocating hug. "We are so, so, so sorry," she crooned. "Emmy, how are you holding up?" Despite the saccharine oozing from her voice, Stan didn't get the sense that Mary felt all that sad. She could see it in the way Mary's eyes assessed the room over Em's shoulder, taking in the clutter and disorganization. Which begged the question—how well did all these co-op farmers really get along?

"I'm okay," Em said, trying to pull away. "I have to be. For the boys."

Leigh-Anne clucked sympathetically. "Of course. The boys. How terrible. You must be feeling so overwhelmed right now!"

"A little," Em admitted, though Stan couldn't tell if she meant by Hal's death or by the outpouring of sympathy.

"And terrified," Leigh-Anne went on. "I mean, these are

things that happen in big cities! New York and Chicago! Not in Frog Ledge." She shuddered. "It makes me nervous and I don't even live in this town. But I feel like it's becoming an epidemic. After all, I'm only an hour away. No one is safe anymore. Imagine, a crazed killer wandering onto a farm and stabbing a farmer! What is our world coming to?"

"It's just unfathomable." Mary shook her head in agreement. "And Amy sends her regrets, Emmy. She had some things to attend to. Don't think she's upset, because she isn't," she added hastily. "She completely understands the police have to do their jobs."

Stan glanced at Em. Em didn't respond. She just gazed at Mary as if to say, *I don't really care if she understands or not.* She folded her arms and tapped her foot.

"Amy?" Stan asked. "Amy who?"

All eyes turned her way. "Amy Fink. Asher's wife," Mary said. "Of course it was very difficult for her to be woken up in the middle of the night to have her husband dragged in for questioning in a murder case. And something about his shoes being confiscated. But of course, we want the innocent people identified early so they can focus on finding the real killer. I, for one, can't imagine who would do such a thing," Mary went on, oblivious to Em's body language.

"Me either," Char broke in, always the peacemaker. "But I think Leigh-Anne's right. This had to be a random, horrible act. You know, Cyril—our newspaperman—has been keeping tabs on a rash of break-ins, both in Frog Ledge and some of our little towns around it. I wonder if this was a burglary attempt gone wrong."

In the corn maze? Unlikely. Stan kept her mouth shut. She didn't want to get in the middle of this discussion, which seemed to have undertones galore. But she was intrigued by the confiscated shoes. What were they looking for? Evidence of dirt? They were all farmers, for goodness' sake. Dirt was a way of life. Stan made a mental note to ask Jake if Jessie had mentioned anything about a shoe to him. Or perhaps a suspicious footprint. But with all the people walking around the farm, that seemed like a long shot.

"They'll find whoever did it," Leigh-Anne declared. "The police won't let it rest. Especially in a close-knit town like this one. Emmy, please let me know what I can do. Especially when you start planning"—she dropped her voice an octave—"the services. Funding them, even. I'm happy to help."

Em bristled visibly. When she spoke, her voice was sharper than the sickle that had killed her husband. "That's lovely of you," she said in a tone indicating it wasn't, "but I'm sure I can pay for my husband's funeral."

Leigh-Anne, to her credit, flushed. "Emmy, that was not an insult. I know what it's been like for you—for all of us!—and I just want to make sure this is as easy as possible."

This was about to get ugly. Time to go. Stan edged nearer to the chair where she'd tossed her jacket, but the doorbell rang again. Maybe she could sneak out in the rush of new visitors. But she couldn't get past Leigh-Anne Sutton to get her jacket, so she gave up and ducked into the front hall and opened the door. Betty Meany, the Frog Ledge librarian, and Lorinda Walters, who worked the research desk, waited. Each held a shopping bag full of more food, if the delightful smells coming from the bags were any indication. Funny how death brought out people's appetites. Or maybe they just wanted to eat because it was such an alive activity.

"Hi there," Stan said. "Come on in."

"Well, hello!" Betty exclaimed.

"Hey, Stan!" Lorinda had dressed for the occasion with leopard print stretch pants and black heels—more five-inchers. Had these women all coordinated their shoes, or was this the new dress code for condolence visits? Stan felt out of place in her running sneakers and yoga pants, although she did look better than Mary Michelli.

Betty pinched Stan's cheek and breezed by, sweeping off her cherry red beret as she entered the kitchen, full of comforting words for Em.

"So awful," Lorinda confided. "I almost don't know what to say to the poor woman."

"I know. Terrible."

They stood there for another minute, pondering the situation, then Lorinda sighed. "I better go in."

"I'm going to have to get going, so I'll just grab my stuff," Stan said. She followed her into the kitchen.

"I don't know what I'm going to do," Em was saying to the mini-crowd gathered. "Leigh-Anne and Mary, I appreciate your offers, but you have your own farms to run. Same with Asher and Ted. The guys and gals can't come over here twice a day and do my chores. I have to do what's right. Not like I haven't been doing it anyway."

Francine, who had reentered the room while Stan had been in the hall, snorted. "Damn right," she said. "You did too much, Emmy. We have to figure out a better way."

"Now, now," Leigh-Anne interrupted. "We are here to help, Emmy. You just stop that right now."

Em ignored both of them. "I know I need help on the farm. Have for a long time. But laborers aren't too hard to find. What I'm really gonna need help with are the dang books. Hal was better with a ledger than I was, let's face it. And I can't have Tyler running over here from college to do it. He needs to do his own homework. I don't even know where Hal left off most of the time."

Stan saw an opening and snuck in to retrieve her jacket, finally.

"It's just too bad I don't have someone with that expertise standing right in front of me," Em said, and then she stopped talking and turned to stare at Stan. The other women's gazes followed.

"What?" Stan said, frozen with one arm in her sleeve.

Em tapped her lip with her index finger. "Didn't you work for a money company?"

"Me?" Stan stared at her. Char turned from the stove now, too, a thoughtful look on her face. "I, um, technically, yes . . . I worked in insurance financial services. But I did public relations. I didn't do *money.*"

"But," Char said, "you're a whiz with investments."

Stan felt her face turning red. It was true. Her financial situation was quite positive even after losing her job, because of her investment savvy and careful money management. She hadn't had to worry about working again and could focus on her new business. Which was, of course, all good. The bad part was, well, people knew it. Which meant there could be no good outcome to this conversation. The theme song from *Jaws* began playing in her head. She felt like prey being circled by the most lethal of hunters.

"I don't . . ." she tried again, but Em had gotten up and was standing in front of her, hands clasped as if in prayer.

"Stan. Would you please help me with the office work? Just until I figure out . . . what I'm going to do. Please. It would mean so much, and be such a big help." Her puppy dog eyes reminded Stan of Scruffy when she wanted something.

Stan felt all eyes in the room on her. What on earth was she supposed to say? No? To a grieving woman who could very well lose her livelihood? She may as well have just put a sign on her front door proclaiming herself the scarlet *U* of Frog Ledge—"unneighborly"—if she did that. Then she could rest assured her new business would spoil faster than a gallon of milk left out in the sun too long.

Stifling a sigh, she forced a smile. "Well, sure, Em. I'd be glad to help out."

"Oh, thank you!" Em hurled herself at Stan and locked her in a hug. Stan took a step back to keep her balance as the other ladies clapped.

"You're such a love," Char said, sliding plates of omelets onto the table. "Sit and eat."

"I really should get going," Stan said. She didn't think she could eat another bite this morning, after Izzy's quiche.

"Nonsense!" Em grabbed her hand and led her back to her chair. "Eat. You're going to need to keep your strength up." She smiled a bit, but Stan sensed something other than mirth. "This place can be a handful."

Chapter 8

"You need to go shopping for overalls." Brenna leaned forward on the shiny mahogany bar that served as the center of McSwigg's, her chin resting in her palm, eyes filled with humor.

"Shut up," Stan grumbled. "I'm just doing the books." She'd foregone her run and gone right to McSwigg's after leaving Em's, hoping for some sympathy.

Clearly she'd come to the wrong place. From his spot behind the bar stacking glasses, Jake guffawed. He turned to look at his sister and they both cracked up. "That's what you think, kiddo," he said when he could stop laughing.

Stan glared at them. "What's that supposed to mean?"

Neither of them said anything. They just continued smiling, which annoyed Stan. She looked around the pub. It was still early. Only a few customers were in the bar. Two young women sat at a table near the window eating nachos and gossiping. A lone man sat across the room with a beer glass and a book, the title of which Stan couldn't see. The place had a much different feel during the day than it did at night when people filled every corner and the music weaved Irish spells over the crowd, but it was still appealing. Jake had revamped the entire building two years ago. He turned the first floor into the bar and pub. The upper level served as the living space he, Duncan, and presently Brenna, called home. Both floors had that wide-open space design going for them. The pub had tall and short tables scattered around surrounded by padded stools in greens and golds, their wooden legs carved with Celtic knots, gleaming wooden floors, and Irish landscapes dotting the walls.

The bar had drop lights positioned every few feet above it. An Irish flag matching its counterpart over the front door was proudly displayed on the far wall behind the bar, and a carved wooden sign with a Gaelic saying hung above it: *An áit a bhfuil do chroí is ann a thabharfas do chosa thú*: Your feet will bring you to where your heart is.

Stan loved that sign. But today, it didn't make her feel any better. Her heart wasn't on the dairy farm, so she had no idea why her feet had landed her there earlier. "I have no clue why they think I'm qualified as an office worker. I don't even know why I'm doing books. I've never done books for anyone in my life. People just assume since I worked in financial services I'm an accountant or an investment manager or something."

Duncan, who had been sitting at her feet since she came in, stood and pushed his face into her hands, watching anxiously to see if she was upset. She rubbed his nose and fed him a treat.

"I think it's sweet. It'll be good practice. You'll have to do books for your business," Brenna pointed out.

Stan thought about that. It was true, but still. Doing books for a five-hundred-cow dairy farm was a bit beyond the scale of her meager little pet food business.

"I'd recommend a heavy pair of boots," Jake said. He

pulled out a knife and began slicing through a pile of lemons and limes. "Gets cold this time of year."

"What are you talking about?" Stan demanded. "I'm not working *outside* on the dairy farm! I don't even think I like dairy farms. Aren't they mean to the cows? That's what Nikki says." She lowered her voice as a couple of members of Jake's staff stopped what they were doing and stared at her.

"Mean? I don't think so," Jake said. "It's not like a factory farm. I don't think cows have the best deal around, but I don't think they're treated badly. It's not like beef cows. Think about it. Even if the farmers aren't as . . . animal-sensitive as someone like you, the cows are their livelihood. If they mess that up, they're just hurting themselves."

"They better not be," Stan said. "Because I don't care about buying local if that's the case. And I certainly wouldn't want to work for a place like that. I just said yes because everyone was watching me and I felt bad for Em. I mean, jeez, she just lost her husband. What was I supposed to say?"

Brenna looked sympathetic. "And once Em gets something in her head, good luck getting it out. Right, Jake?"

"Yep. Once she's got you, she's got you. Trust me, it's happened to us," Jake said.

"Why do you think I used to babysit those kids?" Brenna rolled her eyes and shuddered. "Because of our mother. She promised Em. Danny, the one with the chain saw? That kid was a nightmare."

"Was?" Stan asked at the same moment Jake repeated, "Chain saw?"

"Yeah, I see your point," Brenna said to Stan. To Jake, "He thought it would be funny to greet guests with a real chain saw when they came in for the maze. Almost took Stan's head off." She grinned. "That's nothing. One time when I was babysitting he got his hands on a butcher knife and locked me out of the house. I had to explain that to Em and Hal when they got home. Kid's a piece of work. But I guess we all know where he got that."

"Yeah, Hal was a handful," Jake said, his eyes on the limes he was slicing fast and furiously. Stan watched his fingers, almost a blur as they moved through their task.

Brenna snorted. "My brother, the king of understatement."

Jake filled a lime tray and covered it with plastic, then focused on the lemons with a shrug. "No understatement about it. He was a handful. He spent a lot of time here."

"Like every night. When he wasn't out playing poker or doing whatever else he did for his opening act," Brenna said.

Stan was surprised to hear Brenna, so normally carefree, sound almost . . . bitter.

Jake noticed it, too. "Bren, leave it alone."

Brenna's voice ratcheted up. "Why? It's the truth. And it's about time people stopped pussyfooting around and protecting him. Em doesn't deserve that."

"Protecting him from what?" Stan piped in. Both Jake and Brenna turned and stared at her as if they'd forgotten she sat there.

"Nothing," Jake said.

"Nothing?" It came out as a shriek, startling the other patrons. They all looked up from their tables at Brenna, who appeared to be about to hit Jake over the head with her plate of French fries.

Jake shot her a look. "Hal didn't spend a lot of time at home," he said to Stan.

"He didn't spend *any* time at home. He let Em deal with everything—the farm, the kids, the bills—and all he did was go out and play. We all know what he was like. Why are you defending him?" Brenna shoved her plate away, rose, and stomped off. Stan watched her disappear through the entrance to the apartment she shared with Jake. She hoped Brenna came back, because they were supposed to have a planning session on upcoming batches of treats that needed baking.

Stan looked back at Jake. He met her gaze steadily, still slicing the lemons.

"So Hal Hoffman was . . . not a family man," she said.

"None of my business. Or Brenna's."

"She seems to think otherwise," Stan said.

"Well, she's wrong."

"She's close to the family."

"We're all close to the family. I told you, our mother is one of Em's closest friends. She was there at the crack of dawn this morning, before everyone else showed up with their casseroles. Probably beating pillows with her in Hal's name or something."

Stan had seen Jake's mother around town but never officially met her. Jessie looked a lot like her, so Stan had shied away, wondering if the personalities were the same, too. But she thought she might like a woman who beat pillows in her friend's dead husband's name. "So why shouldn't Brenna have an opinion? If someone was hurting my friend I'd be angry at them, too. What was he doing, anyway?"

Jake used the edge of his knife to push the lemon slices into his tray. His exquisite green-brown eyes were troubled. "Nobody should be judging anyone else's life, even if they think they know what it's like. Brenna cares about them, of course. But she doesn't know the whole story. Neither do I, before you ask," he said as Stan opened her mouth.

Reluctantly, she closed it again. "But he used to hang out here a lot."

"Course he did. It's the coolest place in town." He winked. "Part of being cool means not asking a lot of questions."

Stan didn't agree. In fact, she wanted to ask more questions, but the front door opened. Jake glanced up to see who it was, and his whole face changed—eyebrows drawing together in a slight frown, lips narrowed. She turned to look, too. His sister, Trooper Jessie Pasquale, stood in the doorway, in full uniform. Her eyes roamed the room, assessing her surroundings, before stopping on Jake and Stan. The other patrons watched her entrance with interest.

Great. Just what she needed. Stan sighed inwardly, watched as Pasquale moved to the bar, no nonsense as usual. "I should probably go," she said, but Jake shook his head.

"No need. Jess," he said with a nod as his sister reached them. "I can't say I remember the last time you set foot in McSwigg's. Welcome."

Pasquale's face remained impassive. She didn't acknowledge her brother's comment, probably recognizing it as sarcasm. She nodded at Stan, then turned back to her brother. "Got a minute?"

He shrugged. "Sure. I'm setting up for tonight, but we can talk."

She hesitated. "I meant in private. It's about Hal Hoffman."

Stan saw the annoyance flicker across his face. "I'm busy, but I'm happy to talk here while I'm working."

Stan started to rise, hoping to fade away without them

noticing, but Jake turned to her. "No need to leave. We were in the middle of a conversation."

Her face heated. She perched back on the edge of the stool. "I don't want to interrupt."

"You were already here," Jake pointed out.

Pasquale sighed. "Don't worry about leaving, Ms. Connor. I won't be long. It's nothing you won't hear about anyway."

"Okay, but can you please call me Stan? I mean, now that you don't think I killed anyone anymore. I hope. Oh, God, you don't think I killed Hoffman, do you?" A vicious wave of déjà vu washed over her. It hadn't been that long ago that Pasquale had considered her at the top of the suspect pool for the unfortunate murder of the local veterinarian.

Now Pasquale looked annoyed. She gave Stan the stink-eye for a minute as if to say, *Are you done?* Then turned back to her brother. "I need to know if Hoffman was here yesterday."

"Not sure. I wasn't working. I was bringing Duncan to the birthday party."

"The dog party? At the Hoffmans'?"

Jake nodded.

"You didn't come down at all?"

"For a few minutes, but I was mostly in the kitchen making sure everything was good with the menu. We've got a new dish. Bangers and mash. You should try it."

Stan wrinkled her nose. Her dad's family had been a fan of the traditional Irish sausage dish, loaded with mashed potatoes, Irish beans, and thick gravy. Her mother had never touched it with a ten-foot pole. It was one of those rare instances where she and her mother were completely on the same page.

"Who was on? Was Brenna here?" Pasquale didn't care about the new dish either.

"No. She was helping Stan with the party."

Pasquale shot another sidelong glance at Stan. She seemed to want to ask a question, then changed her mind. "Can you ask your staff if they saw him? I really need to know."

"You can ask them. The waitresses are here already. Travis and Desiree were on the bar. Des is in tonight. Travis is here tomorrow. Do you need an official statement?"

"Don't be a jerk."

"I'm not. I'm just going by what you've told me a hundred times about your work."

"Jake, seriously. I'm not in the mood." Pasquale sounded tired all of a sudden.

"Me either, Jess," he said. "Me either."

Pasquale looked at Stan again, then back at her brother. Stan couldn't help but feel she was intruding.

"I can go," she offered again.

"No. Maybe you can help, too." Pasquale took a deep breath and dropped her voice. "This stays between us. I need to place Hal Hoffman with someone yesterday. It shouldn't be that hard, considering the man's habits. But Emmalee Hoffman wasn't where she was supposed to be yesterday afternoon—her kid's parent-teacher conference— and I have no sightings of her husband after noon. He didn't seem to see anyone, which isn't like him."

"What are you getting at, Jess?" Jake asked.

Jessie leveled him with her most piercing stare. "If Hoffman can't be accounted for, his wife could be in big trouble. Since she can't be accounted for either."

Chapter 9

Jake was used to his sister, and Stan could tell even he was caught off guard. "Wait—what? Em? Jess, stop it. That's going too far."

Jessie shook her head slowly. "It's not me, Jake. My boss is very interested in this case. Probably because he knows my history with the family. He immediately pounced on Em. I've been tracking her day, and . . ." She trailed off. "There are some missing pieces."

"Did you ask her?"

"Of course I asked her. She swears she was at the farm. Forgot about the conference and was running late when she remembered it, so she drove over there but allegedly couldn't locate the teacher. Said after that she returned to the farm, but none of the workers remember seeing her. The ones we've been able to talk to, that is. But the teacher says she was there until at least three-thirty, waiting for the Hoffmans."

"Did you talk to the worker who was at the farm last night?" Stan asked.

Pasquale grimaced. "Sort of. He spoke enough English that we didn't get the translator out of bed, but I think we're going to need a longer conversation with him. Basically he didn't see Hal at all yesterday, because his shift starts in the afternoon. But he didn't see Em either. So you see what I mean. It's not going well." She sat on the stool, a movement that, to Stan, signified defeat.

Jake sensed it, too. He paused from arranging his garnish trays and grabbed a beer mug, filled it with ice and water, and placed it in front of his sister. "Did you eat?"

She shook her head.

"Veggie wrap?"

A nod.

"Chips?"

She hesitated. Jake took that for a yes. "Be right back." He left the bar and disappeared around the same corner Brenna had a few minutes earlier.

Stan was left with Pasquale. *Well, this is awesome.* She picked up her water glass and swirled the remaining ice around for something to do. Pasquale hadn't touched her water. Instead, she observed her surroundings as one would a sleazy alley they'd been forced to walk down in the dark. Either she wasn't a drinker and thought bars were a waste of time, or she had a particular aversion to her brother's place. Stan wanted to ask.

"Do you have any thoughts on who killed him? Aside from Emmalee?" she asked instead.

Pasquale frowned. "I can't discuss the case."

"You were just discussing it," Stan pointed out.

Before Pasquale could respond, Jake came out of the kitchen. "Order's in. You really should eat more than once a week, you know," he told his sister.

She ignored him. "I'm going to talk to the waitresses now."

"Fine. Let me go tell them first." He waited until the two

girls had left their customers' tables, then beckoned them over. "Caroline, Maddy. Can I borrow you two for a minute?"

The girls approached, curiosity apparent on each face. They were both twentysomethings, but on the young end of twenty. "What's up, boss?" the blonde one with the long ponytail asked.

"This is my sister—Trooper Pasquale. She's a state police officer. She needs to ask you two a question about a customer. That okay?"

"Sure," the blonde said. "I'm Caroline." She turned to look at her coworker, a curvy brunette with a tattoo covering her entire forearm.

The girl hung back, apparently wary of this whole exercise. "I'm Maddy."

"What's going on? Is someone in trouble?" Caroline asked.

"Thanks for taking the time, ladies. I just need you to look at a photo." All business again, Pasquale pulled a photo out of her pocket and showed them. "Was this man in here yesterday at all?"

Caroline and Maddy bent their heads together over the photo. Neither of the girls looked disturbed. They must not read the *Frog Ledge Holler*, Stan figured.

Maddy looked up first, shook her head. "I didn't see him."

Caroline lingered over the photo a bit longer. "That's Hal, right? Hoffman?" At Pasquale's nod, she continued. "Sure, he's a regular. Decent tipper, too. He doesn't always sit at the tables. Mostly the bar. But he wasn't in here yesterday. At least not while I was here, and I came in at two. I worked an extra shift yesterday." She tapped her index finger thoughtfully against her lips. "But you know, I do remember . . ." She turned to Maddy. "You know him, too, Maddy. He's usually in here with a group of guys, kinda look like the Mafia? But sometimes with his wife. Wasn't she in here yesterday afternoon looking for him?"

Maddy looked uncomfortable. She shrugged. "I really don't remember. And I think my table's getting ready to leave. Is it okay . . . ?" She motioned over her shoulder with her thumb.

"Go ahead," Pasquale said, reaching into her pocket and producing a card, which she handed to Maddy. "If you remember anything else, please call me. My brother knows how to get in touch."

Maddy nodded and hurried back to her customers. Pasquale watched her go for a minute, then turned back to Caroline, still deep in thought.

"It *was* yesterday she was here," she said, nodding now. "Mrs. Hoffman. I remember, because it stood out. She never comes in here during the day, and never by herself. It sort of looked like something was wrong, you know? She talked to Brenna, and then she left."

"Brenna wasn't working yesterday," Jake said.

"Not officially, but she came down for a bit. We were making plans to go to a movie, but she got distracted. Went and talked to Mrs. Hoffman. Then she left, too."

Pasquale was good—Stan had to give her that. She didn't acknowledge this news as disturbing or curious. She waited to see if Caroline had anything else to add. When she didn't, Pasquale pulled out a card and handed it to her. "If anything else comes to mind, please call me."

"You bet." Caroline tapped the card once against her palm, then slid it into her apron pocket. "All set, boss?"

"Yep. Thanks, Car."

Caroline turned to walk away, then hesitated. "Are the Hoffmans okay?"

Jake looked at his sister as if to say, *I'm deferring to you on this one.*

Pasquale, still with her cop face firmly in place, shook her head. "I'm afraid Mr. Hoffman died last night."

Caroline's mouth dropped open in shock. "What? How?"

"We're still looking into it. Thanks again for your time," Pasquale said, dismissing her.

Caroline looked at Jake again, as if she wanted to say something, then murmured, "Sure," and moved distractedly back to work.

"Don't these kids read the paper?" Pasquale muttered. "And where's Brenna?"

"She went upstairs," Jake said.

"She never mentioned Emmalee was in here yesterday," Pasquale said. "Or that she had talked to her."

"Did you ask?"

"I didn't think I needed to. I figured she would tell me if anything strange happened involving the Hoffmans, considering the end result."

"Maybe she didn't think it was strange."

Pasquale snorted. "Emmalee Hoffman in a bar in the middle of the day? Emmalee in a bar is strange in and of itself. But in the middle of the day? When she was supposed to be at school with her kid?"

"Why don't you go ask her?" Jake suggested.

"Fine." Pasquale shoved off the stool and rounded the corner. Stan heard the door leading to Jake's apartment slam behind her, then the tread of her boots on the stairs.

She looked at Jake. He shook his head, a trace of a smile on his lips. "My sister. I love her, but she makes life hard."

"It sounds kind of weird that Emmalee was in here yesterday afternoon," Stan said. "Wouldn't she need to be on the farm?"

Jake looked pained. "I have no idea, Stan. I try to stay out of my customers' lives. I'm just the bartender."

It was a gross understatement, Stan knew. There weren't many people in Frog Ledge as invested in the community as Jake. But she let it go. Clearly he had feelings about the Hoffmans and whatever had occurred at their farm that he didn't want to share.

Less than three minutes later, Pasquale appeared around the corner.

"That was quick," Jake said.

"She's gone."

"Gone?"

"Must've gone out the private entrance in front."

"Okay. Well, I'll tell her to call you when she gets back. She's working tonight."

Pasquale still frowned.

"What, Jess?"

"I want to know what Em talked to her about yesterday. What was she doing here in the middle of the day? Why was she suddenly so hell-bent on finding Hal?"

Chapter 10

Stan went home to let the dogs out and change into jeans, her new pink blazer, and her sequined ankle boots with cut-out toes. By the time she returned to the bar, Brenna was back, wearing her work uniform—black leggings; tall, flat black boots; and her green McSwigg's T-shirt.

"We're supposed to talk about next week's work, aren't we?" Brenna said when Stan took a seat at the bar.

"We are." Stan smiled.

"I'm sorry." Brenna looked upset. "My sister gets me so mad. Let's talk now. You're getting a lot of orders, right?"

"Yes! Look." She pulled out her iPad and opened a document marked "Orders." "We have five orders for treats, but since we didn't have the party last night, I only need to bake a couple dozen."

"Who are the orders for?" Brenna asked.

Stan ran her finger down the list. "I have two for Nikki, for adoption events. One for the Dogtown Pet Spa and Resort—that new place across town. I think Betty Meany knows the owners and referred us." It was exciting. Already word-of-mouth customers and she'd only been in business a couple of months. "One for Izzy, and one for the woman who owns the food co-op. She says it's one of the only things she's missing—local, organic dog treats."

"Impressive," Jake said. Stan hadn't even noticed he'd joined them at the bar. He'd been setting up for the step dancers across the room.

She flushed a bit. "It's nice to have people willing to pay for my treats."

"It's very cool. You're making a name for yourself already. I knew you'd be a hit in no time." He nodded approvingly and disappeared into the kitchen.

Brenna grinned at her. "I wish you two would just get it over with."

"Brenna!" Stan blushed even redder. "I don't know what you're talking about."

Brenna rolled her eyes. "Sure you don't. Okay, so if I come over Monday afternoon, we can bake?"

"Yes. And then I have to follow up on Benny's party. I don't know that we'll be able to have it at the farm, so I have to think of a place we could do it." She tapped her finger against her lips. "Any thoughts?"

"How about your house?"

"My house?" Stan repeated.

"Yes, your house. It could be fun." Brenna shrugged. "And your backyard is perfect."

"I guess." Stan hesitated a minute, then plunged into the question she'd been waiting to ask. "So did you catch up with Jessie?"

"No." Brenna's voice hardened.

"Bren. Did you see Em in here on Friday?"

Brenna crossed her arms, the ultimate defensive position. "She stopped in. So what?"

"What did she want? Was she looking for Hal?"

"What, are you taking my sister's side now?" Brenna

looked visibly upset. "She treated you badly, too, Stan. Don't forget that. Now she's trying to do the same thing to Emmalee."

"I'm not taking anyone's side, but it could be important to the investigation. Don't you want to know who killed him? And make sure the rest of the family is safe?"

Brenna hadn't considered the crime from that angle, Stan could tell. She pursed her lips and thought about it, then said tersely, "Yes, she was in here. Looking for him. They were supposed to go to the parent-teacher meeting together and Hal never showed up. As usual. There. Are you satisfied?"

"You should tell Jessie," Stan said.

Brenna gathered her hair in a ponytail. "Fine. Whatever. Jake and Desi are gonna have my head if I don't get to work." She slipped an apron on and ducked behind the bar, already fielding orders from her regulars before she even got the strings tied.

Stan slipped her iPad back in her purse and sipped the glass of Merlot Jake had slipped in front of her. He'd already tuned in to her choice of wines. Weird. But nice, at the same time. Her last boyfriend hadn't figured out after four years what she liked to drink. Richard had always been too busy worrying about what he was drinking. She watched Brenna slip into bartender mode, chatting with her customers, deftly pulling pints and mixing liquors. Was she telling everything about yesterday's visit from Emmalee Hoffman? Why had she claimed to be so late for the parent-teacher meeting that she drove over to the school immediately after realizing her error, but really she had stopped by the bar looking for Hal?

The crowd gathered in earnest now, anticipating the step dancers' arrival. Stan watched from her prime spot as people streamed in. Some she recognized vaguely, others she knew from her travels around town. Amazing to see how many locals crammed into the place. It was easy to see why, though. McSwigg's exemplified community. Real community. Stan could see it in the way people interacted. It didn't seem to matter who they'd come in with. Most tables and other seating areas had excess clusters of people gathered around them, old friends catching up or new acquaintances becoming more intimate. Stan caught snippets of words floating around her: "A good topic for the next council meeting agenda . . ." "Eileen is back in the hospital again. Pneumonia this time . . ." "Jacob is doing much better in school, what a difference a teacher can make. . . ."

Stan half listened, allowing herself to float in that space of comfort without feeling compelled to get up and begin contributing to one of the conversations. She'd never been to Ireland, but liked to believe this is what it would be like. Friendly. Comfortable. Safe. And then she heard another half conversation, somewhere behind her. "The bottom line is, Hoffman owed money," a man with a deep voice said. "They'll find a way to get it. Don't matter if he ain't around anymore."

Stan spun on her chair and squinted into the dim room, trying to see who was speaking. The man at the table directly behind her with the Yankees cap on? No. The woman he was with hadn't stopped talking yet. The group of men next to them? They looked rough, with their black leather jackets and oversized bodies. One of them met her gaze. His was not friendly.

At the other end of the pub, the background music went off and someone introduced the step dancing troupe. Everyone clapped. A wave of folks moved forward to get a better view, and the music began again, louder and more compelling as the room filled with the thunderous sound of the dancers hitting the floor over and over. Stan whirled around, pretending not to have noticed the guy looking at her, and focused on the music. The beat matched her pounding heart. Hal owed money? Had the lender killed him? What did that mean for Emmalee and the boys? Were they in danger? She took a swig of wine and tried to calm down. She risked a glance behind her again and noticed the group of men had left. Why? Because they knew she'd heard them?

"What's wrong?" Jake paused on his way down the bar.

"Oh, nothing. I just . . . nothing." She offered him a bright smile.

He tilted his head, observing, trying to decide if she was telling the truth. "You sure?"

"I am. This is a great group. I'm enjoying it."

"Okay, then. I'll be back to fill your glass." He continued on to whatever task he needed to do.

Stan forced herself to concentrate on the dancing. She had a decent view from her bar stool, and the more she watched—and sipped her wine—the more relaxed she became. She tapped her foot along with the beat, unable to remember feeling this content in a long time. Like she had finally found a place she belonged. Home. A different kind of home than she'd ever had, and the one she'd probably have least predicted for herself, but it was true. Here, she didn't have to be "on" all the time, like in her mother's fancy Rhode Island waterfront home, or in the cutthroat financial world she used to inhabit. She was just Stan, who prepared food for animals she loved, and it was perfect.

Perfect. The thought snuck in, unexpected, but instead of startling her like it may have had a few months ago, it didn't. Instead she felt peaceful. And a little warm and fuzzy, which could have something to do with her wine.

"Having fun?" Jake paused in front of her again during one of his endless trips up and down the bar and placed a glass of ice water in front of her. She wondered how many miles he walked the nights he worked. He leaned forward, elbows on the bar, face inches from hers.

That warm, fuzzy feeling flared a little, and she reached for her glass of water to douse it. And managed to spill it all over the bar, and well into her neighbor's lap. The man jumped up, flinging icy water off his clothes. Duncan jumped up, too, from his spot on the floor, thinking this was a fun game, and launched himself at the man's leg.

"I'm so sorry!" Stan grabbed a pile of napkins and thrust them at the man as Jake deftly grabbed a rag and swiped up the water on the bar before it traveled. Stan could see the hint of a smile on his face as he did so.

The man observed her, then looked down at his soggy pants. Without a word, he took the napkins and swiped at himself, shaking Duncan off his leg. He was handsome, with wavy black hair shot through with silver, a tanned face with minimal lines, and a neatly trimmed mustache. He was also annoyed.

"What happened?" The woman seated to his left leaned forward to see what was happening. "What a lovely dog! Why is he in the bar? How did I not notice him before?"

"I'm so sorry to be so clumsy." Stan still felt like crawling under the bar in embarrassment. "And that's Duncan. He . . . works here. Again, I'm so—" She broke off as she recognized the woman. She had been in Emmalee's kitchen that morning. Leigh-Anne Sutton. The farmer with the highest heels of all.

The woman recognized her at the same time. "Oh, you're the lovely little girl helping Emmy out! Stella, wasn't it?"

Stan's jaw clenched and she pressed her lips together. What should she respond to first—the incorrect name, or the fact that Leigh-Anne certainly wasn't old enough to call Stan a "little girl"? She was probably in her midforties—ten years older than Stan.

Behind her, Jake laughed. It turned into a cough when she aimed her death stare on him as he continued to swab at the bar, obviously interested in the exchange.

"It's Stan," she said. "How are you, Leigh-Anne?" There. She should feel bad that Stan remembered her name.

"I should go home and change," the man said to Leigh-Anne.

"I'm so sorry," Stan said again.

Leigh-Anne wrinkled her nose. "Don't be a baby," she told her companion. "It's only water. Go stand under the hand dryer in the bathroom." She pointed toward the rest-room signs. The guy frowned, but obeyed.

"I'm sorry," Stan said again, finally sitting back on her stool.

"Ah, not to worry," Leigh-Anne assured her. "He's just cranky. Most men are cranky. Right, Mr. Bartender?" She winked at Jake, who raised one eyebrow.

Luckily someone waved him over for a new drink, and he simply nodded at her and moved down the bar.

"This is a lovely little place," Leigh-Anne commented. "And such a hunk of a bartender!" She nodded approvingly, watching Jake's every move as he whipped up some fruity drink.

Stan frowned. Forgot about water. Picked up her wine and took a long swig.

Leigh-Anne swiped the excess water off the bar stool her

companion had abandoned and perched on the edge. "This seems like the place to be in town. I figured I'd start checking things out. I'm going to be staying around here to help Emmy during her time of need."

"Oh, really?" *Maybe you should do her books.* She thought Em had declined the offers of help. Maybe she'd changed her mind. "When you say staying around . . ."

"At the B and B. With all the lovely llamas."

"Alpacas, you mean? Char's place?"

"Alpacas, yes." Leigh-Anne snapped her fingers. "My memory just isn't what it used to be. Yes, my farm is about an hour from here, so it doesn't make sense to drive that every day. And who knows how long poor Emmy will need the help, right? So I mentioned as much this morning, and that lovely woman suggested I stay at her place. She gave me a tremendous discount, too. I'm going home tonight to get my things and 'moving in' tomorrow." She winked at Stan. "I thought I'd better check out the nightlife first. But it's such a delightful little town. I haven't been back since the co-op's annual meeting six months ago. I always forget how adorable it is."

"It's very nice here. And that's wonderful of you to come help," Stan said. "What about your farm?"

"What about it?" Leigh-Anne looked blank.

"Who's going to run it while you're here?"

"Oh, that." Leigh-Anne waved a manicured hand. "I have a staff. It will be fine."

"Oh. So what are you helping Emmalee with?"

"Well, whatever I can! There's so much to do. And with the co-op to run, too, well, she'll need all the help she can get." Leigh-Anne beamed at her, then turned her smile on her semidry companion as he returned. He went around her to sit on her abandoned stool, happily leaving Leigh-Anne next to the drink-spiller. "That's Tony," she said to Stan. "I'm sorry he's not being friendly."

"Well, I did spill on him," Stan said.

"He'll be fine." Leigh-Anne turned a pointed stare on Tony, and his whole demeanor changed.

He leaned over to Stan and offered his hand. "Tony Falco. No harm done with the water."

Tony Falco? As in the guy on the election sign? "Nice to meet you. Stan Connor."

"Stan. Interesting name. Do you live here in Frog Ledge?"

"I do, actually."

"Oh, well then." His entire demeanor changed, and charm spilled out of every pore. "Perhaps you've heard of me. I'm running for mayor."

Behind him, Leigh-Anne raised her eyes to the ceiling. "Always campaigning."

Stan smiled. "I have heard of you. Your sign is in the Hoffmans' yard."

Tony Falco sobered. "Yes. Yes it is. Hal is—was—a good friend."

"I know. It's terrible," Leigh-Anne said, shaking her head. "Just terrible."

"So how do you two know each other?" Stan asked.

"Oh, Tony was a dear friend of my late husband," Leigh-Anne said.

"Yes. Good man. Well, lovely to meet you," he said to Stan. "I'm having a fund-raiser on Tuesday. At the hospital. Please come. Although you might've liked the one on Thursday better. It was held at the local winery. Everetts'— do you know it? Anyway, it was wonderful. Don't you agree, Leigh-Anne?"

"Delightful," Leigh-Anne said. "Lovely place. But the hospital will be lovely, too, I'm sure. Do come, Stan."

"I'll try," Stan said, noncommittal. "Nice to meet you, too."

"I'll see you on the farm!" Leigh-Anne tugged a short, purple leather coat on and waggled her fingers at Stan, then followed Falco.

Stan said her good-byes back and watched them walk through the pub to the door. Their seats were grabbed before they even got halfway there. She took the last swig of her wine and thought it might be time to go, too, but before she could commit to that decision, another glass landed in front of her. Behind it, Jake winked.

"The show's not over yet," he said. "Stella."

Chapter 11

"You're *what?*"

Stan held the phone away from her ear to ward off Nikki's high-pitched scream of protest. Stan had called her first thing Sunday morning after she'd finally found the energy to roll out of bed at eight—late for her—with the aftereffects of wine still lingering. She'd had a great time at McSwigg's, and stayed a lot later than she should have. She'd enjoyed the step dancers, chatted with some of her fellow townsfolk, and spent a lot of time watching Jake when he wasn't looking. Hopefully he hadn't noticed. She'd also noodled the conversation she'd overheard among the group of onerous-looking men, dissecting it in the back of her brain, looking for any clues that might help her figure out who they were and if she could find out more about the money Hal owed. There had to be a way. She had access to the books now. Or she would, shortly.

Which was what Nikki was screaming about. Stan had felt compelled to break the news that she'd gotten roped into working at the dairy farm, knowing full well what Nikki would say about it. She'd called early to get it over with.

"How can you work there?" Nikki continued. Her voice

had come down a notch, and Stan hesitantly put the phone back to her ear.

"I'm not really working there. I'm just . . . helping this woman out for a few days. Well, a few weeks, I guess. I'm not really sure."

"That's working there, in my book. Jeez, Stan. Don't you listen to *anything* I say? Hold on." There was a minute or so pause, then Nikki came back on the line. "Check your e-mail. I just sent you a video. You have to see what they do to these cows."

"Nikki. Please. Stop. I love cows. But I don't know what to say. This is a farm town. The woman lost her husband. She has four kids to feed and the cows are here and they need care, too. What else can I do?"

Silence on the other end of the line. Braver, Stan continued. "Even if I did stage a revolution and helped them, where would I take five hundred cows? Where could they go? Seriously. Where do cows who don't live on farms live? Who takes care of them? It's not like we can ship them to India." She remembered Nikki had told her once that cows were treated like holy objects in India.

"I'm not saying you should stage a revolution." Nikki's voice was sullen now. "I'm just saying, it's embarrassing to have my best friend supporting an animal torture chamber."

Stan sighed and rubbed her temples. It was already shaping up to be a long day. "Look. I'm not supporting the farm. I'm not even taking any money. I'm just going to use my spare time to help this woman get through the next few weeks and then I'm done. I'm not condoning the farm. I'm not doing marketing for them. I'm not even drinking milk." She didn't mention the cheese she sometimes bought for her treat recipes. Dogs and cats both loved cheesy treats.

Nikki hmphed at her. "Fine. Don't tell me about it, okay?"

"My lips are sealed," Stan promised, and hung up. Why did she do it to herself? She had a bad habit of needing to explain herself to people, friends and family included. She needed to work on that.

Outside her window, the sky was gray and serious. Probably nice and cool out. She could take the dogs for a walk around the green, then go for a bike ride. Then she could start planning her treat orders. Brenna was coming tomorrow to bake, but she could get a head start today. She glanced at the animals. Scruffy was still sprawled out on the pillow next to Nutty. Nutty didn't even blink. He liked to sleep in on Sundays. From his bed on the floor, Henry lifted his head and woofed at her.

"Morning, guys. You wanna hit the green?"

Henry wagged his tail. Scruffy sat up and handed Stan her paw.

"Let's get on with it, then." She glanced at her phone, which had just lit up with the morning local news alerts she had set up. Weather, cloudy with chance of showers, high forties by noon. A water main had broken in the next town. And an early morning dispute in a Frog Ledge café had sent one to the hospital and one to jail.

Stan's mouth dropped open. A Frog Ledge café? There was only one real café in Frog Ledge—Izzy Sweet's Sweets. Stan scrolled to her contacts and hit Izzy's name to dial her cell. The phone went straight to voice mail.

"Huh," she said to Henry, the only one who was actually paying attention to her. "What do you think of that?"

Henry's tail smacked the floor in excitement.

"I'm thinking the same thing," Stan said. "We should take a walk down there instead of around the green, right?

That way, we can fill up the feral cat food, too." Stan and Izzy were feeding a colony of feral cats who lived behind her shop.

Scruffy sat up and *woo wooed*. Nutty came over and shoved his head against Stan's hand, looking for rubs. "Well, I'm glad we're all in agreement," she said. "Let's go eat so we can roll."

An hour later the cat food was packed up and they were ready to go, Stan in yoga pants and a sweatshirt, Henry in his new plaid vest, and Scruffy in her pink sweater. Nutty bid them farewell from his window spot. Stan knew when they returned he'd be curled up in the sun spot, either on the hall floor or in his cat tree near the window. Being a cat was a pretty good deal. He seemed to prefer having the house to himself.

On the way down the street, she glanced at the house directly next to hers. Amara Leonard's house. Stan hadn't seen the homeopath in ages. Not that it mattered. Amara hadn't spoken to her since the day last summer that she'd come to Duncan's rescue, when he'd shown up sick on Stan's porch. Their falling out earlier this year had been silly, and Stan wanted to wave a white flag and get on with things. Maybe she'd stop by this week. It would be nice to have a friend next door. Especially someone close to her own age.

They hiked down to the corner of Main Street and Darling Lane and crossed over, continuing down Darling. Scruffy led the way, prancing along, stopping to greet everyone she saw on the street—mostly a lot of older folks coming and going from the senior center. Izzy's shop and upstairs apartment was a block farther. Scruffy knew exactly where they were headed. She was used to going to the café to visit Izzy's dogs. She dragged Stan and Henry through the parking lot to the front door.

They came face to face with a CLOSED sign.

"What the devil?" Izzy usually had to be reminded to close, and not at nine in the morning on a Sunday, the day people came to the shop to linger over lattes and the *New York Times,* and refill their mugs. Stan cupped her hands around her eyes and peered inside. No one. Lights off, no delightful coffee or pastry smells drifting through the door. Stan knocked. Nothing. Then, from a distance—probably upstairs in the apartment—the faint sound of dogs barking.

Maybe Izzy was sick upstairs or something. But why wouldn't the shop be open? She had help. Stan pulled her phone out again and redialed. Still voice mail. Concerned now, she pondered what to do. But before she could come up with her next move, a teenager with a green stripe down one side of her hair and various piercings in her face strolled around the corner with a trash bag.

"Hey. We had to close, uh, unexpectedly. Sorry 'bout that. We're back tomorrow," the girl said when she noticed Stan.

"Thanks. Is Izzy okay? Are the dogs?"

The girl grinned. "She's cool, but I'm not sure about the other guy. He wasn't lookin' too hot after she threw the chair at him and they had to call an ambulance. The dogs? I think they're fine. They were out back until the cops came."

Stan gaped at her. "Izzy? Threw a chair at someone?"

"Yeah, well, the guy was messing with her. I'da done the same thing. I was gonna help her, but, you know, the other guy called the cops."

"Do you know who they were? Were they assaulting her?"

"Nah, just came in asking her questions. She didn't wanna answer them, I guess."

"Where is she now?"

"That lady cop took her away." The girl hefted her trash bag to her other hand and gazed wistfully at the sweet shop. "I hope they don't throw her in the slammer for long. I mean, like, I gotta pay my tuition soon."

Chapter 12

"Can you find out from your sister how much bond they're holding Izzy on?" Stan demanded. After her conversation with Mya, Stan had put her home-cooked food out in bowls for the feral cats and immediately called Jake. Brenna had warned her he was sleeping, but she didn't care how grouchy he was.

"Izzy?" Silence. She could picture him, still in bed, rubbing his eyes, trying to focus and understand what she was talking about this time. Then she blushed. *Stop picturing Jake in bed, for the love of God.*

"Yes, Izzy. She threw a chair at someone at the café today and got arrested. The place is closed."

"Threw a chair at someone?" He sounded more awake now.

"That's what her employee said. The guy's friend called the cops and your sister arrested her."

"What, they didn't like her blueberry muffin and wanted their money back?"

Stan sighed. "Seriously, Jake. I'm worried about her.

I'm gonna run home and get my car and drive down to the barracks."

"Stan. Stay out of it. You do not want to get involved in another one of my sister's cases." He didn't say it, but she heard the unspoken *again*.

"I'm not. I just want to make sure Izzy's okay. Never mind. Sorry to bother you." She disconnected and pocketed the phone, urged the dogs on. "Come on, guys. We're gonna go home and get the car."

The dogs obediently jogged with her as she headed for home. She heard her phone ring, distantly, but ignored it. But just as they reached her driveway, a truck careened down the street. Much too fast for this neighborhood. Jake drove up behind her. Duncan hung out the window, mouth wide open, tongue lolling, smiling at her.

Stan stared at him. "What are you doing?"

He sighed. "Get in the truck."

"No. I was taking the dogs with me for the ride."

He muttered what was probably a curse, then got out. Came around and opened the double door of the pickup to make the backseat accessible, grabbed Duncan's collar, and motioned to the dogs. "Come on, guys. Jump in."

Henry didn't need a second invitation. Gracefully, he launched his stocky body into the truck and kissed Duncan. Scruffy looked up at Stan. She scooped the smaller dog up. "I know, too high for you." After placing her in the truck with the boys, she jumped into the passenger seat. Jake slammed both doors, went back around, and climbed in. He took off down the street like he was in a NASCAR race.

Stan grabbed the door handle as he careened around the corner and back up the other side of the green. "So what brings you here at this hour?"

He glanced over at her. She could see a laugh tickling the corners of his mouth as he tried to hold it back. "Funny."

"Hey, I'm a big girl. I can find my way to jail on my own."

"Yeah, we know."

"There's no need to be snarky." Stan also didn't want to be reminded of how close she'd come to being arrested for murder this past summer.

"So what did Izzy do this time?"

"I'm not sure. There was some fight at the café. She threw a chair at some guy and he had to go to the hospital." Duncan stuck his head between the seats and stared at Stan adoringly. She rubbed his head.

Jake shook his head. "I knew that girl was nuts."

"Oh, come on. She's not nuts. Plenty of people deserve to have chairs thrown at them. It's kind of admirable to find someone who'll actually do it."

He gave her a sidelong glance. "You're a weird chick, you know that?"

"I do. So what are we gonna do when we get there?"

"We? What 'we'? I'm just driving you. I'm not taking my sister on this early in the morning, after I've had about four hours of sleep."

She glared at him. He stared straight ahead.

"I didn't need a ride. I need someone to deal with her while I bail Izzy out."

"You're bailing her out?"

"If she's arrested, she'll need to be bailed out. That's not important. Stop distracting me. You need to come in and talk to your sister."

"Yeah, yeah. Fine."

Caught off guard, Stan opened her mouth again, then closed it. Looked over at him. "Fine?"

"Yeah. I was just messing with you."

"You're such a jerk."

"I know. And Izzy will keep reminding us both of that on the way home." For some reason Stan hadn't yet figured out, Izzy hated Jake's guts.

Jake pulled into the barracks parking lot and lowered the windows enough for the dogs to stick their noses out to sniff. "There better be a coffee shop near here."

They walked silently into the dingy gray building. The last time Stan had been here, she'd been taken in through the back, where they brought the criminals. She hadn't seen this tiny, ugly room, with two chairs and a rickety table covered in magazines that may have been from the nineties. Behind dark, bulletproof glass, a trooper watched them.

Jake went to the window. "I'm looking for Trooper Pasquale. It's Jake McGee."

The cop picked up a phone and said something Stan couldn't hear, then pointed at the chairs.

"They don't know you here?" Stan asked him in a low voice once they sat.

"I don't exactly hang out here. On normal days."

Before she could think of a retort, a door next to the bulletproof glass opened. Jessie Pasquale appeared. She observed both of them, then focused on her brother. "What's up?"

He rose from his chair, the worn plastic creaking in protest. "Did you arrest Izzy Sweet?"

Pasquale crossed her arms. Defensive. "You came all the way here to ask me who got busted today?" *Translation: Why do you care?*

"No. I came down to see if she needed bond posted."

Pasquale cocked an eyebrow. "Seriously? The woman despises you."

Stan covered her outburst of laughter with a cough. It

was the most personality she'd ever seen Jake's sister demonstrate.

"I'm not posting it." Jake jerked his thumb at Stan. "She is. So, come on. Can she post bond?"

Pasquale's lips thinned as her gaze flicked to Stan and back. "Izzy won't need bail. She's cooling off. The guy dropped the charges."

"Really?" Stan vaulted to her feet. "Can she leave, then?"

"She can do whatever she wants. Until the next time she assaults someone in her own store." Pasquale turned and disappeared, letting the door slam behind her.

Stan looked at Jake. "She definitely didn't get the social skills in your family."

"Yeah. Good thing she's not the bartender."

"So now what?"

"I guess we hang out and wait."

Stan sighed and sat again. It seemed to be hours, but when she checked her phone only fifteen minutes had gone by. When the door opened again, she braced herself for another go-round with the disagreeable trooper.

But it was Izzy who appeared. She was alone. She looked exhausted.

"Hey!" Stan exclaimed, jumping up. "You're free to go?"

But Izzy didn't look delighted to see them. Tossing her long braids over her shoulders, she crossed her arms and glared at Jake. "What is *he* doing here?"

Stan frowned. Izzy's issue with Jake was none of her business. She probably didn't even want to know what had triggered it, especially if it had to do with some torrid love affair between the two of them. But today he'd come at Stan's request to help, and he didn't deserve to be treated like that. She took a step forward, hands settling on hips. "What's he doing here? We came to bail your butt out after we heard you were acting out a *Jerry Springer* episode. That's what he's doing here, and if you continue to be rude, you can call a cab back to Frog Ledge. The dogs are in the truck and we'd like to leave."

"Stan, really, it's fine," Jake started to say, but she shook her head.

"It's not fine. I don't know what the deal with the two of you is, and I'm pretty sure I don't care, but at the very least she can be civil to someone who comes to help her out. Do either of you disagree?" She looked at both of them.

Jake shook his head. Izzy still looked annoyed, but chastised. The dispatcher behind the bulletproof window stared at Stan. When she met his gaze he quickly dropped his head.

"Good. So, are you free to go?"

Izzy nodded.

"Would you like a ride?"

"I'd love one," Izzy drawled.

"Fine. Let's go."

Jake, biting back a smile, rose and headed outside. Stan pushed Izzy in front of her. "You want to tell me what happened?" she asked in a low voice.

"Nah. Later." Izzy shoved her hands in the pockets of her jeans. "It's stupid."

"Well, throwing a chair at someone doesn't seem like the best way to solve a problem," Stan said. "Did you know these people?"

"Sort of." Izzy clammed up as they reached the truck. Jake unlocked the doors and wordlessly opened the passenger side. Izzy climbed in back, trying to fend the dogs off as they threw themselves at her.

Stan settled in the front seat. "I went by the shop. The

dogs were barking upstairs. Your employee told me what happened."

"Mya?" Despite herself, Izzy grinned. Stan caught a glimpse in the rearview mirror. Now that looked like her friend. "Mya was ready to jump right in and help."

"Yeah, she told me."

"So, uh, hey. Thanks for picking me up," Izzy said as Jake swung out into traffic and headed back to Frog Ledge. "Both of you."

"Don't mention it," Jake said, and Stan couldn't tell if he was being sarcastic.

"I can relate," Stan said. "Well, not the chair part. But the being dragged out of the café part. You're lucky they didn't press charges."

"I guess. Whatever, I'm tired of the whole stupid thing." Shutting up abruptly, Izzy leaned back against the seat and closed her eyes. Jake glanced at Stan, who shrugged.

Izzy didn't say another word until they pulled up in front of her place. Leaning forward, she muttered another "thank you" to Jake, then climbed out of the truck.

"Call me later. We can go for a walk or something," Stan said through the open window.

Izzy nodded. "We'll see," she said, and Stan thought she looked incredibly sad. "Thanks again, okay?" And she hurried inside, leaving Stan staring after her.

Chapter 13

All the remaining leaves seemed to have abandoned their trees overnight. When Stan looked out the bedroom window first thing Monday morning, her yard was covered with reds, oranges, and yellows. The sight of them, blown in colorful drifts across the grass, made her clap her hands in delight. It had been years since she had raked a pile of leaves and jumped into them. Her dad used to do it for her and her sister when they were kids. Maybe today she would do that, in her dad's memory.

Nutty jumped up and wedged himself in the window between her and her view of the yard. His fluffy tail tickled her nose.

"Hi," she said. "What did you do with the dogs?"

Nutty refused to answer, so she went looking. Nutty trailed behind her. He looked disappointed when she located Henry and Scruffy on the back porch. Henry lounged on the floor, his fox skin toy hanging out of his mouth. Scruffy nestled up against him adoringly, but bounded to her feet when she saw Stan. Henry woofed at her.

"I'm getting breakfast now. Let's go to our places."

The three obediently followed her to the kitchen, Nutty

leading the way. They sat in their usual spots—Scruffy and Henry right next to each other on the floor, Nutty on the counter. It was a bad habit he'd gotten accustomed to when he first moved in with her. Stan felt bad making him get down. So they compromised: Nutty only got on the counter to eat, and sat in the same spot. No need to spread out the mess.

Stan prepared a bowl for each of them with pureed chicken, vegetables, rice, and calcium powder. Leaving them immersed in their breakfasts, Stan made herself a healthy green smoothie and a hard-boiled egg and ate while reading the latest *Frog Ledge Holler*. After he finished his breakfast, Nutty leapt onto the table and settled down next to her, resting his paw just on the edge of the paper. He often did that—when he wasn't sitting directly on whatever she was trying to read.

The edition was a big one at seven pages. The front page headline announced a meeting at town hall Tuesday night where the council would hold a public hearing on the petition for the property at 82 Main Street. Stan recognized the address. It was the former veterinary clinic that had been damaged earlier in the year. Amara Leonard, her homeopath neighbor, her fiancé Vincent DiMauro, a traditional veterinarian, and the town animal control officer, Diane Kirschbaum, wanted to buy the property. According to Cyril Pierce and the paperwork filed with the town hall, they hoped to create a veterinary practice offering both allopathic and homeopathic treatment, and expand the clinic to add animal sheltering capabilities.

Stan let out a low whistle. "Wow, Nutty. That would be a great thing for Frog Ledge," she said to her cat. Nutty stared at her, blinking his big eyes in acknowledgment. "You think so, too? Good." She nodded approvingly. She was all for it. But she wondered how the town officials felt about it.

It was no secret the town's animal control facility was sorely lacking in both space and quality, but the town powers-that-be probably wouldn't agree because it would cost money to renovate. Tucked away in the back of a large park on the outskirts of town, the facility was difficult for most people to find if they did want to look at the animals. And the quarters, even though Diane kept them clean and as friendly as possible, were old, run down, and dark. Stan felt certain the animals were sad, even though Diane did everything in her power to get them adopted. Yes, an upgraded sheltering facility would do a world of good. But would it have to be separate from the town quarters? Would she run both? Would they be consolidated? Or would this be Diane's personal venture?

Stan hadn't been to a council meeting since she'd moved to Frog Ledge. Tomorrow night seemed like the perfect time to check one out. She'd go, and show her support for the project. Maybe it would even help repair her relationship with Amara.

She flipped the page and scanned the other headlines. A small blurb on Hal Hoffman's untimely death, but no new information. The coroner had ruled it a homicide. Police were investigating. A statement from Trooper Pasquale deemed there to be no public threat, which meant she thought the killer knew Hal. Below the article was Hal's obituary.

The picture was the same as the one that had run the day after the murder. Stan stared at the tanned, smiling face, smoldering eyes, the shadow of stubble apparent on his chin, and wondered what secrets were hiding there. Who had killed him and why?

"What do you think, Nutty?" she asked her cat. "His wife seemed to hate him, his business partners weren't thrilled with him, and he partied a lot. Any number of things from that list could've gotten him killed. And, he may have owed someone money."

Nutty flicked his tail at her and rested his head on Hal's picture. The obituary described Hal as a loving husband, father, son, and brother who had lived in Frog Ledge his entire forty-six years and had grown up on the Happy Cow Dairy Farm, taking it over from his parents, Lester and Camille Hoffman. Lester had passed ten years ago. Camille Hoffman lived in Stowe, one of Frog Ledge's neighboring towns. Stan skimmed the part about Hal being survived by his wife, Emmalee; sons Tyler, age eighteen, Danny, fifteen, Robert, ten, and Joseph, four; a sister, Hillary; and a brother, Lester Jr. Hal had an MBA from the University of Connecticut.

Impressive. Stan didn't know if that was typical for a second- or third-generation farmer, but she guessed it might not be. She had heard people crediting his good business sense, even if he wasn't necessarily into the manual labor. He was also the chairman of the Connecticut Milk Promotion Board, to which he'd been appointed by a local senator. He'd been an avid fisherman and part of a men's hockey league. His funeral service would be held on Wednesday at St. Augustine Catholic Church, right across the green. There would be no calling hours. Burial would be in the Frog Ledge Cemetery.

Well, there were her Wednesday morning plans. She'd have to adjust her baking schedule accordingly. She smiled as she glanced out the window into her backyard at a bird that had just landed at one of her feeders. Six or seven months ago, her Wednesday plans would not have included baking, or even thoughts of baking. Her days used to consist of bolting out of bed, downing nearly a pot of coffee, showering, dressing in a designer suit, and hitting the road. Then, she wouldn't see the light of day for almost another ten or twelve hours. Unless she had a lunch meeting. If someone asked her tomorrow what exactly she'd done for all those hours, every single day for more than ten years, she didn't think she could answer them.

It made her sad to think she'd traded so much of her life for something she'd thought was so important just to learn that it wasn't. But, better late than never. Stan flipped the paper shut and looked at Nutty. He eyed the pieces of yolk that had escaped from her egg. She slid the dish over and let him lick it clean. When he was done, he rubbed his head along her arm as if to say thank you, and jumped down to find a sunny place for a nap.

She collected everyone's dishes and started upstairs to dress in her running gear. Before she could, the phone rang.

"Izzy got arrested yesterday?" Char demanded before Stan could even say hello. "Why didn't anyone call me?"

Stan chuckled. It wasn't like Char could've done anything useful if she had been called. She just wanted to be in the know. "Good morning, Char. And no, the person dropped the charges."

"Huh. Really." Char paused for a minute, probably to stir her Bloody Mary. "I can't imagine what would persuade Izzy to throw a chair at a customer. Did they not like her coffee?"

Similar to what Jake had said. "She actually didn't tell me why, although I don't think that's it. Her employee said the men were asking her questions. I don't think they were normal customers."

Char whistled. "Do you think it's the FBI?"

"The FBI? What would the FBI want with Izzy?" Stan started to laugh it off, then stopped. Stranger things had happened in real life. And what about that movie with the family of American terrorists who lived in a nice neighborhood and blew up the FBI building and framed their neighbor for it? *Arlington Road*. The movie had given her the creeps.

Oh, seriously. What was wrong with her? Izzy wasn't a terrorist.

"Maybe we should find out," Char said.

"Well, I was hoping she'd tell me after things died down, but I haven't been able to get ahold of her."

"That's odd," Char said. "Keep trying. Let me know what I can do."

Stan agreed and hung up. She finished getting ready, pocketed her gloves, popped her earbuds in her ears, and headed outside. Henry and Scruffy tried to follow her out the door.

"Nope. Sorry, guys." The last time she'd tried to take them on a run, Scruffy had spent the first quarter mile trying to make friends with other dogs on the route, and Henry had wanted to stop and take a nap every ten feet. She finally had taken them home and started over solo.

The fall morning air snapped its fingers in her face. Stan took a deep breath, grateful for the weather. She savored the clean air for a moment, then started a slow jog to the green.

When she paused to let a car pass, she heard her name behind her.

"Stan! Good morning!"

Turning, she saw Emmalee Hoffman coming from the back of the house, waving at her.

Shoot. Should've crossed already. Stan pushed the

uncharitable thought out of her mind and waved back. "Morning, Emmalee. How are you?"

Emmalee shrugged, pulling off her hat. "Doing fine. Just working, you know. Anyway, what time are you coming?"

"Coming?" Stan repeated.

"Yes. To work in the office. You are starting today, right?"

"I, um . . . Honestly, Em, I didn't know you needed me today. I have a few things to do this morning and some treat orders to fill."

"Oh." Em fiddled with her hat, swinging it around on her hand. "I'm sorry. I shouldn't have assumed."

"Is, uh, Leigh-Anne around yet? I bumped into her last night and she said she'd be staying at Char's so she's nearby to help you."

Em tried to hide the disdain that passed over her face. "Yes, she sure is," she said. "All moved in and already coming by. Right now she's taking inventory of the farm equipment. Inventory. Can you believe that? Because she thinks there are things we need. Or need to upgrade. I highly doubt she's gonna buy them for us, though."

Oh, boy. Stan could see herself getting caught in the middle of those two personalities. She sighed inwardly but pasted on her best accommodating face. "I'm happy to come later this afternoon."

Em brightened. "Oh, would you? I'm afraid the work has been piling up already. Hal had been so . . . busy lately. Bills need to be paid and I have no idea where some of my feed is. I'd love it if you could."

"Okay, then. I'll see you later."

Em waved and went into the house. Stan jogged across the street, her feet slapping the ground in time to her self-berating thoughts. *Why in the world did you agree to this in the first place, Stan Connor? There's that impulsive streak again.*

The impulsive streak her mother never hesitated to remind her about. Her mother. Despite the situation, Stan bit back a giggle. If she ever told her mother she was helping out on a dairy farm, Patricia Connor would die. It was not a Rhode Island socialite thing to do.

Chapter 14

"So, I got a new order today. Along with all that"—Stan pointed to the handwritten list she'd taped up on the fridge for Brenna, who was in charge of treats while Stan covered the farm—"we need two batches of cat-shaped treats that are cheese-and-veggie-flavored and two batches of apple and cinnamon. No shape preference, although Pookie supposedly has a thing for fire hydrants." A friend of Char's had called this morning begging for dog treats by tomorrow. She said she'd heard everyone raving about them around town and she *must* have some.

It had been a lovely phone call to receive.

Stan laid ingredients out on her counter and handed over the cookie cutters. She'd found a great place near Nikki's house in Rhode Island that sold all shapes and sizes of dog treat cookie cutters. Heaven on earth. She couldn't wait to try out the one shaped like a burger. She wasn't fond of the cat-shaped cutter since she didn't like to think of dogs eating cats, but she'd bought it after a ton of requests for cat-shaped cookies. And for the cats, the store had fish and mice and balls of yarn and birds for shapes, and they were getting new ones in every week.

Brenna shook her head. "Pookie has never gone near a fire hydrant. They just say that because Pookie's a dalmatian."

Stan laughed. "Well, if it makes her happy, let's just use the fire hydrant. So I'll stay while you mix the batter and then I'll head to Em's, okay?"

Brenna pinned her long hair up in a bun and smiled knowingly. "That's fine. I know you'll want to taste the batter."

Stan felt her cheeks grow warm. Was she that transparent? "No, I just . . . the dogs are picky," she finished lamely.

Now Brenna did laugh. "The dogs aren't picky. You are. And there's nothing wrong with that. In fact, I think it's pretty cool. Not many people care about how things taste for dogs, never mind how healthy it is for them. That's why I'm so excited to be working with you. So." She rubbed her hands together. "Where are your mixing bowls?"

An hour later, Stan left the house in a flurry of doggie good-bye kisses. Henry and Scruffy followed her to the door, trying to get her to take them, but soon forgot about her when Brenna called them to lick bowls. Nutty sat on his tree next to the window in the hall. He gave her the paw. Stan stopped to give him a kiss and ruffle his fur. "I'll see you soon, okay? Go wait in the kitchen for some treats."

Nutty gave her face. He did that when she left sometimes. Stan wasn't sure if it meant he didn't like hanging out with the dogs, or if he would miss her. Either way, she was sure all three of them would barely remember her in about half an hour when the treats came out of the oven.

She strolled down the street, enjoying the sights of Halloween. The spirit here was fantastic. Every yard had pumpkins, mums, and cornstalks. The real enthusiasts had orange lights, graveyards, skeleton families, or other spooky accents in their front yards. One house on the other side of the green had small skulls hanging from every bare tree branch, and skeletons guarded the front door. Spiders dangled from webs and jack-o'-lanterns lit up every window as soon as dusk hit.

Stan wore jeans and her silver ballet flats, a snub to Jake and Brenna for their teasing. *Hip-high boots, my rear end.* There were limits to friendship and community, and slinging cow manure fell into that category. Did people really sling cow manure, anyway?

But when she entered the yard and noticed the sign haphazardly leaning against the fence that read CORN MAZE CLOSED UNTIL FURTHER NOTICE, she felt bad. This wasn't about her. A man was dead. His family was in shambles. She took a deep breath and rang the bell at the old farmhouse. No answer. She knocked in case the bell was broken. Nothing. She went into the yard. Samson sat on the grass. Stan stopped to say hello and fished a treat out of her purse. The dog took it and chewed contentedly, then licked her hand. She continued on.

The Hoffmans had a lot of acreage. Directly behind the house was the gated patio where the doggie party had been set up. Beyond it was a substantial yard. It was barren except for an old-style swing set perched unsteadily in the grass, a few kids' toys scattered about, and a bike on its side. And then, the corn maze. It looked less threatening today, but Stan still felt creeped out looking at it.

The other side of their land was the farm. She turned left and hurried toward the cow barns. The sides of the structure were up today, and she could see a row of black and white behinds, tails swinging lazily. Despite herself, she smiled. She liked cows. They were so chill. She remembered hearing stories of cow tippers when she was a kid and wondering how anyone could be so mean.

Yeah, well, that's nothing compared to a dairy farm, Nikki's voice chided in her head.

Stan commanded the voice to silence and moved closer, wondering if she could say hello to one of them. How did cows react when people came near them? She had no idea. While she pondered it, a human head popped up from in between a couple of the largest residents. A young man, barely as tall as the cows, stared at Stan.

"Yes?" he said in halting English. Stan recognized him—it was the guy who had been working the night Hal died.

"Um, hi. I'm here to see Em—Mrs. Hoffman."

He nodded and motioned her to follow him. He led her to the barn where Brenna had sent Danny to put his chain saw away just three nights ago, when everything was different. Pushing open the barn doors, he made a sweeping motion in Stan's direction, as if presenting her to an audience.

Emmalee Hoffman looked up from where she was working on a tractor wheel. She had a wrench in her hand and dirt all over her and Stan wondered again what in God's name would possess anyone to want to own and work on a farm. But, it wasn't really for her to judge. Not to mention she'd just volunteered to work on said farm, and she didn't own it.

"Hey, Em."

"Hi!" Em jumped up, letting the wrench fall with a clatter. "Thanks, Enrico."

Enrico nodded and backed out of the barn.

"Enrico's great," Em said. "If you need anything, just ask him."

Might be tough since he can't speak much English. Stan nodded obediently.

Em paused and pushed a strand of gray-brown hair out of her eyes. She looked like she hadn't slept in a week. "Well, haven't I just lost all track of time. Sorry about that. The tractor wheel is busted. Come on, I'll take you to the office."

Stan forced a smile. "Great."

Em surveyed Stan's outfit. "You should really find a pair of boots to wear, honey," she said, taking in Stan's glittery silver shoes. "You don't want to get those lovely little slippers dirty. And aren't your feet cold? It's chilly outside this time of year."

Stan gritted her teeth, trying not to make it obvious. "Well, yes, but I figured since I would be in the office I wouldn't have to run around in the mud."

Em chewed on her lower lip. "Wait one second." She veered over to a corner of the barn that looked like it could be home to many different species of wildlife. Stan heard clanks and thuds as Em tossed tools and equipment around. She returned looking puzzled. "I was going to give you the spare pair of boots Hal keeps . . ."—she faltered—"kept out here. But they seem to be gone. I wonder who would've taken them." She stared into space for a moment, then shrugged. "They would've been fine for you to wear around the farm. I'm sorry they're not here."

"Oh, Em, don't worry. They probably wouldn't have fit me anyway," Stan said. *Thank God.* "And I really don't think I'm going to need them."

Em waved a callused hand and led Stan out of the barn and around the back of the house. "Farm life is so unpredictable. You never know what can come up." She stopped in front of a door next to the bulkhead. Fumbling in the pocket of her overalls for a key, she unlocked it and pushed it open. But before they could enter, Stan heard someone calling her name.

"Yoo-hoo! Stan! Emmy!"

Stan turned to see Leigh-Anne Sutton making her way across the grass. She wasn't wearing her heels today, but she still looked like a fashion plate in her jeans, North Face jacket, and pink designer hiking boots. "What are you girls up to?"

Stan could feel Em's whole body clench, even standing a few feet away. She turned to face Leigh-Anne with more of a grimace than a smile.

"Taking Stan to the office. She's starting today."

"Fantastic!" Leigh-Anne clapped her hands. "I'd love to help. Please let me know what I can do."

If possible, Em stiffened even more. "It's mostly a matter of getting organized. After that, Stan will be fine. She comes from financial services, you know," she said, as if Leigh-Anne should be impressed.

"That's right! I do remember you saying that." Leigh-Anne leaned forward, her eyes alight with interest. "Stockbroker? Investment banker? Do tell!"

The truth sounded lame. "Actually, I did PR." She smiled. "Not terribly exciting, I know. Certainly not like working on Wall Street."

"Oh, but it still must have been wonderful. I think that whole world is so exciting. Money makes our country run, after all." Leigh-Anne glanced at Em, who was watching with disdain. "Well, I don't want to keep you, though I would love to hear more about that. So, Emmy. Let's sit later and talk about what you need most from me. I'm at your service, after all."

Em sniffed. "I need help with the stalls. But you're going

to get those pink boots all dirty walking around in this muck."

"These?" Leigh-Anne glanced down with a look of surprise, then chuckled. "Emmy. These are work boots. Just because they're pretty doesn't mean they can't get the job done." She winked at Stan. "We can't let our duties get in the way of our fashion sense, right, Stan?"

Stan couldn't help but smile. She agreed completely. It vanished quickly when Em turned dagger eyes on her. Behind Em, Leigh-Anne rolled her eyes.

"I'll go get to work. Come find me if you need me. Remember, I'm here to help. Em set me up in a little office over in the milking parlor." With that, she waggled her fingers at Stan much like she had at the bar Saturday when she made her exit with Tony Falco, and turned back in the direction of the cows.

Emmalee muttered something under her breath that sounded suspiciously like *God help us,* then motioned to Stan to follow her into the office.

"Here we are," she announced. "Where everything happens."

Stan stepped in behind her and looked around. The room was about the size of her guest bedroom closet, and that was being generous. It looked like it had been a laundry room at one time. The hookups were still on the far wall. The linoleum floor was cracked in most places and missing in some. Stan could see dust bunnies skittering along, pushed around by the breeze Em had let in. Boxes were stacked along one wall. Someone had slashed the words "Files" in black Sharpie across the front of each. The wall itself looked like it used to be white, but was now grayish. An out-of-commission washing machine was jammed in front of another door—a feeble attempt to block the entrance to what Stan presumed was the main house. There was a desk shoved up against the front wall. It looked like an antique, what Stan could see of it. Piles of paper and folders were stacked so high they tilted dangerously. One wrong move and they would all go crashing to the floor.

Em followed Stan's gaze around and shrugged, her smile sheepish. "I'm sorry, I didn't get in here to clean yet," she said. Her tone was light, but Stan could feel the seething behind the words. If Hal was alive, Em probably would've torn him a new one at the condition of the room. Stan wondered how long it had been since Hal had actually worked in this office.

"Don't worry about it. I can help get things organized while I'm here." *Why do I keep digging this hole deeper?*

"I don't want you to waste your time," Em said.

"Em. I would have to at least dig through the files on top of the desk to get anything done," Stan pointed out. "So just tell me what I'm supposed to be doing and I'll tackle it as I can, okay?"

To her dismay, Em's eyes filled with tears. "I don't deserve wonderful friends like you," she said, her voice wobbly.

Stan hated seeing people cry. "Oh, Em, of course you do. Listen. Why don't you go back outside and get your stuff done. I'm sure the kids will be home soon, right? And in the meantime, I'll just start organizing some things." How hard could it be? Find some bills, write some checks. Maybe call and order some feed for the cows. Simple. And this way, she could stay away from the actual farm operations, and possibly avoid Nikki's wrath.

"Of course, the kids." Em wiped her eyes with the back of her hand. "I just have to go get that tractor squared away. Ted is coming over later to oversee the evening milking.

Roger has been here since five this morning—I can't ask him to stay too late. And Tyler is doing what he can to help out. He's not much for getting dirty, though. Maybe he can help you sort through some things in here?"

"Sure, whatever works," Stan said. She was anxious to get going on a few tasks. She really didn't want to be at the farm all night.

"Okay." Em took a deep breath and pulled her gloves back on. "I have to go to the funeral home and drop off a suit for Hal to wear. The funeral's Wednesday." She looked like she would rather stay here and scoop cow manure. "Do you have any experience with funeral homes?"

Please don't let her ask me to plan a funeral, too. I only do animal parties. "No. When my dad died, my mother handled the details."

"I'm sorry to hear that. Was it recent?"

"No, almost eight years ago now." Had it really been that long?

They were both silent for a minute, thinking of the ones who had left them. Stan wondered if Em's thoughts of Hal were as generous as hers for her dad.

"Well," Em said briskly. "I'll send Tyler in shortly. He's just finishing something up for me in the house. But he'll know the most important vendors to pay and the other critical tasks."

"Great," Stan said. "In the meantime, I'll . . . try to find the desk."

Chapter 15

Only one of the three piles of papers had fallen when Em shut the door behind her. Already a small victory. Stan gritted her teeth again—she had to stop doing that—and yanked the chair away from the desk, hoping not to see bugs scurrying for safety.

She didn't, so she bent and picked up the first stack. An invoice on top from Sal's Feed and Grain for $800. An electric bill. Her eyes widened at the amount: $4,567.93. That had to be a mistake . . . didn't it? The door slammed behind her and she jumped.

Leigh-Anne Sutton gave her a sheepish smile. "I hope I'm not interrupting, but I just didn't feel right not offering to help." She glanced over her shoulder as if afraid Emmalee would throw her out if she discovered her in the office. "Is there anything I can do?"

"That's very nice of you to ask. Honestly, I don't know." With a helpless laugh, she looked around. "I guess I have to sort through the paperwork first."

Leigh-Anne gazed doubtfully at the stacks. "That looks like a big job."

"Sure does," Stan said. "If you're not busy—which it

sounds like you are—you could always help me with this. But if you have other things to do—"

"Nonsense," Leigh-Anne interrupted. "I know what it's like to be put in this situation with no guidance. In my case, I took over for my husband when he passed away. It was a learning process, and a lot of it was painful. If I can help even make sense of anything for you, I should do that."

"Okay," Stan said. "Great, then. Want to take this stack?" She passed over a pile of files.

Leigh-Anne took them from her. They worked in silence for a while, creating piles of statements, old bills, current bills. One invoice was addressed to Pristine Fields Dairy Farm, Attn. Ted Brahm. Stan held it out to Leigh-Anne. "What do I do about this?"

Leigh-Anne studied it. "Ted must've bought some parts for Hal for the feed truck. That has to be paid. Looks like it's overdue, though." She pursed her lips and sighed. "Ted hates overdue bills. That should go at the top of the stack."

Stan put the invoice to the side. "Is that common? In co-ops, I mean. To buy stuff for each other."

"Sometimes. Different partnerships do things differently. In our group . . ." She trailed off, looked behind her again. Dropped her voice a notch. "Our group could be difficult. We don't all see eye to eye."

"But it works—doesn't it?"

"It works . . . in different ways. Take Ted, for example. So laid back. Loves dairy farming. Perfectly content to let Hal run things. Now, Peter, on the other hand . . ." She shook her head. "Peter fought Hal tooth and nail every step of the way. He only signed on because his farm was going under. He had no choice. And his wife was about to kill him." She stopped, covering her mouth with her hand.

"What a poor choice of words. Anyway, you know what I mean."

"Sounds like Asher fought with Hal, too," Stan said.

"Asher." Leigh-Anne smiled. "It's complicated with Asher. He's very rigid. Put it this way: Hal wants to make a buck. Asher wants to do everything right. You see how they could disagree?"

"I do." Stan placed an empty folder in a new pile for recycling. "How did you feel about Hal's style of running the business?"

"Oh, putting me on the spot now, eh?" Leigh-Anne crossed her pink boots and smiled. "Honestly, I understood Hal. Businessman through and through. Smart, smart, smart, too. He'll be missed."

They both spun as the door clattered open again. Tyler Hoffman walked in. His gaze went to Leigh-Anne first, assessing, then slid away without acknowledging her. He looked at Stan, nodded. "S'up."

"Hey, Tyler. How's it going?" *Why am I asking this kid how he's doing when his father was brutally murdered a few days ago?*

The boy looked different than he had Friday night after the murder. He had been jazzed up then, worried about his mother, full of angst and impatient to see the police solve the case. Today, he looked weary. Beaten down. Like he'd rather be anyplace but where he was.

But he didn't articulate any of that. "Going fine. My mom said you needed help, but it looks like you have it."

"Oh, no," Leigh-Anne said. "I was just keeping Stan company until you got here. I have to get back to a few other things anyway." She stood, handed Stan her remaining folders. "Thanks again for helping." And she slipped out, catching the door behind her so it didn't slam.

Stan watched her go. Tyler didn't. He looked around the room the same way his mother had. He looked like Emmalee. His brown hair, cropped short, was her color, and he had the same facial features. Full lips, big, dark, expressive eyes. Stan figured Em had been attractive, at least when she was younger. Now, she looked old beyond her years. But her son was very handsome.

Tyler shook his head ever so slightly and headed for the desk. "I'm not real sure what my dad did in here."

"Does he have a computer?" Stan asked.

Tyler looked around again. "He had a laptop. It's not here?" He peered around the files on the desk's surface, checked in the rickety drawers. No laptop. Tyler swore under his breath, then caught himself. "Sorry."

"I have been known to use foul language on occasion," Stan said dryly. "No apologies necessary. So. What do we do if there's no computer?"

"I'm gonna go check in the house," Tyler said. "But if you want to look through those papers for any recent bills, that's where I would start. Then we can figure out if they ever got paid. I doubt it. I think my dad was a little behind."

"So he wouldn't have marked them 'Paid' or filed them somewhere special?" Stan asked.

"Doubt it."

Well then. "He must've been busy," Stan said.

Tyler smirked. "Yeah. He was busy all right. None of it had to do with the farm, though." He closed his mouth abruptly, as if he'd said too much. "Be right back." Instead of using the door, he vaulted over the washing machine and into the basement, giving Stan a glimpse into the darkness beyond. Stan heard him pounding up the stairs.

She busied herself with the first stack. A lot of the papers were packing slips. She separated those into a pile with a sticky note she'd found in one of the drawers and wrote "Toss?" The monthly bills—and there were a lot, most over-due—went into their own pile. Repairs, food, gasoline, the insane electric bill. After Stan was sure she'd gotten all of them, she went through and totaled them up using the cal-culator on her iPhone. When she hit the equal sign, her jaw dropped. The farm owed about fifteen thousand dollars by the end of the month. Less than two weeks away.

No wonder Em was hosting doggie birthday parties and running corn mazes.

Stan picked up the top folder of another pile. It was crammed with bank statements. She glanced at the top statement and checked the balance in the checking account. Nine thousand dollars. That wouldn't cover the bills. Per-haps there had been deposits since then. Stan put the folder into its own pile. She looked around for a filing cabinet. Nothing. *How did they keep any records around here?* Silly question. She was looking at the system they used—and it was sorely lacking. And since no one could seem to figure out how Hal had been attending to business, exactly, she was limited in how she could help.

So, she'd do what she could.

She went through the next few folders and found notes from board meetings with the other Happy Cow farmers. Those looked like they might be interesting, so she tucked them under her coffee mug to remind her to go back and read. A pamphlet of information on large animal veterinar-ians. Hal must have been considering changing providers. She found drawings of the buildings on the farm, and draw-ings of what looked like new buildings. Maybe Hal had planned to upgrade pieces of the facility, or expand it. Maybe the co-op was doing well, and Hal saw that as his farm's future. Stan wondered what Emmalee thought of that. She didn't get the vibe from Emmalee that she was overly excited to be milking by committee.

It was another ten minutes or so before Tyler returned with only a checkbook in his hand. "I'm gonna have to track down the laptop," he said. "It might be in his car. How long are you here?"

"I'm not sure." Stan checked her watch. It was already four. Did she get to knock off at five like the rest of the population of office folks? "Did he back up to a cloud? That way, if you have the passwords, it can be accessed from any computer."

That smirk again. "I don't think my dad was that computer savvy. But I'll ask my mom. In the meantime, here's a checkbook. But I doubt there's money in the account."

"I just saw the last bank statement. If everything is reconciled, there's some, but not enough to cover."

"Don't count on it."

"You mean there's more than it says? That's great news."

"No, I mean don't count on there being much money in there in the first place."

Stan's mouth dropped open. "What do you mean? How do I pay the bills if there's no money? How will the farm run?"

"My mom probably thinks there's plenty of money. I'm telling you how it really is. There probably isn't any."

"How do you know this?"

"I just do."

Stan watched him carefully. He spoke very matter-of-factly. Stan couldn't help but wonder if he was the reason there was no money. If Hal didn't pay attention, which seemed to be a fair observation, would his oldest son take advantage? She immediately pushed the thought out of her head. She didn't know this boy and she had no right to think he would hurt his family and their business like that. Then again, when you considered all the crazy stuff you heard on the news every day, nothing was a stretch. Or, was he telling her that Hal had spent all the money?

He watched her, those dark eyes unreadable. Stan suddenly felt uncomfortable in this tiny room alone with this angry boy. And, he was blocking the exit. Unless she wanted to vault over the washing machine.

When she spoke, she tried to make her voice low and soothing. "Tyler. If there's something your mother needs to know—"

"My mother doesn't need to know anything," he burst out. "She's got enough going on. Besides, she should know how bad it's gotten. She just doesn't want to admit it. Why do you think we have a corn maze now? And those parties where she rents out the yard? It's absurd. Every day she works on this damn farm. For nothing." Tyler's eighteen-year-old frustration with his family was clear. Stan could also tell he'd left his teenage years behind a long time ago. It couldn't have been easy, growing up like this.

"I don't think it's for nothing, Tyler. She seems to love it here."

"Yeah, well, she does," he said bitterly. "And I don't get it. She loves it more than he ever did, and it was his family farm. She's getting too old for this crap. She has to get a knee replaced. We don't even have health insurance."

"No health insurance?" Stan was horrified. How did they take care of the kids? "Did your dad at least have a life insurance policy?"

Tyler jerked his shoulders in a shrug. "My mother won't talk about it."

"Maybe she's not ready. This has to be killing her. Killing all of you, actually."

Tyler watched her for a long moment, appraising. "She has to be ready," he said. His voice was harsh. "This is her reality. I loved my dad, but he had other things going on. Things that didn't include us. I think he hoped those things were his ticket out of here. But he never made it."

Chapter 16

Stan walked home slowly as dusk fell around Frog Ledge, her mind spinning as she replayed her conversation with Tyler Hoffman. The boy was sharp, and he seemed to have a lot of insights into his father's life that even Em may not have had. Would he eventually share those with her if she kept coming around? Clearly this kid understood his parents did not have a storybook marriage, testimony that would not bode well for Emmalee if Jessie Pasquale continued down her current path of investigation—which she would have to, if that's where the evidence led.

As Stan climbed her front porch steps, she heard Henry's and Scruffy's frantic barking from inside. It made her smile.

Stan pushed the door open and had to brace herself to withstand Henry's bulk as he launched himself at her, his tail wagging and his tongue nearly drowning her. Scruffy, much smaller in size, had to settle for standing up against Stan's thigh and *wooing* at her.

"Hi, guys! I missed you, too." She dropped to her knees and gathered the dogs in hugs. "Where's Nutty?"

"Begging for treats." Brenna appeared in the doorway. She'd found one of Stan's aprons and carried a wooden spoon. "The treats came out rockin'. Wanna try one?"

Stan laughed and got to her feet. "That's good news. I'd love to try one. It's funny; I know they're made with ingredients humans eat, but I don't usually tell people I sample the animal treats. It makes me think of that saying about people who don't save for retirement and have to eat Alpo when they're old."

Brenna stared at her for a second. "You're kinda weird."

"Yeah, I know. I'm good with it."

"Jake's kinda weird, too, so it's a good match." Brenna winked and turned to go back into the kitchen.

"Hang on a second." Stan hurried after her, the dogs trotting obediently behind her. "What's that supposed to mean?"

"Oh, you know. You two will eventually stop dancing around each other." Brenna slid a tray of cookies out of the oven.

"How do you—" Stan was about to argue the point—she'd never admitted to anyone that she sort of liked Jake—when she noticed the batches and batches of treats heaped on the counters. "Holy cookies. How many batches did you bake?"

"I got a little carried away," Brenna admitted. "They were coming out so good. So I foraged in your cabinets and came up with a few more experiments. Nutty and the dogs have been willing guinea pigs. But I think all the orders are covered. And some extras. Maybe I can bring a few home for Duncan."

"Of course. Wow, Bren. Thank you. I didn't expect you to bake *all* of them." Stan saw Nutty then, lounging on his side on her kitchen table, waiting for the next kind to be done. He lazily cleaned his paws, eyes not meeting Stan's.

"How many cookies did you have, Nutter? Jeez. You guys sure know how to party when Mom's not home."

"Yeah, they like a good party. So how was Em's?"

Stan wasn't sure how to answer that. "She set me up in the office, which looked like Hal hadn't set foot in it in a year. Leigh-Anne came in to help. Then Tyler showed up and Leigh-Anne left in a hurry. Tyler realized the laptop was missing and went on a mad search for it. Couldn't find it. So I ended up sorting through the piles of paperwork and pulling the bills that needed paying. But when I asked how they wanted me to pay them, he told me there probably wasn't money in the account. It was very strange."

"Really?" Brenna turned the oven off. "Wow. I knew things were bad but . . ." She shook her head. "I know you're not supposed to speak ill about the dead and stuff, but I'm sorry. Hal didn't deserve his family. He was a jerk."

"Yeah, I got that from you yesterday. What was he doing with all their money?"

Brenna kept her back to Stan and pulled a batch of treats out of the oven. "Who knows. Probably spending it on girl-friends. Definitely gambling. He went to the casinos at least once every week. And 'investing' in real estate." She spat "investing" like it was dirty.

"How many people in town agree with your assessment?" Stan tried to keep her voice light, but her brain had accelerated into overtime. If Hal wasn't popular, that should widen the suspect pool pretty quickly. And that might save Em—unless she really did it.

"Not enough," Brenna said bitterly. "He had quite the following. But there were some who saw right through him.

Look, I just know he didn't treat his family right. I babysat for them, remember? I saw a lot of things no one probably thought I saw."

Stan pushed a bit. "So did your sister get what she needed from you about Em?"

Brenna snorted. "My sister needs to get a life."

Stan stifled a chuckle. A few months ago, she'd shared exactly the same sentiment, but it probably wasn't wise to voice that. "She's just doing her job, Bren. And it seemed like she was trying to find every way possible to alibi Em. I don't think she really believes Em would kill her own husband."

Or maybe Jessie did believe it. Stan didn't know. For her, it was hard to imagine, despite the fact Stan hadn't known Em that long. But Em looked like such an *ordinary* person. Then again, just because someone lived in an idyllic small town and sold yummy cheese didn't mean she couldn't have a dark side. Another thing Stan had learned the hard way when she moved to Frog Ledge. But now the thought freaked her out. She imagined being trapped in that tiny office, no exit besides jumping over a washing machine through a doorway into an unfamiliar house, with Em deciding she had to protect herself. . . .

Stan shook the thoughts out of her head. Her imagination was going wild.

Brenna had turned back to the counter, and now she stacked cooled treats in containers. Her movements were almost manic. "Em is one of the sweetest people I know. Her life isn't easy. Her kids are a handful. Danny's always in trouble at school and Robert has some learning disabilities. And Joseph is still so young. . . ." She shook her head.

"She doesn't deserve this. Although I personally wouldn't blame her for murdering that man."

Tell me how you really feel. "Brenna. If there's any chance—"

"No way," Brenna interrupted, seemingly insulted at the insinuation. "Of course Em wouldn't do such a thing. I'm just *saying* she had every *reason* to." Her carefully enunciated words suggested Stan was even more coldhearted than Brenna's sister.

But Stan sensed Brenna was holding something back. "What's up, Bren? Something else is bothering you."

Brenna's hands stilled, hovering over the top container. She turned slowly, not quite meeting Stan's eyes. "Nothing. I can't say."

Stan got up and perched on the edge of her counter so Brenna would have to look at her. "You can tell me. I won't say anything. Unless, of course, you tell me you know who killed Hal." She was only half kidding, but grew alarmed when Brenna's eyes welled with tears.

"Maddy called me. After Jessie went in to talk to them. She didn't know what to do." Brenna sniffled, grabbed a paper towel and blew her nose. "She didn't tell Jessie, but she went outside for a smoke that day. When Hal died. She saw Em leave, but Em left her car in the parking lot and took off on foot back down the street."

"Okay," Stan said slowly. "To where?"

"She doesn't know." Brenna wiped at her eyes with the towel then threw it at the trash can. Sighed when she missed it and bent over to pick it up. "I promised her I wouldn't say anything. Please don't say anything to anyone."

Stan thought about this. Had Em stashed her car, walked home, and killed her husband? Then hurried over to her parent-teacher meeting? "Was she having car trouble, maybe?"

"Oh." Brenna visibly brightened. "Maybe!"

Stan didn't point out that at some point Em must have driven the car away. Unless no one had noticed a tow truck in the parking lot. Regardless, she didn't know if she wanted to continue down this path. She filed the information away as "potentially useful" and changed the subject. "What new kinds did you make?"

Brenna hesitated a moment, then her shoulders relaxed. "I tried blueberry yogurt and carrot ginger. Oh, and apple pie."

"Those sound delicious." Stan was impressed. "You just came up with the recipes on your own?"

Brenna shrugged. "Thought I'd experiment. Hope it's okay. I checked all the ingredients to make sure they were safe for dogs."

"It's great," Stan assured her. "We can bring some to Char and Ray's open house next weekend." With all the tourists coming through the area, Char and Ray wanted to showcase the farm and help boost the local economy. They were serving food and conducting tours, and having a sale on the alpaca clothing they sold. And they figured if they could get people to check in at the B and B, they could send them along to the farmers' market, Izzy's café, and some of the other local shops.

"You want me to come, too?"

"If you're not working at the bar, I'd love for you to come."

Brenna smiled, finally. "I'm not working until Saturday night."

"Good, because the open house is from ten to two. Maybe we can pick up some new orders."

"You'll need to borrow my brother's kitchen at the rate you're going," Brenna said.

Jake again. It always seemed to come back to Jake. *What the heck,* Stan decided. "So what's the deal with your brother, anyway?"

"What do you mean?" Brenna blinked innocently at her.

"I've heard about his . . . dating habits, but I've never seen him with anyone. Not that I'm paying that much attention," she hastened to add.

"So you heard he's a player?" Brenna chuckled as she wiped the counter down. "I'm not sure who told you that, but nothing could be further from the truth. I think a lot of women wished he was a player." She tossed the sponge, and it sailed with a splat to land in Stan's sink.

"Really?"

"Yes. He doesn't even go out that often. He's always at the bar. And I know, 'cause I live and work with him." Stan could sense that fiery Irish temper brewing again. "He does his own thing. He dated someone from college for a long time, but she never wanted to stick around here, and he always did. They did a long distance thing for a while and it didn't pan out." She shrugged. "Don't get me wrong—he goes out here and there. But I don't recall anyone who made it past date two. There's plenty of other people I'd call players before my brother, believe me." Her tone went sour on that note, and Stan couldn't help but wonder if Hal Hoffman was back on Brenna's mind. "Who told you that, anyway?"

Stan didn't want to throw Izzy under the bus. "I don't know. I just remember hearing it when I first moved here. I shouldn't be listening to people I don't even know."

They finished putting the treats away in silence, each left to their own thoughts. Stan's mind wandered away from

Jake and back to the murdered farmer. Had he really been out every night, partying and boozing it up? Seeing other women? If that were true, the whole town should know it. Or at least a few really plugged-in townsfolk.

She was willing to bet Char had some intel. Maybe she'd see if she and Ray wanted company for dinner tonight.

Chapter 17

"A lawsuit? His own brother? Wow." Stan scooped up another spoonful of steaming hot New Orleans shrimp gumbo—Char's specialty and Stan's favorite request when she had dinner with them—and followed it up with a piece of corn bread.

"Oh yeah. Those two never missed an opportunity to be nasty to each other." Ray wiped his mouth with his napkin and tipped his chair back so the front legs lifted off the floor. "See, Lester and Hal parted ways on the farm before Hal created the co-op piece. And really, that's been more fruitful than just running the farm had been. Lester was always angry that he didn't get a piece of it."

"And he turned their mother against Hal, too," Char chimed in from the counter where she was checking on the monkey bread, Stan's other favorite. "How's your food, Stan?"

"Delicious, as always." Stan patted her tummy. "I've had to double my exercise routine since moving here. Thank you so much for cooking for me."

Stan always marveled at Char's domestic skills. From the

time Stan had put in a casual phone call to her friends around six, Char had whipped up her favorite dishes, set the table like it was a special occasion, and had martinis ready and waiting on ice. A fire crackled pleasantly in the kitchen fireplace. Soft jazz played through the sound system piped throughout the house. And it was barely eight.

The two couples staying at the B and B had gone out for the evening. Leigh-Anne Sutton, already settled in for her indefinite stay, had also gone off somewhere, so it was just the three of them. Although dinner wasn't included in a stay, people loved Char's cooking so much they usually joined them for meals instead of venturing out. The food, atmosphere, and company were all lovely. If she didn't love her little house so much, Stan would move in. The place was so darn cozy and . . . Southern. She surprised herself with the thought. She'd always preferred living alone. It was another reason why she and Richard had lasted so long. He was set in his ways and she was set in hers, and they had been careful not to rock the boat.

Now things seemed different.

"Don't mention it," Char said in response to her thanks. "Look at Savannah! She looks wonderful." Char gazed at her yellow Lab, curled up contentedly in the corner after wolfing down the organic local beef and vegetable dinner Stan had brought her. "Her tummy problems and skin allergies are nearly gone. You are a miracle worker with your food, missy."

Stan blushed. "You're too nice."

"She's telling the truth," Ray said.

Still not great at taking compliments, Stan changed the subject. "You said Hal's brother turned his mother against Hal? How did he do that?"

"I'm not so sure that's true, dear." Ray liked to discuss

other people's business almost as much as his wife. "Hal had a tendency to . . . alienate his loved ones. His momma was no exception. Plus, she's a tough old bird. Not easily swayed. Even by her own sons. Hal at least was charismatic, bless his soul. Lester, not very."

Char plunked the tray of monkey bread down on the table. "Lester's just plain nasty. Y'all are delusional if you think otherwise, Raymond."

Ray held his hands in front of him in surrender and let his chair fall to the ground. "No argument there, dear."

Char nodded, satisfied that he'd agreed with her. "Want coffee, Stan? I've been working on a delicious Irish coffee recipe I found. It's taken me a few tries to perfect it, but the trials have been fun." She winked.

Stan slurped the rest of her gumbo and broke another corner off a piece of corn bread. She'd go for a run tomorrow, but she couldn't resist loading up on Char's delicious food. "I'm about to be really full, so I'll take a rain check on the coffee. Not the monkey bread," she said around her mouthful. "So Hal didn't get along with his family?"

"No. Well, his sister is harmless. But Lester and his mother, forget it. And Emmy had no use for them either," Char said. "Emmy's a very generous woman, but she really disliked those in-laws."

"What happened with the lawsuit?"

"Still pending," Ray said. "But I guess now he'll be fighting Em."

"What about the Happy Cow co-op? What happens to that now?"

"Well, I don't think anything, except they might choose to vote on a new president. I think the leadership defaults to Emmalee, but I would venture she doesn't want any part of it." Ray snagged a piece of monkey bread and popped a

chunk into his mouth. "That was Hal's baby. Emmy thought
it was nonsense. In her mind, it was more people to deal
with, more decisions other people had to weigh in on.
Emmy's a private person. I may be speaking out of school
here"—he glanced around guiltily, as if expecting someone
to be listening—"but she has been very resistant to the
whole thing."

"What other choice does she have?" Stan asked. "She
needs the income, clearly."

"I believe she does," Ray said. "My opinion, it's a point
of pride for her. She wants to be able to say she and Hal
made a good go of their farm. I always said, kudos to Hal.
He didn't want to do the dirty work but understood he
needed to keep the farm, and this was a way to bring in
more income without the headaches of expansion. And truth
is, the farmers need each other. And for all their spats, that
group is dedicated to farming."

"So they don't get along?"

"More gumbo, Stan, before you dig into the bread?"
Char called from the counter. It was the time of night when
she drank more martinis and pushed more food on people.
Stan felt her stomach groan in protest.

"No. Please. I have to rest. Ray, you were saying?"

"I think they get along well enough." Ray shrugged. "It's
like any business. Some don't see eye to eye, but most are
out for the common good. I'm curious, though, to see how
Emmy will handle it. Especially with Leigh-Anne taking
such a proactive role. She's got a head for business, too, that
one. Like Hal, she stays out of the muck and digs into the
money."

Stan hesitated. She wanted to talk about Em being in the
state police's sights, but didn't want the news all over town.

Curiosity won out. "It sounds like Em might have to explain where she was the day of the murder. Have you heard that?"

Ray and Char glanced at each other. Ray sighed and snapped one of his suspender straps. "I sure was afraid of that."

"The spouse is always the first in line as a suspect," Char added. "Goodness, Ray, don't ever go and get yourself murdered. I couldn't stand the scrutiny!"

Stan waited for the withering look. Instead, Ray nodded thoughtfully. "Of course, dear. That would be very inconsiderate."

Stan stifled a giggle. She'd never met a man like Ray. That was probably because there wasn't another man like Ray, anywhere in the world. "Do you think she could've done it? I heard Hal was . . . not the best husband."

Ray leaned forward in his chair, his eyes wide. "Emmy? Oh, goodness, no. And Hal was just a typical Irish boy. Sowing his oats."

Char sent him a dirty look over her shoulder. "I agree that Emmy didn't do it. She doesn't have time to go to jail for that kind of nonsense. She would simply ignore him until they could part ways."

"Really? You don't think she could've had a dark side?"

Char giggled. "Everyone has a dark side, honey. That's not how Em would use hers. Trust me."

Kelly Clarkson ran through Stan's head. She decided to let that go. "You don't think Hal was that bad then, Char?"

Char snorted. "I didn't say that. I'd probably have killed him if I were married to him, but I'm a different kind of lady than Emmalee. Right, sweetheart?"

"Righto, dear," Ray responded.

"I thought so," Char muttered. "Have y'all been over to

help Emmy out yet, Stan?" She mixed herself a new martini, using her long green fingernail as a stirrer.

"I actually went over today. Things are . . . a bit disorganized."

"Well, that's not a surprise," Ray said, at the same time Char sighed and said, "I was afraid of that."

Stan looked from one to the other. "Why?"

"Well, that's just Hal's way," Char said, pausing to sip her drink. "And Emmy got tired of picking up after him. She started letting things slip, just like he did. But now it's gotten out of hand. I hope she lets Leigh-Anne help her. But it's good you'll be in there helping with the day to day details."

"Hal was a phenomenal businessman, but he counted on other people to keep track of the details," Ray added. "He's what I believe you corporate types would call the 'idea guy.' But he was running low on detail people. Em didn't have time to keep track of all that and run the farm while Hal was out working on new deals."

"New deals? Like what?" Stan was intrigued.

Char made a tsk-ing sound. "He had more deals than Carter had liver pills. Go on, eat your monkey bread while it's still warm, Stan."

Stan couldn't help it—she burst out laughing. She hadn't heard that saying since her dad passed away. Impulsively, she got up and kissed Char's cheek on her way to put her plate in the sink. "I would love some monkey bread. Thanks, Char."

"Our Hal loved to try new money-making schemes," Ray said with affection. "Some worked well, like the co-op. And the gift shop out near the school. Others, like the rehabbing, well, that didn't work as well."

"Rehabbing? What do you mean?" Stan slid back in her

chair and accepted the new plate of food. Her stomach was already screaming in protest. She should run home to shed some of it, but she hadn't worn running shoes. And she'd probably throw up.

"Hal got it in his head that he would help out the local economy—and his own wallet, I'm sure—and started buying some of the old buildings in town. Had grand plans to fix them up and turn them into wonderful places. He had visions of establishments like Jake's bar, for example, and a new movie theater. He was convinced if there were enough fun new places to attract younger folks, the entire town would be revitalized. Can't say his vision was a bad one. He was passionate about it," Ray said with affection. "And he focused on people with new ideas, who hadn't been around town forever, which I'm sure angered some of the old-timers. Even had a deal going with Izzy Sweet."

"With Izzy?" Stan stared at him. "What deal?"

"Now, this was some time ago, remember. Funny enough, a bookstore. Funny because Hal wasn't much of a reader. Izzy loves books. And it went so well with her café. But our locals, God bless 'em, they didn't see any use for it. 'We got all we need,' they liked to say. People around here, well, it takes them a while to accept change. If they accept it at all."

"So what happened to the deal?" Stan asked.

"We're not really sure," Ray said. "It never came to light. Hal lost a bunch of money. I'd suspect our Izzy did, too. But for all the things she tells us, she never did speak of that again."

"Huh." Stan sat back, thoughtful. "She never mentioned it to me either." *Was that why she'd been so distraught at the news of Hal's death? Was it a money thing?*

Stan didn't get to push them on it, because the front door

blew open and Leigh-Anne Sutton swept in, offering a high-wattage smile when she saw the three of them around the table.

"Good evening! Is this a party? I do love parties! Hello there, Stan! Survived the farm, I see?"

Stan smiled. "I did."

"Did y'all have a nice evening? Come, sit, join us." Char rose and began clearing plates. "Who wants a game of cards?" she asked.

They were done talking about Izzy, apparently. Stan wondered if there was more to the story and neither Char nor Ray wanted to tell it—or didn't want to tell it in front of Leigh-Anne.

"I could go for some rummy," Ray said, clearly up for the change in topic. "How about you, Stan?"

"Thank you, but I can't. I still have a few things to do tonight. There's a lot to starting your own business, I'm finding out."

"Ha! Don't we know it," Leigh-Anne declared. "What is your business again?"

Stan explained Pawsitively Organic Pet Food.

"She makes the best food ever for dogs," Char piped in. "Saved our Savannah's tummy."

"Really? What do you prepare?" Leigh-Anne propped her chin in her hands and gazed at Stan, as if fascinated by the whole business.

"I do meats, veggies, and usually rices. Or fruits. I'm learning more, so I'm experimenting more."

"Where do you buy your meats?"

"I've been picking them up at the food co-op as I need them."

"Well, I'll tell you. If you're interested in buying straight from a farm, please consider Stubenville Farms." She beamed. "It's Zen Garden's sister farm," she added.

"You have two farms?" Char asked. "I had no idea."

"I do. Both from my husband's family, God rest his soul." She crossed herself. "I lost him last year. That's when I inherited the farms."

"I'm sorry to hear that," Char said.

"Thank you, thank you. Yes, it's been hard." Leigh-Anne sighed. "I'd never been part of the farming piece, really. Just helping out with business plans and some marketing. But I had to step up and learn pretty quickly, because I didn't want to disappoint him. Anyway, Stubenville is a meat farm, obviously. The dairy farm is separate."

Ugh, was Stan's first thought. She wasn't a meat eater herself, but all her customers were carnivores. And the meat, as long as it was organic and grass fed, would be better for them.

"All free range, excellent quality," Leigh-Anne said, as if she'd read Stan's mind. "Let's talk."

"That sounds great," Stan said, glancing at her watch. "I'm going to get going, okay, Char?"

"Of course, dear. Let me pack up some monkey bread."

A few minutes later, while her hosts and Leigh-Anne settled in for some Irish coffee and that game of rummy, Stan let herself out the front door of the B and B with a package of leftovers and a lot of questions. Izzy and Hal in business together? Not just in business, but a deal gone south. And the most Izzy had said about Hal was that he'd given her a discount on eggs and milk as a local business. Why hadn't she mentioned the proposed bookstore? Embarrassment? Another reason?

Stan strolled home, despite her inner voice telling her to power walk off the big dinner and dessert she'd just inhaled.

It was so convenient to have friends and everything else she needed within walking distance. And it was definitely a night to take advantage of the nice weather.

The regular crew of skateboarding teenagers lurked ahead, taking up residence in an empty parking lot near the green. Her street was quiet otherwise. Stan could see the lights at the farm up ahead, past her own house. Would the farm survive without Hal's business sense? What would happen to the co-op? Would Em run it, or would she turn it over to one of the other farmers? Would they force her out if she didn't want to play nice in the sandbox?

As she let herself in her front door to the happy licks and wags of her pets, she marveled again at how one person's life could touch so many others and leave so many secrets in its wake.

Chapter 18

Tuesday morning, and Stan had a full day ahead: cooking a batch of Amish chicken with spinach and cranberries for Savannah and figuring out how to host Benny's birthday party at her house. Brenna's suggestion made sense. Stan had run it by Nancy, who'd loved it despite her initial hesitation about pit bulls.

So now she was doing it, like it or not, next Sunday. And she had to bake a cake. And treats. And get more cow trachea chews. And deliver all the treats from Brenna's baking frenzy yesterday.

Before she could do more than pour coffee, Nikki called. Stan winced. Either her friend was calling to give her an earful about the farm, or she was looking for her treats. She tried to head her off.

"Morning! Hey, I have your treats."

"My treats? That's good, but I wanted to see how you were," Nikki said. "Any developments in the murder?"

"Plenty, actually." Stan multitasked her way through what she'd learned yesterday about Hal, including the tidbit Char and Ray had mentioned about the development deal

Izzy had allegedly been involved in. Nikki listened intently until Stan stopped talking, then let out a low whistle.

"Izzy's definitely not telling you everything about her relationship with the dead farmer." Nikki's voice came over the line crisp and clear, despite the fact that she was most likely running around her backyard with a hose, filling up doggie water bowls, or serving breakfast to her current residents. "Why didn't she tell you about the business deal?"

"I don't know. Could be because it wasn't a deal anymore. Sounded like it was over." Still, she could've mentioned it. Wait, why did she care? She usually hated when people shared too much. This town was making her soft. "I'm worried about the men in the café, though."

"Do you think it had anything to do with Hal's death?" Nikki asked.

"I wondered," Stan said. "If they killed him or know who did, Izzy could be in danger. But it doesn't explain her reaction to his death."

"Well, I've met this girl. She seemed like a tough cookie. So why would she be so upset over him dying? Was he giving her that much of a break on milk, for crying out loud?"

"I have no idea." Stan turned the oven to bake and slid the chicken in. "And she had nothing to say about it on the way home from the police station. I don't know if that's because Jake was there."

"Huh. Maybe she was blackmailing the farmer for money. Although, there could be more to this real estate thing."

"Blackmailing, Nik? Come on. He didn't even have any money."

Nikki apparently had come to terms with mankind's tendencies. "Why not? Anything's possible. And you don't know what he had on the side. Tell me about the deal, though."

"They wanted to buy an adjacent building and turn it into a bookstore. Expand Izzy's offering, I guess."

"So why did it go south?"

"I can't get a good answer. Char and Ray talked about it. Then they stopped, like they realized they shouldn't. They definitely know more than they're saying."

"Gideon! It's not time to play ball. Gimme that. Hold on, Stan."

Stan heard a lot of static and barking as Nikki retrieved the ball from one of her charges.

"Okay, sorry." She came back on the line. "If I were you, I'd flat out ask Izzy. If you want to know."

"You think that'll work?"

"If not, she'll just throw a chair at you." Nikki laughed at her own joke. "Come on. People can't keep secrets like that forever. If there was something going on with money or blackmailing or whatever, they'll eventually look at her as a suspect, right? If they can't come up with anyone else."

"Yikes." Stan hadn't thought of that. "They already suspect his wife."

"Yeah? Did she do it?"

"I have no idea." Stan didn't need the little voice to remind her that she didn't know anything about Em. And again, even if she did, that was no guarantee, even though Char and Ray swore up and down she was innocent. "She was supposed to be at a parent-teacher conference the day he died and she never showed up. And she was in Jake's bar that afternoon looking for him—which people around here say is extremely out of character."

"Hey, people get pushed to a point. Who knows? Maybe

that's the day she found out there was an affair. Happens all the time, Stan, unfortunately. You read the papers."

"I guess." The doorbell rang. Stan glanced up, surprised. She wasn't expecting anyone. Henry and Scruffy went barreling down the hall, their barks a mixture of alto and soprano ringing through the house. "Hey, Nik, I have to run. Someone's at the door. I'll call you later, okay?"

"Yeah. And hey, keep me posted," Nikki said. "Now I'm intrigued. Oh, and can I meet you somewhere to grab the treats?"

Stan agreed to meet her for lunch Thursday at their usual midway point, then hung up and hurried to the door, half expecting Jake, or even Char. But she didn't get either of them. Instead, she came face to face with her mother. Whom she hadn't seen since she'd moved to Frog Ledge over the summer. And whom she certainly didn't expect to see right now. On her doorstep, separated only by the screen door. With a suitcase.

"Mom." She cleared her throat and tried to force some enthusiasm into her voice. "What are you doing here? I mean, it's great to see you. Is everything okay?"

"Kristan. Why does something have to be wrong for me to visit my oldest daughter?" Patricia Connor's lips tilted in the closest thing she had to a smile. She pointed at the porch. "Are these your cats?"

Stan leaned out the door and smiled when she saw Lucy and Ricky, the cats from the house to her right. She worried about their frequent trips outside, but they often landed on her front porch sniffing around for treats. "No, these are a neighbor's. They're looking for snacks." She reached into the treat jar she kept next to the door for that purpose and handed them each a cookie. The cats plopped in the sun to enjoy.

"Come on in, Mom."

Patricia took a step into the door, then stopped abruptly when Henry came around the corner. "My goodness. I didn't know you had an attack dog. Are things that frightening out here in the country?"

"Attack dog?" Stan laughed. "Henry is far from an attack dog. Right, Henry?" She patted his head and pulled the door wider so Scruffy could get past Henry to say hello. Her mother eyed the small dog with the same level of wariness.

Stan sighed. "Do I need to put the dogs outside?" Her mother and sister had never been animal people, whereas Stan and her dad had always loved animals. It ran in that side of the family—her dad's mother, her favorite grandmother, had been the one who introduced Stan to the idea of cooking and baking for cats and dogs. Many of Stan's happiest childhood memories had taken place in her grandmother's kitchen, where they concocted healthy treats for the neighborhood cats and dogs who often came to visit. She hadn't realized she'd inherited the gift until she'd begun cooking for Nutty.

"If you don't mind." Her mother's tone indicated she didn't care if Stan did mind.

Stan gritted her teeth. And reminded herself not to. "Come on, guys," she said. Henry immediately followed her. Scruffy continued to *woo-woo* at her mother in hopes of getting some pets. She was unsuccessful. The little schnoodle finally dropped to all fours with a huff, then turned and pranced down the hall after Stan and Henry. Stan let them out the back door and returned to the hall. Her mother had finally entered the house. She now eyed Nutty, who had gotten in on the act. He rubbed all over her tall leather boots. Stan swore she saw that glint in his eye that said, *I know exactly what I'm doing.*

Suppressing a smile, she reached for her mother's bag. "Sorry, I'm not putting the cat outside. That's Nutty. He's an indoor cat. Come sit." She led her mother into her living room, a bright, sun-filled room. She rarely used it despite the comfy setup she'd created, with an overstuffed sectional, strategically placed tall glass tables topped with pots brimming with bright, inviting flowers. Right now it screamed Halloween, with black and orange streamers around each window and light-up haunted houses on each small coffee table. Usually, when she wanted to watch TV or read she curled up in the smaller den, which she'd painted cranberry red and accented with gold drapes. The den was her favorite room. It had a gas fireplace and built-in bookshelves, and she didn't want to share it with her mother yet.

"Can I get you something to drink? I have iced tea and lemonade. Made with organic lemons."

Her mother settled carefully in one corner of the couch, smoothing her cream-colored suede skirt over her knees. "Iced tea, please. Thank you."

"Sure." Stan squared her shoulders and headed into the kitchen. *Just calm down and see why she's here. Maybe it's a good visit. Maybe she's changed.* Then, that other voice: *Sure. And when you look out the window, you'll see a couple of the Hoffman cows flying.*

Stan poured the iced tea, put some cookies on a plate, and checked to see what the dogs were doing outside. Scruffy was digging a hole and Henry was supervising. Satisfied, she gathered her refreshments and took them into the living room. Stan handed her mother a glass and set the cookies on the table, then took a seat on the opposite side of the couch. "So what's up? I have to admit, you were the last person I expected to see today. I didn't realize you knew how to get here." *Or even remembered the name of the town.*

"Well, I do have a GPS," her mother said, sipping her tea. "I must admit, it's quite picturesque out here. If you go for this type of setting."

Meaning, it didn't hold a candle to the rich, oceanfront area of Rhode Island she called home. Stan shrugged. "It's not the ocean, but it's pretty in its own right. And the town is lovely. Wonderful people." Except for whoever had murdered Hal, but no need to go into those details. "What's with the suitcase?"

Her mother nibbled a cookie. "I had some free time from my volunteer work this week and I thought I'd stay for a few days. I took a chance you'd be free," she added dryly. "I hope I'm right."

"Stay? Here?" Stan repeated, then realized how she sounded. She forced that enthusiasm back into her voice. "What a wonderful idea, Mom. Not that I'm necessarily *free,* since I am running my own business. But I'm free in the sense of being flexible."

Patricia still hadn't gotten over Stan's decision not to return to a "real" job after her position had been eliminated. She also couldn't understand why that situation had led to Stan's retreat from the Hartford area to her new haven and the realization that corporate America no longer held any appeal. She'd already heard all about it, and now she refused to take the bait. Billy Joel made an appearance in Stan's head singing "My Life."

"Your own business? Oh, you mean the dog food. Yes, I recall Richard mentioning that."

Stan stiffened. "Richard? You've spoken to him?" She hadn't talked to her ex since they'd parted ways last summer.

"Not in a bit, dear. He did tell me about your . . . decision. To stop seeing him. He was quite disappointed, but felt you two had drifted apart. And he did mention your new hobby. But that was months ago." She waved a hand as if dismissing the whole conversation, and took another cookie.

"My decision?" Stan chuckled. "Yes, it was, but his affair with the office's version of Pamela Anderson had a lot to do with it."

Her mother wrinkled her nose. She didn't usually like to get into those kinds of details. Dirty laundry had no business being aired. "Sometimes a fresh start is a good thing. So those dogs live here?"

"They do." *Maybe that meant she wouldn't stay.* "They're both adopted. One was from Nikki and the other from the pound here in Frog Ledge. He was saved from a bad breeder situation."

Her mother didn't really have any concept of rescue versus bad breeders, so she had no comment on that. "And they . . . behave?"

"They're terrific dogs," Stan said. "And they both love Nutty. And Nutty loves them. Most of the time." She grinned at her cat, who had climbed up on the couch next to her mother just to be a brat. He sprawled with his tail resting on her leg. Nutty opened one eye and seemed to raise his eyebrow at Stan, probably disagreeing with her assessment of his feelings about the dogs.

"Well, the house seems quite nice," her mother said, gazing around. "Aside from all these . . . decorations. Are you having a Halloween party?"

Stan had gone all out for her first Halloween in her new house. She'd strung up her own orange lights along the farmers porch and on the shrubs right in front of it. A ghost that responded to motion hung next to her front door. After dark, when someone walked past it (or when the wind blew it), it made ghostly noises. Fluttering in the breeze was a flag featuring a black cat watching a witch fly past the moon on her broom. Her pumpkins sat on the railing, waiting to be carved. But she'd really let loose on the inside. Every room had black and orange garland, bat garland, spider webs, pumpkins, witches, pumpkin-scented candles.

Too bad her mother didn't like it.

"No plans for a party yet. I just like Halloween. You do remember that, right?"

Patricia chuckled. "Of course I know that. Are you going to show me the rest of the house?"

"Sure," Stan said, putting her iced tea down with a snap. "I love showing off the house. Don't you love Victorians?"

Patricia made a noncommittal sound and rose. "Shall I leave my bag here?"

"I don't think anyone's going to steal it," Stan said.

"Oh, Kristan. Always such a wise mouth. I meant, will the cat lay on it?"

"Probably."

"Oh." Her mother looked like she didn't quite know what to do with that.

"Mom, it will be fine." Stan stood up impatiently. "Do you want to see the house?"

Patricia followed her to the kitchen. "The colors are very nice. Did you paint it yourself?"

"Not this room. The previous owner had just redone the whole kitchen. I love it. Don't you?"

"It's very bright. I like the wine rack up there." Patricia pointed to the rack built in over the refrigerator. "So tell me about the dog food. What do you make?"

Stan described some of the treats she made and the meals she was experimenting with as she took her mother through the downstairs. They were almost having a nice conversation when the doorbell rang again.

"Hold on, Mom. Today's the day for unexpected guests." Stan hurried to the front door, and this time found Char holding a box.

"Hi! What have you got there?"

"A package for you that came yesterday. Janey, the UPS driver, knows we're friends and asked me to sign for you so you wouldn't have to wait for her to come back. I forgot to give it to you last night. How are you, honey?" Char squeezed her and stepped back, handing the box over. "Oh, hello."

Stan turned to find her mother trailing after her. Patricia looked at the flamboyant red-haired woman in the doorway, her mouth pinched tightly shut in what Stan assumed was shock. "Char, this is my mother. Patricia Connor, Char Mackey. She owns the B and B down the street."

"Hello." Patricia offered her manicured hand.

"Well, how delightful it is to meet you!" Char ignored the hand, stepped forward and squeezed her mother into a giant hug. Squished against Char's ample bosom swathed in an apple green tunic, her mother looked slightly horrified. Stan turned away so she didn't laugh out loud. "Stan, honey, you didn't tell me your momma was coming to visit!"

"I didn't know. Come on in, Char. Oh, these are my new cookie cutters!" Stan squealed in excitement as she read the return address on the box. "All my holiday designs. Some new Halloween ones, and Thanksgiving and Christmas. Yay!"

Char finally let Patricia go, but held on to her hand. "How long are you in town for?"

"Well, I was going to stay a day or two, but I'm not sure."

"Not sure? You changed your mind already?" Stan

laughed, but she had to admit she was hurt. She wasn't entirely thrilled about an extended visit, but her mother clearly had reconsidered. After barely an hour.

"Well, I wasn't expecting the dogs. Truthfully, I'm a little nervous around them." Patricia clasped her hands together. "I'm sure I'm being silly, but—"

"You're afraid of dogs?" Stan stared at her. She'd thought her mother just didn't like animals that much because they made messes and were loud. She'd had no idea fear was a factor.

"Well, not afraid, but—"

"Oh, well, don't you worry about that," Char declared. "I have the perfect solution. I have an extra room at the B and B this week. Why don't you come stay with me?"

"Stay with you?" Patricia looked from Char to Stan and back.

"Yes! It is a B and B, after all. It's a little ways down the street. That way, you both can have your space but still have a nice time visiting. And the dogs won't be a problem. I have a Lab, but she's outside with the alpacas most of the time. Never with the guests, unless they ask for her." She beamed and clapped her hands. "Problem solved! What do you think?"

Stan and Patricia were both silent. Then Patricia smiled. "I think that's a lovely idea. Thank you for offering."

Stan's mouth dropped open. She coughed to hide it. What was up with her mother? She normally would never set foot in a small-town inn. It was high end or nothing. Something had to be going on that her mother wasn't telling her. Had her house gone into foreclosure? Had she fallen prey to some scam? Had the stock markets crashed and she hadn't heard? She better check her accounts.

"Excellent! I'm delighted." Char enveloped her mother

in another bear hug. "And I'm going to run home right now and make sure your room is all set. Stan, will you bring your mother over when she's ready?"

"Sure," Stan said.

"And I'll make you both dinner. This is lovely. What a week this is going to be!"

Char was pleased. Patricia looked happy, too. Stan pulled out her old corporate standby face, the one she would assume when the world was turning upside down around her and she had to pretend she had everything under control, and beamed at them. "Yep," she said. "It's gonna be quite a week, that's for sure."

Chapter 19

After Stan got her mother settled into the B and B and left her happily eating butternut squash soup with Char, she made her rounds in town to deliver her treat orders and headed to the farm. A Jaguar was parked in the driveway next to a beat-up pickup truck. She rang the bell at the house first. No answer. She went around into the yard and headed toward the barn. The sides of the barn were raised, allowing the cows fresh air. With everything open, she could hear voices—and they didn't sound happy.

"We need someone here for twelve-hour shifts. The four-hour overlap is necessary," a voice she didn't recognize argued.

"Well, those were bad staffing decisions on Hal's part. We can't be expected to staff his empty slots because one of his illegal aliens was deported." Another unfamiliar voice.

Curious, Stan inched closer to the pens. She couldn't see the speakers yet and wanted them to continue their conversation.

The first guy's tone had chilled to frosty. "Watch your tone. We have no illegals working here, Peter. And no one's been deported. Frankly, I'm worried about the kid. He's a good worker, and I don't know why he hasn't shown up. But I don't believe we've asked anything of you since this crisis began, and Ted, Asher, and even Leigh-Anne have stepped up to assist because we're all in this together—at least we thought so. Leigh-Anne's here right now trying to put a better schedule together. What are you doing to help?"

"You don't have any right to speak to me that way," the other man began angrily, but a shout interrupted them.

"Yo, Stan! There's a new bull. Wanna come see him?" Danny noticed her as he came around the corner. Two other men stepped into view behind him. One of them was the head herdsman, Roger, who Em had pointed out on her first day. He was tall, lanky, and wore a cowboy hat over a leathery, serious face.

The other man's arrogance showed all over his face, especially in the arch of his eyebrows. He had salt and pepper hair and looked more like an accountant than a farmer. Peter, Roger had called him. As in Peter Michelli, the other co-op farmer. Stan had met his wife, Mary, at Em's the day after Hal's murder but didn't recall seeing Peter before.

Stan waved back at Danny. "A bull?"

"Yeah." He looked at her like she was really dumb. "A baby. You know, a boy?"

"Oh! Is that what they call baby boy cows? Sure, I'd love to."

Stan felt herself blushing at Roger's chuckle. Now they all thought she was clueless. Which she was, actually, when it came to cows, male or female. She walked toward the group. Roger tipped his hat at her. Peter didn't acknowledge her existence.

"Hello," Stan said anyway.

"Miss," Roger said. "Anything I can do for you?"

"No, I was just looking for Em. But, Danny, I'd love to

see the baby first." She smiled at the teenager, who was waiting impatiently for her answer.

"Well, good, then. I'll be in the barn if you need me. Peter, let's talk in there," Roger said.

But Peter turned away. "I don't need to talk anymore. I'm leaving."

Roger shook his head. "That's your choice. But this business still needs to be run. It's your responsibility, too."

"Well, once the collective group stops scratching its head and figures out who's running it, maybe we can talk," Peter shot back, and walked away. Stan heard what she presumed was the Jag roar to life and zoom out of the driveway a minute later.

Peter's farm must be doing better than Hal's, if he drives a Jag, Stan mused. She looked at Roger. "He didn't seem happy."

Roger tilted his chin in acknowledgment. "Enjoy the visit with the bull," he said. "They'll take him away soon enough." He turned and walked toward the barn.

Stan watched him go, then turned to Danny. "What does that mean?"

"What?" Danny's energy had long since stopped him from paying attention to adult conversation. He leaned over the pen, stretching his fingers out to the baby bull.

"What Roger said. That they'll take him away soon."

Danny shrugged. "That's what happens to boys. They take him to another farm."

Stan tried to keep her feelings off her face as she observed the baby bull, huddled in the corner. He was adorable. She had a sneaking suspicion what kind of farm he meant. She wasn't a meat eater, hadn't been in years, and this was one more reason why. She felt Nikki on her shoulder, disapproving, and didn't blame her one bit.

Danny looked at her. "What?"

"So he doesn't get to stay with his mom?"

"Nope. Not after she cleans him off. Then we have to do stuff with the babies. Like feed them stuff so they don't get sick. My dad used to let me do it." His smile faltered, then fell away. "I don't know if Roger will let me."

Stan felt bad for the boy. And for the baby bull. Nikki was right—helping out here wasn't such a good idea. "Maybe we should let him be, Danny, you think?"

"I guess." That sullen, teenage tone had started to creep back in.

"Maybe you can ask Roger for a different chore," Stan suggested, but Danny didn't want to hear it.

"I don't want to ask Roger for another stupid chore!" he shouted, and turned and ran for the house.

Now she'd done it. Stan sighed. Why was she involved in these people's lives?

"The boy is having trouble. Don't take it personal." Roger appeared from behind a row of cows, his face thoughtful.

"Oh, I know." Embarrassed he had overheard, Stan brushed it off. "I just feel bad for him. I had trouble losing my dad as an adult, never mind as a fifteen-year-old kid."

"It's tough." Roger nodded. "Hal and Danny were close. And Danny has some . . . other problems, too. So you're helping out for a while?"

"Yes, for the short term," Stan said quickly. "While Em figures stuff out. It's only my second day."

"That's right neighborly of you. Did anyone show you around?"

"Around the farm? No. I've been in the barn with Em, that's about it. And the office."

"Well, why don't I give you a tour. It might be helpful if you're gonna be working here."

"Oh, no, that's not necessary," Stan said. "I'm only going to be helping in the office anyway."

Roger's expression didn't change, but Stan got the sense that she'd insulted him.

"It'll help you to get a sense of things. How will you know what's important if you don't know how anything works?" he asked.

Stan didn't have a good argument for that, so she relented. "You're right. Absolutely. Are you sure you don't mind?"

"Heck, no. I'm the official Happy Cow tour guide anyway."

Stan couldn't tell if he was serious or not. "You are?"

"'Course. When we open to the public, someone's gotta be in charge. Mrs. H isn't a big people person, and Hal wasn't around much. So I got the job. S'okay. I like it fine." Roger glanced at her feet, noted her sequined flats. "You gonna be okay in those shoes? It's muddy out back."

Stan sighed. No one was going to lay off about the boot thing, apparently. "I'm fine," she said. "Let's do it."

Roger shrugged. "Okay." He waved toward the pen where the baby bull sat. "That's the pen for the new babies. We're expecting another, any day now. Someone experienced on staff always has to oversee the birthing. I was here extra early today to be with Momma. Since we're down a guy." He looked unhappy about that.

"Still no sign of Enrico? He just stopped showing up without a word?" Stan asked.

"Nope. Nothing. He worked Friday, worked Saturday. Had Sunday off, never showed up Monday."

Guilt over Hal's death? Stan wondered. She didn't ask

Roger's opinion on that. "So where's the momma cow?" Stan looked around at the pens.

"Right there." Roger pointed at a cow by herself in another pen. "She's fresh, so she'll be in there by herself for a bit."

"Fresh? Like she's mean to other cows?"

A glimmer of a smile appeared on Roger's stern lips. "No, ma'am. Fresh meaning she just gave birth."

"Oh." Stan felt the red creep up her neck. "That makes sense."

Roger nodded. "Sure does. And then we divide the rest of the ladies based on their lactation cycle." He led her through the next gate into the larger penned areas. "Over there's our dry pen. Those are the cows that have run through their cycle. They won't give milk for about a hundred fifty days. They're the ones we take out to the pasture over there, let them have their alone time." He pointed outside, to the vast green area at the back of the farm. Where Stan's dogs could look at the cows from her backyard.

"So the other cows don't get to go for walks?" Stan glanced at the other side of the enclosure. The cows' lazily swinging tails indicated they hadn't a care in the world, but that pen seemed so confining.

Roger watched her, and Stan saw that ghost of a smile again. "These cows are treated very well, miss. Trust me. They're the Hoffmans' livelihood. Not to mention, Hal loved these creatures. You want to see his wrath, do something he didn't like to the cows. There were no second chances."

Stan flushed again. She hadn't meant to be so transparent, but Nikki would kill her if she didn't ask. And she liked cows. They were so gentle, and seemed so Zen. She hated to think of them sad. "I'm sorry, I didn't mean to insinuate—" she began, but Roger shook his head.

"No apologies necessary. It's good to ask questions. Otherwise, how will you know what to tell others when they ask you? Come on, now. Still more to see." He led her back out and around the cow enclosure to the other side. "Now, cows don't like heat. That's why we have fans and sprinklers here in the barn. And speaking of heat, another part of my job, along with having good cow sense, is the breeding part."

"Breeding?"

"Yes'm. Watch for cows in heat, then breed them. Artificial insemination." He winked. "No boys allowed on this farm."

Stan thought of the baby bull. "I guess not."

"And this"—Roger pointed, walking around to the other side of the barn—"is an example of how innovative we are here at Happy Cow. See that?"

Stan squinted at the metal blade, which looked almost like a spackle tool, running along a track in the floor. The cows stepped over it lazily as it ran by, as if they were used to it. "Yes. What is it?"

"An alley scraper." Roger puffed his chest out proudly. "I presented the idea to Hal after studying up on it. Saved him some money," he said. "Eliminated a staff person, along with a good stretch of time."

Wow. Job eliminations happened at dairy farms, too. Stan felt a moment of empathy for the poor immigrant kid who had lost his job because of the nefarious alley scraper, remembering her own mortification at losing her job earlier this year. She tuned back in to Roger, who was still talking.

"All the manure gets pushed into this tank here." He pointed to the end of the track where a large pipe waited. "It takes it down there to the manure separator where the liquids are separated from the solids. Then we can use the solids to make beds for the cows."

"Beds? They sleep in . . . their own poo?" Maybe she should rethink the feeling that these cows weren't too miserable.

Roger chuckled. "It's not what you're picturing. It's like peat moss. See? That brown Swiss right there is sitting on one." He pointed the cow out.

Stan surveyed it suspiciously. It certainly looked like peat moss, but still. Eww. Roger was watching her with that amused look on his face. He was having a few laughs at her expense.

"And then the liquids go there." He pointed across the field at a circular structure that looked like an above-ground swimming pool. "The manure tank."

Stan glanced doubtfully at the structure. The walls were slightly higher than the above-ground swimming pool her grandma had when she was a kid. There was no fence around it. A steel ladder with about five steps on it was attached to the side, leading up to a tiny steel platform. A large pipe ran down the side.

"Manure tank. That sounds lovely," Stan said. "What do they do with it from there?"

"That there's how we keep our grass growing." Roger smiled. "It gets spread over the farm. Emptied three to five times during the year. It's a dirty job, but someone's gotta do it." This time, he laughed out loud at his own joke. Stan could see why they made him the tour guide.

"That's wild. Has anyone ever mistaken it for a swimming pool?" Stan asked. "Like new staff, late at night in the summer?" She was kidding, but it apparently wasn't a good joke, because Roger sobered immediately.

"Actually, that's the number two dairy farming accident

that kills folks," he said. "People fall in that thing and the gases kill 'em before too long."

"My God. Really?"

"Yep. Happened to a farmer in Attawan, not far from here, year before last." Roger shook his head and made a sign of the cross.

Stan had no idea what to say to that. "So what's the number one killer, then?"

"Augers in the equipment. Sharp blades," he explained at her blank look. "Nasty job they do on a human body, too. The manure tanks have those, too, so it's a double whammy."

"Ugh." She blanched, pushing that visual out of her mind, and changed the subject. "So what do the cows eat? Do they eat grass? Is it good for them?" She felt like a schoolkid again, asking endless questions.

"They eat feed. We got a feed guy who mixes the grain, hay, and silage. His job's pretty important 'cause we don't never want to run out of feed. Hungry cows aren't happy cows, and they're not healthy cows either."

"Do they eat grass, too? Is the grass safe?"

"Yes, ma'am. The grazers eat the grass, you know, the ones I told you about who aren't lactating? They head down that hill back there onto that pasture and graze away. No one else ever goes back there, so the grass is pristine. They love it."

"So how many people work here?" she asked. She hadn't seen anyone else on the farm since they'd started their tour.

"We have nine employees. The feed guy, someone who raises the calves, a few milkers, a few pushers—"

"Pushers?"

"Corralling the cows in and out of the milking area. Got a mechanic, part time. He mows the lawn, too, does general maintenance work. The rest of the guys work twelve-hour shifts. There's a four-hour overlap. Or should be." He glanced at his watch again and then looked around the farm, the annoyance apparent on his face. "Most of our workers are good. Enrico is—was—our best guy. Speaks some English but he knows cows. Wish I knew where the Sam Hill he was." Roger shook his head, then turned back to Stan. "Let's go. I'll show you the milking platform."

They rounded the corner and entered the next building. Stan saw a bunch of cows high up on the platform in stalls, machines and tubes hooked up to their udders, a bar keeping them in place. Milking time. She felt bad for them again, although none of them looked bothered. Two boys who looked remarkably similar—short, skinny, Latino features—worked each aisle, making sure the milk flowed into pipes. They looked at Stan curiously, but neither spoke. Roger said something in Spanish, then turned back to Stan.

"Timing with milking is everything," Roger said. "These boys need to be real good. Within sixty to ninety seconds after they touch the udder, the milk flows. That machine better be hooked up by then, or the milk's spilling."

Which meant money was spilling, too. "Are they good at it?"

Roger shrugged. "Some better than others. That was one thing Hal was a major stickler on. Milk is a precious commodity on a dairy farm. When it spilled, he wasn't happy. He didn't speak any Spanish, but he got his point across. The guys were very careful not to make Mr. Hoffman angry."

Stan thought about the farm staff. Young men doing manual labor for probably very little money. Even more unappealing when someone was yelling at you about spilling milk. Had one of these guys gotten fed up with it? They had to be strong if they worked at the farm. And you didn't need that much height or strength to stab someone in the chest with a sickle. Especially if they weren't expecting it. She shivered.

"Did the police finish questioning the staff?" she asked.

Roger nodded. "Questioned all of us. They brought in a couple translators for the guys and questioned each shift. They didn't come up with anything."

Even if the police had, they wouldn't have told him. Stan wondered how she could find out. Jessie wouldn't be telling Brenna anything, not as close as she was to this case. Would Jessie discuss it with Jake? Stan needed to figure out who Jessie's friends were and get friendly with them. But even the couple of times she'd seen Jessie out at town events, off duty, she had either been alone or with her daughter, Lily. The three-year-old loved Scruffy.

Stan forced her attention back to the farm. "Where does the milk go?" She watched the bars keeping the cows in place lift, allowing them to move again. They all backed out of their stalls as if they had been doing this whole routine for a long time. Which they probably had.

"Excellent question. That's our next stop." Roger led her around the stalls and into a hallway. They passed a small office with his name on the door. Unlike Hal's, it was neat and tidy. It even had a comfy-looking chair tucked in the corner. Why did Hal work in the dreary laundry room while the head herdsman had a nice office in the middle of the action?

Stan followed Roger around the bend and they entered a narrow room with a stainless steel tank that nearly reached the ceiling.

"This is our tank room," he said, flicking on the light. "Holds four thousand gallons of milk."

"Four thousand?" Stan repeated.

"Yep. The milk gets cooled as it goes through the pipes, down to fifty-five degrees. Comes out of the cow at a hundred and one. And goes in here." He motioned to the ladder running along the front of the tank. "Go on up and lift the lid, take a peek. Just don't lean too far. There's augers in that tank."

Stan observed the ladder suspiciously. It didn't look very steady, especially for a man the size of Hal, or Roger. How dangerous was this place? She grasped the sides of the ladder and climbed the few feet. Augers in the tank. She pulled the lid off and peered inside. Milk churned slowly within, the steel blades just visible. She reset the lid and climbed down. "Do you guys make cheese here, too?"

Roger frowned and shook his head. "No, ma'am. This farm ain't that fancy. Only two of our farms have the cheese-making facilities. Ted's and Leigh-Anne's. She's got the ice cream piece, too. And she don't let no one forget it." For as much as he smiled when he said it, Stan could taste the bitterness under his words. Clearly Roger wanted Happy Cow, the founding farm, to be the best farm in the co-op. And it wasn't.

"How come you guys don't do it, too? The more you produce, the better the profits, right?"

"Well, sure," Roger said, pulling off his hat and scratching his head. "But Hal didn't have no interest in expanding. Which never made no sense to me, other than the initial cost. But milk, well, milk ain't no gold mine. We get twenty bucks for every hundred pounds of it. That's the price the state sets, end of story."

"Twenty dollars? That's it?" No wonder dairy farmers looked exhausted and beaten down. How did anyone make a living on that? And how did they pay their staff? Stan didn't know for sure, but she was willing to bet a guy like

Roger didn't make a lot of money, and probably hadn't had a raise in a while. Did he see a brighter future for a bigger farm? It sounded like he'd encouraged Hal to expand the operations. Would he have killed Hal over his denial?

She jumped a foot as the door clanged open behind her. One of the workers stood there. He tipped his hat to Stan and addressed Roger.

"Excuse me," he said in halting English. "No break?"

Roger swore under his breath and immediately looked at Stan. "I'm sorry. Not the right language in front of a lady."

"Don't worry about me," Stan said with a smile. "I'm afraid I've used worse."

"It's so frustrating when people are irresponsible and don't show up for work. Go ahead and take your break, Hector. I'll cover."

Hector tipped his hat again and disappeared. Roger motioned Stan ahead of him and they exited the tank room. He pulled the door shut tightly behind him. "That's the end of the line anyway. I hope you enjoyed the tour. At least you'll have a better idea of how things work 'round here."

"It was excellent. Thank you, Roger. I appreciate it. I'm going to head over to the office now." She bid Roger good-bye and left the building, cutting across the grass to the house. The back door was unlocked. Stan let herself into the chilly room and immediately turned the thermostat up. She hated being cold when she was pushing paper. She'd always kept a blanket in her old office. When she needed alone time, she'd shut her door and wrap herself in it. She got a lot of work done that way.

Not that she'd get a lot of work done here, since there was still no laptop, no clear indication of how much money was in the account to pay bills, and no other direction except to straighten out the piles. She sighed and dug into one. Official paperwork in this file. Stan spent a few minutes thumbing through the dairy farm licensing information, mortgage information, and the co-op agreement. Then Em appeared at the door. She looked disheveled and upset.

"Stan, I need your help," she said, her voice dangerously shaky. "Can you come now?"

Chapter 20

Please don't let it be another dead body. "What's going on, Em?" Stan asked, hurrying to keep up as she followed her across the yard.

"We're down a man and it's putting everyone behind." She sounded completely frazzled. "I need you to help. We need a pusher."

"I'm sorry, I said I'd do the books, not deal drugs." Stan's lame attempt at a joke fell short when Em turned and stared at her. "Yes. A pusher. You want me to go get someone?"

Em snapped the straps of her overalls impatiently. "So you know what a pusher is?"

"Roger took me around and explained, yes. Whoa, wait a minute." She held up a hand as it dawned on her what Em was asking. "Listen, Em, I'm happy to help, but I don't know how to push cows. I mean, do cows even like to be pushed?"

"You'll do fine. The cows know the drill. Roger is tending to the expectant mother and assessing whether another cow is ill, and I have to make sure the other boys get their break. If we get behind on our milking schedule, the rest of the week will be off." Emmalee wrung her hands, the stress of the last few days manifesting in her face. "Please?"

How in the world did I get myself into this situation? Stan gritted her teeth and forced a smile. "Sure, Em. I'll come push cows." She glanced down at her flats, already crusted with mud and God-knew-what-else from her earlier tour. Her jeans weren't her best pair, but they weren't her worst, either. Well, that's what she got for trying to be fashionable at her new "job."

"Oh, thank God." Em stepped forward and clasped Stan's hands between hers. "Roger will be over to help you if he can. And I have a call in to Ted and Asher. Come on now." She tugged Stan to the barn. "Roger! Stan's going to help."

Roger's head popped up over the stall. "Great. Remember how I showed you the groups of cows? The holding pen is the small group on the left. Just lead them out and up the ramp. You're just an escort, really. They know the drill." He disappeared again.

"You're a dear!" Em called out, already heading back to whatever she'd been doing. A minute later, the door closed, and Stan was alone with the better part of five hundred cows.

"Well, that's just great," she muttered. "Move to a farming town and become a farmer. Who would've thought?" She stepped hesitantly over to the row of cows waiting patiently for their trip to the milking area. "Hey, guys," she said. "Want to, ah, head over here?"

None of them moved. A couple swiveled their heads at her and gave her what she believed was the stink-eye. So much for them just going right along. She took another tentative step forward, feeling the muddy, manure-y ground squish around her feet. *Awesome.*

"Come on," she tried again. "We're just going to go right

up the ramp here." She pointed, hoping a couple of them would be accustomed to leading the pack.

Nothing. The *Mission Impossible* theme song played in her head.

She glanced around. No one else in sight. She wished she had some treats right now. That might help. Did cows like treats? She had no idea. And it might contaminate the milk if she fed them treats anyway. Nope, on to Plan B. Not that she had one.

Hands on hips, Stan surveyed the group. Some of them were still looking at her, kind of like how the problem kids used to look at the substitute teacher in school. The others were blatantly ignoring her. Well, time to get serious. If the milking got off schedule, it would be her fault.

"Okay, who's going to go first?" She clapped her hands. "How about you?" Moving to the front of the pen, she swung the gate open. The cow closest to it eyed it, but didn't move. She rested one hand tentatively on the cow's flank.

The cow whipped her tail up and smacked her in the face. It was like getting hit with a lasso flung by a particularly strong cowboy. The pain stung, setting her face on fire. Stan stumbled back, tripped, and fell on her rear right in the mud. Or manure. Her luck, probably manure. She pulled her left hand out of the muck, sniffed tentatively. Eww. Pulled her other hand out, not bothering to sniff. The cow, looking smug, sauntered through the gate toward the milking pen as if she'd planned to do it all along. If she could talk, Stan imagined she would say, *Welcome to the farm, sucker!* One by one, the others followed. Stan leapt to her feet to avoid being trampled by any of them, only to find Roger hanging over the pen laughing.

"I'm sorry," he managed when he realized she'd seen

him. "That was priceless. Nice job getting the cows through the gate, though."

Stan wiped her filthy hands on her filthy jeans. "Glad I could help."

"You're a good sport." Roger nodded. "There's a couple more shifts to move. I hope you can stick around for a bit."

Two hours later Stan walked home, hoping she wouldn't bump into anyone on the street who could smell her. She hadn't actually gotten anything done in the Happy Cow office, but she'd finally gotten the hang of cow pushing and had helped get the last few groups where they were supposed to be.

If her corporate friends could see her now. From PR mogul to cow pusher in just six months. It was so absurd she giggled a little, then frowned when she glanced down and saw her ruined shoes. These would have to be thrown out.

As she turned into her driveway, she slowed. Char and her mother sat on her front steps, laughing. *Her mother. Laughing.* Stan hadn't seen that in years. What were they doing at her place? And why did her mother have to show up when Stan looked like she'd taken a dip in the Happy Cow manure tank?

Sure enough, when her mother spotted her the smile faded a bit. She stopped talking and stared. Stan pasted a smile on and waved. "Hi, ladies. What's going on?"

"Heavens to Betsy, Stan, whatever happened to you?" Char asked.

"Oh, this." Stan flicked a hand at her dirty clothes, dismissing them. "I was helping Em out. Doing some things I hadn't planned on."

"Like what? Shoveling cow poop?" her mother asked.

"No, Mom. I didn't shovel it." *Just fell in it.*

"Well, Kristan, I won't dare ask again. Something tells me I don't want to know."

She absolutely wouldn't. Which is why Stan told her.

"At a dairy farm? Have you lost your mind?" Her mother couldn't have looked more horrified if Stan had told her she'd taken a part-time job as a prostitute.

"Now, Patricia, she's being a lovely neighbor and helping that poor woman at the farm," Char said, sending Stan an anxious glance as if to say, *Don't fight.* "Her husband was killed the other night." She leaned close to Patricia and said in an exaggerated hush, "Murdered! Have you heard? We're trying not to discuss it at the B and B. We don't want to upset our guests."

Patricia's eyes widened. "Murdered? Here?"

"It's terrible." Char shook her head. "And Stan here, well, with her financial background, she jumped right in to offer her expertise."

Stan had to laugh. "Char. I spent the day herding cows. That has nothing to do with financial expertise."

"How was he murdered?" her mother asked.

"Stabbed with a sickle," Stan said. "It was ugly."

Her mother's hand flew to her mouth. She looked pale. "In this neighborhood?"

"Two doors down."

"Why in the world were you herding cows?" Char broke in, an attempt at drawing Patricia's attention away. "I thought you were doing books."

"They were shorthanded. Listen, do you guys want to come in? I really want to shower."

"Sure, we'd love to." Char stood. "We stopped by to see if you were going to the council meeting tonight. Your mother decided to tag along with me and I thought it would be loads of fun if we all went together. I figured you were going since this is your topic, right, dear? Animals, shelters, and vets?" She beamed like a kid delivering a handmade card to a grown-up and now expected high praise.

Shoot. The town meeting. She'd forgotten. Stan pushed past them and unlocked the door. "Scruffy and Henry, sit," she commanded. They obeyed. "Yes, I'm going."

"Kristan." Her mother got up and followed her inside, giving the dogs a wide berth. "This doesn't sound like a safe neighborhood. There was that other murder when you first moved here, too. Maybe you should think about moving back to Rhode Island. I can help you find a house near ours."

"Oh, Patricia, don't be silly! This is a lovely town. It's very safe, normally. There've just been those couple of unfortunate incidents since Stan moved to town." Char shut the door behind her and waggled her fingers at Nutty, who sat on the windowsill. "Besides, Stan loves it here. Don't you?"

"I do. Make yourself at home. There's lemonade in the fridge. Fresh squeezed, organic." She kissed Nutty's head and patted each of the dogs. "I'm going upstairs to wash off the cow poop."

Chapter 21

Showered, refreshed, and cleaned up, Stan dressed in a new pair of jeans, a blouse, and comfortable flats. She'd bid her other pair of shoes good-bye and resigned herself to wearing a pair of hiking boots next time she ventured to Happy Cow. Not that she planned on accepting a permanent promotion to cow pusher, but just in case. Which made her think about Hal's missing boots from the barn, and Asher Fink's confiscated shoes. She needed to ask about that. She left her long blond hair loose and dried it enough to give it waves, spritzed some perfume, and applied some eyeliner, mascara, and lipstick.

Downstairs, her mother, Char, and Nutty lounged in the kitchen. Nutty sat on Char's lap as she fed him treats from Stan's treat jar.

"I just adore this cat," Char told her as she walked in.

Her mother wrinkled her nose but didn't speak. Stan ignored her.

"He's a good boy," Stan said. "I think he's getting fat."

"Nonsense. He's big boned." Char checked her watch. "Well, the meeting's at seven. Do you want to go to Izzy's for dinner first? She's got a delightful pumpkin soup on the menu this week."

Stan looked at her mother. "Mom?"

"Wherever you ladies would like," her mother said. Stan knew what she was thinking. She usually only ate at fancy restaurants, not sandwich shops in little podunk towns.

"Izzy's it is, then," Stan said. It might give her a chance to pin her friend down and ask about the business deal with Hal. Izzy had been strangely absent since Stan and Jake had dropped her off Sunday after the chair-throwing incident.

But Izzy wasn't at the cafe. The soup was phenomenal, though. Not even Patricia could resist it. She was the first to finish her meal. After, the three of them headed over to the town hall, a brick building with a stately white steeple on top. The building blazed with lights. A hopping place to be on a Tuesday.

"The meeting's on the second floor," Char said. "Do you want to take the elevator?"

Stan, perusing the directory next to the front door, shook her head. "Why don't you go on? I need to make a quick stop," she said. Before either of them could question her, she headed down the hall in search of the resident state trooper's office.

She'd been in the town hall twice—both times to license her dogs. Never to Trooper Pasquale's office. She checked the directory and set off toward the back of the building. Stan had no idea if she was even at her desk at this hour, but it was worth a shot. She rounded the corner, stopped in front of Pasquale's office door, and knocked.

"Come in," Pasquale commanded from the other side.

Stan pushed the door open, smiled. "Hi."

Pasquale stared at her. "Ms. Connor. Please don't tell me you're coming to report another dead body. I can't take the excitement."

Funny, she echoed Stan's earlier thought when she was at the farm and Em had run in panicked. "No, actually, I was here for the meeting and thought I'd stop in and see how the investigation was going."

"It's going fine."

"Any news?"

"You know I can't discuss it."

"Well, I thought maybe you had gotten somewhere with the farm staff." Stan slid into the chair in front of her desk. "I was over there today and Roger mentioned the interviews, so—"

"So you thought you'd come see if you could bounce some theories around with me?" Her tone was somewhat amused, but she still wore her cop face. She had the best cop face Stan had ever seen. Not that she'd been around any other cops for a good amount of time, but anyone who could hold her face in such a blank position for so long deserved some kudos, however grudging.

"I wanted to see what you thought of the missing worker."

Pasquale's face didn't change. "Missing worker?"

"The guy who was there the night of Hal's murder. Enrico. He never showed up for work Monday."

Pasquale was silent for a moment. Taking the information in or formulating her nonanswer, Stan couldn't tell.

"Listen, Ms. Connor," Pasquale said finally. "I appreciate your . . . enthusiasm, and the information, but this is a murder case. It's our top priority, and I'm very confident in our ability to solve it. Please don't hesitate to give us any information you come across, but also, please don't expect me to consult with you."

During Stan's corporate career, she'd met many people like Jessie Pasquale. Self-righteous, condescending, and convinced they were smarter than everyone else. Well, she had news for her. She was plenty smart. And now she was annoyed.

"Listen. I've been over at the farm helping Em, and there are a lot of people who were unhappy with Hal. The staff was afraid of him, and that guy Peter Michelli—"

"Ms. Connor," Pasquale interrupted. "I'm well aware of who was unhappy relating to Mr. Hoffman, and I'm going about my investigation as carefully and thoughtfully as possible. I will get to the bottom of it. People don't just go around stabbing farmers—or anyone else—with sickles in my town and get away with it. But I don't need your help. Am I clear?"

Stan stood up and put her coldest corporate face on. "Crystal," she said. "Best of luck to you. I hope no one else gets stabbed before you figure it out." She turned on her heel and swept out of the office, pulling the door firmly shut behind her. Never slam it—it showed vulnerability.

She headed back around the corner to find the stairwell. A door to her right leading to another meeting room was open. About to pass, she heard a familiar voice and halted before coming into view.

". . . for your own good, Emmy." Leigh-Anne Sutton's pleading voice. "We need to make sure this business stays strong. For the good of all of us."

"Leigh-Anne's right," a man's voice said. He sounded somber. "Emmalee, you're grieving. You have your boys. You're trying to keep the farm going, and I heard you're missing an employee. Let us help."

"That's not helping," Em snapped. "You're just trying to take away what Hal created. Because you wish you'd thought of it yourself. Admit it, Peter. You didn't give a hoot about Hal. Why, I wouldn't be surprised if you were the one who stabbed him!"

Stan gasped, then quickly covered her mouth with her hand and pressed against the wall. What was happening? Was Peter trying to wrench the Happy Cow co-op from Em and her family? It certainly sounded like it.

"If anything, it should be a partnership," a new male voice interjected. "I don't think it's a wise business decision for Emmalee to cede her ownership. But I do think you could use some help, Em. And Leigh-Anne has such a good business sense. We should agree to give it a try, don't you think?" He sounded like he was cajoling a little kid.

Em didn't agree. "Ted, if anyone had told me you'd take their side, I'd have punched them in the nose and called them a liar," she said, her voice as frigid as the iceberg that had taken down the *Titanic*. "But I guess I'm outnumbered. Asher? Do you want to put your two cents in?"

Silence. Stan leaned closer, anxious to hear Asher Fink's response.

His solemn voice resonated into the hallway. "I agree with Ted. We should vote on electing Leigh-Anne as the co-lead of the co-op in partnership with you, Emmalee, and Ted as the manager of daily operations. Who wants to make a motion?"

"I will." Peter's voice was matter-of-fact despite the callous removal of Em as the head of the business her husband had started.

"Second," Asher said. "All in favor?"

Ted and Leigh-Anne's simultaneous "Ayes" drifted into the hall as Em barged out of the room, eyes blazing. Her eyes met Stan's and she said nothing, just glared at her, too, and hurried for the door.

Stan didn't stick around for the rest of the group to disperse. She found the elevator and hit the button. The doors slid open right away and she stepped in, her mind racing. If she interpreted what she'd just heard correctly, Em had been ousted as the head of the co-op. All of the partners had voted against her remaining the sole overseer. Was this the second half of a diabolical plan the group had cooked up? Had Asher tried to be the voice of reason with Hal the day he died, when they'd met in that parking lot? Clearly it hadn't gone the way Asher had planned, if the conversation had deteriorated into a shouting match. Had he gone back to the farm later, startled Hal, and stabbed him with his own tool as he pruned his corn maze? Or had Peter shown up and done the deed after Asher reported back that Hal wouldn't budge? And were they now trying to get final control of the business?

The doors slid open on the second floor. Exiting the elevator, Stan found herself facing the large room that served as the town council chambers. Seven seats were set up on the dais. The rest of the room was filled with benches reminding her of the church pews of her youth—straight backed, unfriendly. A table in the corner had a printed sign that read PRESS. Cyril Pierce was the table's only occupant.

Stan scanned the room looking for her mother and Char. They were sitting up front, heads bent close together, giggling like schoolgirls. Weird. She needed some time alone with her mother to find out the real story about her visit. Patricia wasn't the type to drop in on people, even her daughter, especially when said daughter lived in a small town out in the middle of nowhere. Patricia Connor was usually lost if a decent afternoon martini wasn't within reach at some fancy bar. Although Stan would bet Char's drinks would rival any served at her mother's hoity-toity places.

She headed to their row and slid in next to her mother. "Hey."

"Hello there. Find what you needed?" Patricia asked.

"I did," Stan said.

Char leaned over. "Good timing. It's going to be packed! I guess everyone is interested in a new vet clinic. This will be a great meeting!" She rubbed her hands together with glee.

Stan had to smile at her enthusiasm. Char made everything fun. She looked around, trying to get a sense of attendees. There was Betty Meany, with a couple of folks from the library. Another group of people she recognized from the War House clustered together near the back, not far from Cyril Pierce's press area. Stan wondered if any other journalists ever showed up, or if Cyril's only competition was his own pen.

The War House volunteers were almost unrecognizable tonight. The four men and two women were dressed in regular clothes for your average seventy- or eighty-year-old, whereas they normally wore period costumes from Revolutionary War times. Most days they took turns sitting in front of the historical building, encouraging people to come in for tours. They often staged reenactments of Revolutionary battles on the town green, as a tribute to the war activities of the past. Frog Ledge had been an integral site during that time. Tonight they looked like regular citizens from the present.

Huddled together in the front row were Amara Leonard, Vincent DiMauro, and Diane Kirschbaum. No sign of Jake, but Jessie Pasquale had come in and stood near the back. Made sense as Diane's boss. Stan wondered how she felt about this shelter proposal. Or if she was there to investigate Hal's murder and didn't care, given the close eye she had on Asher Fink, who had also come up after the co-op meeting ended. Stan wondered why. He didn't live in town. There was no sign of Ted Brahm, Peter Michelli, or Leigh-Anne Sutton. Or Emmalee.

Stan leaned over to her mother again. "Are you sure you want to sit through this, Mom?"

"Of course I'm sure, Kristan. It's interesting." Patricia squeezed Stan's hand. Stan almost fell off her bench. What had come over her mother?

Then, all of a sudden, Patricia's gaze shifted. Her hand clenched Stan's tighter, an unconscious motion. Stan followed her stare. Tony Falco stood just outside their row, speaking to a woman with blond curls tighter than a standard poodle's and a suit that had seen better days in the eighties. His smile came so easy it seemed fake.

"What's wrong, Mom? You know that guy?"

Her mother didn't answer, but clamped her lips together and looked away. She turned her body back to Char and said something. Stan looked at the man again. He was still talking to Poodle Woman, but his gaze had gone to her row. Specifically, to her mother. Did they know each other?

A door to the side of the council seats opened and the town officials filed to their chairs, causing the rest of the still-chatting stragglers to disperse and take their own seats. To the far left, on their side, was Mona Galveston, the mayor. Stan liked Mona. She would definitely vote for her on election day in a couple of weeks. She had no idea who Tony Falco was as a candidate—her own fault. But he hadn't been overly friendly in the bar. Which could be chalked up to the spill.

The other councilmen and -women, many of whom Stan

hadn't met, turned their attention to Mona as she rapped her gavel. "Good evening, ladies and gentlemen of Frog Ledge. Thank you for joining us tonight for our public hearing about the property at Eighty-two Main Street, the former Frog Ledge Veterinary Clinic." She glanced down at some papers in front of her. "According to the paperwork filed with the town clerk, there is a group of citizens in town who wish to buy the damaged clinic and renovate it. The building will house a veterinary clinic offering both allopathic and homeopathic traditions. A request was also filed to extend the rear of the building for shelter space, to house animals in need of homes." Mona smoothed the papers, folded her hands on top of them, and surveyed the crowd. "Do we have that group of citizens here?"

The three stood. Only Diane looked nervous.

Mona nodded. "Would you care to say anything before we open the public hearing?"

Diane immediately shrank back, like she'd rather do anything but. Amara and Vincent both stepped out of the aisle and over to the microphone set up at the front of the room.

Amara spoke first. "Thank you for having us, Mayor Galveston and council." Her voice rang out, strong and sure of herself, in the crowded room. She'd dressed for the event. She wore a long flowy beaded skirt in tones of brown and black, with black ballet slipper flats peeking out from under it. A black tank top with a sheer lacy blouse completed the outfit. She'd curled her short brown hair into full waves. The pointy frames of her red eyeglasses reminded Stan of cat's eyes.

"For anyone who's not familiar with our proposal, we're looking to purchase and expand the former Frog Ledge Veterinary Clinic. As most of you know, the clinic was subjected to a series of . . . unfortunate events over the summer, including the loss of its proprietor. As such, our town has been without an official veterinarian. Dr. DiMauro," Amara nodded to her companion, "has owned his own traditional veterinary practice for the past ten years in the area. And many of you are aware of the homeopathic veterinary services I provide. We're looking to partner and offer residents both services in one place. In addition, we'd like to expand the building slightly to provide cage space for animals in need of homes as they wait to be adopted."

"Thank you, Ms. Leonard," Mayor Galveston said. "Any commentary from the other parties?"

Vincent DiMauro leaned over to the mic. "I would like to add how excited I am at the prospect of serving the residents of Frog Ledge and their pets. With the kind of complementary treatment options we offer, I'm confident we'll add a lot of value to the town. And, we'll be able to carry on the very fine tradition the Morganwick family began so many years ago with their clinic."

Stan nodded approvingly. DiMauro was a smooth character. He understood the politics of small town Connecticut and the resistance to change, and he'd addressed it head on. By acknowledging the long-standing presence of the Morganwick family, despite what anyone may have felt about their standards of care, he'd tempered the probability of old-timers complaining that they were trying to move in and wipe out their legacy.

Vincent, Amara, and Diane took their seats. Mayor Galveston opened up the public commentary portion of the meeting. A man in back immediately stood and moved slowly to the mic. He looked ancient, and moved that way. His thinning white hair was combed over the age spots on his head, and he was bent over slightly at the waist. His pants hung off him, like he'd lost a lot of weight recently. When he spoke, his voice had the quaver of the aged.

"Myron Davenport, Frog Ledge," he said. His posture made it seem like he was looking at the floor. "I hope the council will give good thought to anything that will raise taxes, especially for the senior citizens in town. There have been so many promises of development in this town, and when it don't come to fruition, we're paying the bills." Myron Davenport nodded, as if he agreed with himself, and shuffled back to his seat.

Mayor Galveston suppressed a smile. "Thank you, Mr. Davenport. Anyone else?"

A woman Stan recognized from Izzy's café rose. "Sheila Costanzo. I think it's very progressive to have a practice with both kinds of care. I, for one, will embrace it, and I believe it will attract others from surrounding areas as well and be good for the economy."

The parade of residents continued, most in favor of the proposal, some grumbling about taxes and money and hippies coming to town. Cyril Pierce was furiously pounding away on his keyboard, alternating with scribbling notes in the steno pad next to him. He had a lot of material at his disposal. Stan was impressed with the amount of people investing their time to come to the meeting on behalf of the town. Although maybe it was normal in a place like this. She didn't know. Not that she was proud of it, but she had never bothered to go to a town meeting any other place she'd lived to compare.

Then Tony Falco stood and walked to the mic. He turned on a thousand-watt smile, pausing to make sure every member of the council was included in it, then spoke. "Good evening. Tony Falco, Frog Ledge."

She cast a sideways glance at her mother. That same odd look was on her face as she watched him speak.

"I want to commend this trio of good citizens for their efforts to move Frog Ledge forward and contribute to the revitalization of the town," Falco continued. Stan could swear Mona Galveston rolled her eyes as she watched her opponent. "But a question does arise, mainly regarding the expansion portion of the proposal. As the town already oversees the Frog Ledge Dog Pound, which includes operating costs and the salary of our very talented animal control officer, Ms. Kirschbaum"—Falco swept a hand in Diane's direction, in case anyone wasn't sure who she was—"I'm curious, then, who would be funding and staffing the sheltering portion of your proposed facility. I would imagine it's not something the hardworking residents of Frog Ledge would be expected to pay for. Thank you." Falco took his seat and looked expectantly at Diane, who had turned redder than the candy-apple-colored convertible Stan's dad used to drive.

Stan felt for her. She knew how stressful speaking in public was, especially when you were put on the spot. It had happened to her many times in her early years in corporate America, and she'd hated it.

Amara nudged Diane, who gritted her teeth and began to rise. But before she could get to the mic, Trooper Jessie Pasquale strode down the aisle and took it.

"Trooper Jessica Pasquale, Frog Ledge. As many of you know, I oversee the animal control function of Frog Ledge as part of my duties as resident state trooper, as the town doesn't employ its own police department. I'd like to address Mr. Falco's comment." She gave Falco a sidelong glance that made Stan think she'd take pleasure in arresting him after the meeting. "As many of you in town are aware, our facilities are less than optimal, both for the animals in our care and Ms. Kirschbaum and her volunteers. But since we're not interested in raising taxes for the town, we're making do. However, I'd like to point out that any additional steps Ms. Kirschbaum is interested in taking to better support the animals of our town is her personal choice as a resident, and while those steps don't require town funding, they do have my full support."

And with that, she moved back to her spot against the wall in the back of the room. Wow. Pasquale had just stuck up for Diane and the animals. And the new vet clinic-shelter. Maybe she really did have a heart somewhere after all.

Amara nudged Diane again to get up, which she did, and stumbled through an explanation of how she planned to bring in more volunteers and work at the new shelter on her off time. After she sat down, Stan rose and went to the mic.

"Stan Connor of Frog Ledge. I just wanted to add that I'm thrilled this kind of establishment is moving into Frog Ledge. I think it will give people convenient, healthy veterinary care options. I'm a steadfast homeopathy client myself, and I've seen the difference it's made for my cat. And I commend Ms. Kirschbaum for her selflessness and dedication to the animals, for using her spare time to make their lives better. Thank you."

She went back to her seat. Diane turned and gave her a big smile as if to say *thank you*.

After that, the comments stopped and Mayor Galveston announced the public hearing closed and a decision to be brought back to the council after the next town zoning meeting.

Stan, Char, and Patricia waited until people filed out before leaving. "Well, that was eye opening," Stan said.

"I never thought Trooper Pasquale would stick up for anyone like that!"

Char laughed. "Oh, Stan. You just had a bad first experience with Jessie. She's a lovely girl, if not a little reserved. But she means well."

"What an interesting bunch of characters," Patricia said. "Is this how all small towns work? It's fascinating."

Fascinating? What had come over her mother? Twilight Zone theme song. She pushed it out. "I have to say, I'm surprised, Mom," Stan said as they left the chambers, opting for the stairs. "This doesn't seem like your cup of tea."

"It's fun to try new things," her mother said dismissively.

Since when? Stan wanted to know, but bit her tongue. As they walked back toward Stan's house, she had to ask the burning question. "So, Mom. That guy Tony Falco. You know him?" She glanced at her mother, but couldn't see her face well in the darkening night.

"Which one is that?" her mother said in a tone that Stan had heard before. It meant, *I'm completely avoiding answering you.*

"The man who asked about funding the new shelter. Who also happens to be running for mayor," she said.

"Hmm. I don't quite remember, Kristan. You'll have to point him out to me if we see him again." And with that, she turned to speak to Char, leaving Stan wondering what her mother was hiding.

Chapter 22

"So what do you know about this Tony Falco character?" Stan asked.

She, Char, and Ray filed into the church the next morning for Hal Hoffman's send-off. Char was dressed appropriately in a long-sleeved black dress, but had tied one of her signature orange scarves around her neck and topped off the outfit with flaming orange pumps. She couldn't help herself. Stan had chosen a simple black sweater dress. Ray still wore his overalls, but had changed to a clean shirt.

"Ray's been out all morning with the alpacas," Char had confided on the way. "It was hard to pull him away, but Hal was a friend."

Char stood on her tiptoes to survey the crowd as they paused in the back of the church. "Good turnout," she said approvingly. "What do I know about Tony Falco? Not much. Except that I wouldn't vote for him."

"No? How come, if you don't know much?" Stan asked.

"Well, for that reason, sugar. Not to be mayor. I'm all about welcoming new folks to town, but I have reservations about putting them in charge too early when they don't know us. Plus, I'm delighted with Mona's mayorship. She knows this town and she's a good person to have in charge. Now, Hal was a fan of Falco—if you couldn't tell from that big, honkin' sign in front of his yard. But Hal—God rest his soul—was a Republican, like his candidate. And Tony Falco's stump speech is all about saving the dairy farms. He was a lobbyist before, I heard. Lobbied at the federal level for better milk prices. So, Hal's loyalty is understandable. But there's something about him that just doesn't gel with me. Why do you ask?"

"My mother seemed to know him. Or at least know of him. Did she say anything to you?" Stan asked.

"Why, no. I can ask her later," Char said. "She's delightful, you know. She seems to be enjoying herself very much. She had breakfast with me this morning and even came out to see the alpacas."

"That's great." And surprising.

"We should find a seat," Ray said in a properly subdued voice. "Come on, Stan." With his hand at each of their backs, Ray herded them down the aisle and turned them into the first pew with enough room. Stan found herself uncomfortably close to a woman with long, stringy gray hair topped with a black flower. She had a hankie pressed against her face, into which she repeatedly blew her nose. Stan slid as far over against Char as she could.

The church filled almost to capacity before the priest started the Mass. Stan hadn't been to church in a very long time, but was still able to recite the words to almost everything in her head. Scary. The priest, Father Henry, had been in Frog Ledge for a long time—Ray leaned over to whisper—and knew Hal and his family well. During his sermon, he spoke directly to Emmalee and the boys, sitting right in front, about Hal's devotion to them and how they could take comfort in knowing Hal would watch over them for the rest of their lives. To which Em and one of the younger boys started to cry, but behind her Stan could hear snickering.

"Devoted. Like hell," she heard a voice directly behind her mutter. Trying to be stealth, she stole a glance over her shoulder. Who had said it? The pretty brunette with the low-cut blouse? Or the woman next to her, who was filing her nails in her lap? She couldn't tell. But she did see a familiar face at the back of the church. Izzy Sweet, dressed completely in black, including a hat, stood alone against the back of the church, a wad of tissues clenched in her fist. Crying.

What on earth was that about?

Stan stopped by the after-funeral lunch, mainly to see if Izzy was there. She was not, so Stan slipped out and went home to eat. She changed, checked her messages, and returned a call to a woman named Sophie Grasso, who was friends with Lorinda from the library. Sophie had twin cats who were turning five, and she wanted to have a party for them. Would Stan be interested?

She'd never done a cat party before. It sounded fun. She did wonder how the rest of the guests would feel after being transported to the party. Most cats hated a car ride. Nutty was a prime example. But when she called Sophie back, she found out the rest of the guests lived in the house already. Sophie had rescued ten cats from local shelters over the past few years, and while she was used to throwing them parties, "I want this one to be special," she explained. "These guys had a hard life before they joined my family."

Stan agreed and set up an appointment for the following week to go meet the cats, Wilma and Fred, and talk through what kinds of treats they would like best. Then, since farmers never got a day off, Stan headed over to the Hoffmans'. It didn't look like Em was back yet. She hoped Em could forego work and spend the rest of the day with family. She'd looked exhausted and beaten down at the funeral. Stan figured she would try to get some things done for her today, even if it was just cleaning up.

After checking in with Roger and learning that two cows were sick and in quarantine pens and the baby calf was doing well, she headed to the office. It looked exactly as it had yesterday when Stan left. Which was unfortunate. She'd half hoped Tyler would've come through and sorted through some of the stuff after their conversation on Monday. But she hadn't seen him on the farm since then. The poor kid was dealing with a lot.

But there was a new accessory. Petunia the calico cat blinked at her from the middle of the desk and swished her tail, spilling a pile of folders and their contents onto the floor.

"Well, hello there," Stan said.

Petunia purred. Stan loved calicos. She wondered if Petunia had ventured down to the office to keep Hal company while he worked, or if he preferred the dog. Had he loved his animals? Did they miss him? Or did he have the typical farm mentality, that animals were just there, and expendable? She hoped not. Petunia and Samson were too cute for that.

"You're welcome to hang out. And I think I have something you'll like." She rummaged through her purse and pulled out a Ziploc bag of treats—albeit a bit crushed, but still enticing to a cat, she hoped.

They were. Petunia inhaled the first few pieces and looked up expectantly for more. "Excellent. I'm flattered."

Stan emptied the remainder of the bag out and let the cat enjoy. When Petunia finished, she curled up in a ball on the corner of the desk she'd cleared off and promptly went to sleep.

Stan scooped up the fallen papers. As she went to shove them back in the stack, she noticed a couple of pictures in the midst. Expecting to see family photos, perhaps pictures of the kids as they grew up, she pulled them out.

She was wrong. These were postcards, all of faraway places. San Diego. San Francisco. Napa Valley. A ski resort in Vail, Colorado. Horses in a pasture. None of them had messages on them; rather they seemed to be mementos. Or wishes. Stan shuffled through them slowly, thinking of Hal Hoffman the man. Until now, she'd only thought of him as Hal Hoffman the dairy farmer, or the failed real estate mogul or the bar hopper. But first and foremost, he was a man with dreams and hopes and desires, many of them probably secret, stored away until they were almost forgotten. Reduced to a pile of yellowing pictures stuffed in a folder next to receipts for the cows' veterinary care. Stan wondered how many of those dreams—if any—actually mirrored the life he'd just left behind. She remembered Tyler's words that first day, about his dad looking for a ticket out of town. But he hadn't made it. Now those dreams were buried for good, along with the man who owned them.

But the farm remained. Stan picked up the checkbook and flipped through the register. The last recorded check in the register was dated August 13. There were a few checks missing since that one, and no noted balance. She hadn't run across any recent bank statements either, so those were probably arriving via e-mail. Perhaps they had gone to an online system. It had to be easier. But then she was still out of luck, because there was no sign of a computer.

Well, no use dwelling on something she couldn't change. Better to do what she could.

Stan tackled the piles with vigor and determination and within an hour she'd gotten through one third of them, written out checks for all the September and October bills she could find, and filed the rest. Whether she could mail them or not was a different story, but she'd recorded the amounts to ask Em.

Standing to stretch her cramped legs, Stan wandered around the tiny room. Why hadn't Hal kept an office out in the farm building? She couldn't imagine the appeal of being down here in a room that was dark even on the brightest of days. The one small window was so dirty the sun seemed to have a filter on it.

Petunia woke from her nap, jumped down, and wandered to the back of the room, kicking up clumps of dust as she went. Stan watched her wend her way around the ratty chair and the filing cabinet, out of sight.

"Petunia?" Stan called. She didn't want her to get stuck somewhere in this room where no one ever looked. She'd have to make sure the door to the house was shut when she left so Petunia didn't come back in.

Stan peered behind the chair. No cat. "Want a treat?" Stan tried, shaking the bag. She moved around the chair to check behind the ancient filing cabinet and cursed when she tripped on something. Bending over, she saw the corner of something metal sticking out from under the chair. She reached down and pulled it out.

A lockbox. One for a laptop, it looked like. She tried the lid. Locked. Which made sense but didn't help her any. She tested the box. Heavy, so something was definitely inside it.

Why had Hal locked up his laptop if he used it for farm

accounting? Perhaps he was just cautious, especially with so many workers on the property, but still. Locked and shoved under a chair? It seemed odd.

She set the box on the desk and checked the drawers for a random key. Nothing. Petunia emerged from under the chair and wended her way around Stan's legs, purring. "Were you trying to show me this?" Stan asked. The cat rubbed her ankle. "Thanks. Now show me the key."

Petunia gracefully hopped onto the washer and vanished into the house, her job done. "Great," Stan muttered. The key had to be here somewhere, she hoped, and not buried with Hal. She checked the filing cabinet. Nothing. She slammed the drawer in frustration. She could wait until Em got back, which could be much later. She could try to bust into it, but she was no lock picker. Or she could just leave it where she found it and go about her business.

The third option seemed smartest.

Instead, she hopped over the washing machine herself and headed into the basement. If Em came back, she could always say she was thirsty and went to get water.

Great. Now I'm breaking and entering a dead man's house. . . . What's wrong with you?

She ignored the condemning voice and climbed the stairs to the main floor. The door to the house was cracked. She pushed it open the rest of the way and found herself in Em's hallway. Samson trundled in to greet her. At least he was making her feel better about being in the house. She found the den that Em and Pasquale had used the night of Hal's murder, thinking it might be a good option for keys. But her search yielded nothing. She wasn't ready to snoop in their bedroom and didn't know where else to look.

Maybe she'd get that water after all. She headed to the kitchen. There was a pile of dirty dishes in the sink and on the counter. She found a clean glass in the cabinet, the last one, and filled it with ice and water from the fridge. As she drank it, she glanced around the room. Em really needed a housekeeper. But Stan was keeping her mouth shut about that one. She didn't want that job, too. She finished the water and washed out the glass. Then, because she couldn't in good conscience leave the mess, she filled the dishwasher and ran it. Straightened up as much as she could and swept the floor with the broom in the corner. As she put it back, she accidentally hit the keys hanging on a ring near the door. Bending to pick them up, the lightbulb went off.

He probably kept the key on his ring. These had to be his keys, since Em had her car. Score.

She hurried back down the stairs and sorted through the keys. There were three small ones. The first one was too big. The second one fit but didn't turn. And the last one worked perfectly.

"Yeeah!" Stan pumped her fist in the air. She unlocked the box, confirmed that there was a laptop in it, and raced upstairs to return the keys to their hook. She went back through the basement, grabbed the laptop, closed the door to the main house so Petunia didn't come back in, and left.

Chapter 23

Stan went straight home where she could snoop out in the open. She was supposed to call her mother at six so they could have dinner. It was only five. Plenty of time to take a look at her booty. She poured herself some organic lemonade and grabbed some almonds for a snack, then went into the sunroom so she could let the dogs out and keep an eye on them.

The lockbox itself was high quality, steel, with padding inside. Given the condition of everything else she'd seen at the Hoffmans'—gently and not so gently used, inexpensive— this stood out like a sore thumb. Hal must've really wanted to protect this machine.

She pulled the laptop out. A small, leather-bound book fell out in its wake. Stan put it aside and checked out the computer. It wasn't anything special either. A PC, at least a few years old. As a Mac girl, Stan wasn't impressed. While she waited for it to boot up, she picked up the book. A calendar. For this year. She flipped through. It was the kind with lines next to each date and one page at the beginning of each month showing all the weeks. Stan thumbed through the calendar until she got to October 17.

The day Hal died. There was one entry on the page: "11, Bruno's." Nothing else. No parent-teacher conference noted. The rest of the week also had no entries. The present week had a lot. All just times and names of places, or times and initials. All meetings Hal had missed. One meeting with the Department of Labor. She thought of the argument between Peter Michelli and Roger about the alleged illegal workers. Enrico's disappearance. Had he been an illegal and somehow knew about the meeting? Had he taken off so he wouldn't be deported? Had Em made the meeting?

She went ahead to the next week. The day before Halloween showed an interview scheduled with Carmine, a mechanic. In November, Election Day was highlighted with the initials "TF" noted—Tony Falco. Flipping back through to past entries, she noticed Hal had a number of meetings with TF, or had simply noted, "campaign headquarters."

The end of November had no entries. The next entry Stan found was a reminder for December 8, Danny's birthday. She didn't see anything about board meetings, or other Happy Cow business. She flipped back to October 17. . . . Bruno's. Stan drummed her fingers on the desk and tried to think if she'd ever come across a Bruno. This could reference a person's name, or some kind of business. She didn't remember either from her travels around town. Pulling out her iPhone, Stan did a Google search. The name turned up a match in the nearby town of Willard, seven miles outside Frog Ledge. Bruno's Pub, the "friendliest place in town," according to the listing. Right around the corner from Bruno's Pizza. Knowing what she'd heard about Hal, a pub seemed logical. Somehow she doubted Hal would've chosen the pizza shop over the pub for his meeting.

The laptop had finally turned on. She searched the list of programs for QuickBooks or some accounting software.

Nothing. Where would it be? She scanned the folders and documents on Hal's desktop. Spreadsheets of feed and farm vehicle parts. A PDF of grain delivery schedules. Photos of the Hoffman kids in various stages of farm work. A cute photo of the littlest one kissing a cow. Someone was holding him up—Stan could only see forearms in the picture— while someone else snapped the photo. She opened the "My Documents" folder. Not much in there either. A Word document with a list of numbers and dates. Some were starred, others crossed off. She had no idea what they represented. She closed the document and moved on.

Next was a letter Hal had written to Tony Falco, endorsing his campaign. Stan skimmed it. In it, an articulate Hal had written about his admiration for Falco's commitment to farming and his work on policy to keep milk prices fair. Stan wondered what position the present mayor, Mona Galveston, held on those issues. Did she see farming as a thing of the past, not worth much campaign time?

The last folder had the standard PC title "New Folder." She figured it was probably empty but checked anyway. It was not. Inside were eight documents, all labeled with only dates. The earliest was August of the previous year. The most recent was last month. She clicked on the earliest. A screen popped up asking for a password. She tried the next one. Same thing. Same for all eight. Stan propped her chin in her hand and drummed her fingers on the desktop. What had Hal password protected? She halfheartedly tried a couple of combinations based on the kids' names and the street number of the farm. No go.

Drumming her fingers on her table, Stan pondered the implications of a dead man's password-protected documents. They could simply be bank information, something to do with the farm's finances. She could ask Emmalee about them. Or they could be Hal's personal documents, untitled and protected so his family didn't stumble upon them. Business dealings, most likely. Perhaps love letters from someone other than Em, although that was a wild assumption.

But what if they had something to do with his death? She should call Trooper Pasquale and alert her to the documents. But what if she didn't think it was important? Pretty much everyone in the world password-protected something, and hardly any of them were murdered.

She wished she could take a peek, just to see.

"Ugh," she muttered, frustrated. "There's gotta be a way." Then she sat up straight. She'd nearly forgotten Justin. Nikki's boyfriend, surfer dude extraordinaire, diving teacher—and computer wizard. He could help her get into the documents with minimal effort, she was positive. She pulled out her phone and dialed Nikki's number.

"Where's Justin?" she asked when her friend answered.

"Hi to you, too," Nikki responded. "He's on a dive trip in the Caribbean."

"Shoot."

"What's up?"

"I need his help with a computer thing." Stan didn't elaborate.

"Oh. Send him an e-mail. Maybe he can help over the phone. Otherwise, he's due back Saturday."

"Okay, will do. Thanks, Nik." She hung up before Nikki could probe. She connected Hal's computer to her wireless Internet and e-mailed the documents to Justin with a copy to herself. Hopefully he could take a look soon, but if not, Saturday was only a couple of days away.

She was getting hungry. And it was nearly six. Her mind drifted back to Bruno's and pizza. Maybe she'd go pick one up for her and her mother to enjoy. She'd been meaning to try out some different pizza shops locally. And she could always pop her head into the pub while her pie cooked and ask around. Maybe someone would mention being Hal's date for eleven on the day he died.

Her mother wasn't interested in going out for pizza. Stan had to pick it up and bring it to her. Patricia also had directed her to pick up a large salad, in case the pizza wasn't very good—which meant she had expected a different kind of dinner.

But investigating had to come first. Maybe Bruno's would offer a good lead.

On impulse, Stan called Izzy's cell. She still hadn't been able to track her friend down to see what was going on with her. "You want to have pizza tonight? My mother's in town and we're going to have dinner."

"Your mother?" Izzy sounded exhausted and distracted, such a difference from her usual demeanor. "Why do you want me intruding if your mom is in town? Oh, wait a second." She chuckled, sounding a little like herself again. "You don't like your mother, do you?"

"Not true. My mother's fine. And I haven't seen you in a while. I think you're avoiding me."

"Not avoiding anyone, babe. Just not feeling well. Where you gettin' pizza from?"

"Bruno's, in Willard? Ever hear of it?"

Stan heard Izzy suck in a breath. She didn't respond immediately, and when she did, her tone was cautious. "Where did you hear of Bruno's?"

"I heard about it around town and wanted to check it out." The lie rolled easily off Stan's tongue.

"Where around town?"

"Oh, there was a pizza debate going on in the library when I was there the other day. I heard someone say it was the best pizza around." Lie two. What was happening to her?

"Really." Izzy's tone was flat. Weird.

"Yeah, why? The garlic kind sounded great. Award winning." Fleetwood Mac's "Little Lies" should be her song tonight.

"Award-winning, my ass," Izzy said. "You're lying. And I thought we were friends."

Taken aback, Stan was speechless for a minute. Izzy used her pause to continue her tongue lashing. "Why do you really want to go there? And don't give me another line."

"I thought we were friends, too," Stan said, recovered and angry. "So maybe you should tell me what you know about Bruno's. And why you've been acting so strangely since Hal died."

Silence on the other end. Then Izzy hung up.

Stan stared at the silent phone, then looked at Scruffy, who sat on the floor watching her.

"That didn't go so well, did it?"

Scruffy wagged her tail cautiously.

"Now I really want to go and see what the deal is. I think Izzy knows Bruno's all too well. You guys in?"

"Woo woo!" Scruffy jumped up on Stan's leg.

"That settles it." She grabbed the dogs' leashes and kissed Nutty's head. He reached a lazy paw up to touch her cheek, as if to say, *I'll miss you.*

She loved that cat.

She and the dogs piled into the car and headed out. Stan had MapQuested the address on her phone. Frog Ledge was such a small town the main road leading in and out was a two-lane country highway. She followed this road for about five miles in a direction she'd never taken since moving to town, and came to a bridge with a sign: ENTERING WILLARD, EST. 1682. The bridge crossed a river. On the other side, ramshackle buildings lined the street. Some were boarded, some were abandoned, and some were tagged up with graffiti. People were outside, but it wasn't the same crowd she was used to seeing in Frog Ledge. Teenagers walked along the side of the bridge, some alone, others with one or two friends, some with pit bulls that made Henry look like a runt. The kids were all dressed in red and black and looked like they were trying to be gangsters. None of them looked friendly; most looked like they were on a mission. Henry and Scruffy didn't seem to like the looks of them either—they started barking and howling at the window, resulting in glares from the street.

"Hush, guys," she hissed, rolling up the windows as they drove through. Frog Ledge was such a cute little town, with well-cared-for common areas and people who truly seemed invested in their community. Willard, so far, seemed run down and not as loved. But maybe this was just a bad area and it would improve in a few blocks. Every town had one.

Her phone told her to take a left onto Browning Street. It was as seedy as the neighborhood she'd just passed through. Possibly more so. Along the way, attempts at sprucing up the area were apparent—a cupcake shop, a café, an art co-op. But payday loan shops, thrift shops, stores with Spanish names, and boarded up windows surrounded those few places. Yikes. What business did Hal Hoffman have around here?

Bruno's was ahead on the left. She could see a neon sign blinking pinkish red with the name. She cruised up slowly and assessed the situation. The neon sign was for the pub. The pizza shop was much more low key. She'd hit the pub first, get some info, then swing over to the pizza place. If the pies looked nasty, she could pick something up at McSwigg's for her mother. Or she could just beg Char to feed them.

She parked and glanced at the dogs. "Okay, guys. I'm not going to be long. Keep an eye on the car, okay?"

Henry looked at her, his sweet brown eyes worried. He was so sensitive. She could almost hear him say, *Why don't you leave this to the police?* In hindsight, she probably should have called Pasquale and handed the calendar over. Scruffy sat ramrod straight at the window, alternating between barking at people passing by and looking at Stan with that same concerned face. Did the dogs know something she didn't about Bruno's?

It's fine. Go. Stan pulled down the visor and opened the mirror, checked her hair and makeup. Acceptable. Okay. She grabbed her purse and got out of the car, beeped it locked. The dogs watched balefully through the window as she made her way to the door. The top pane of glass had a large crack in it. The door had barely any weight to it when she pulled it open. It banged shut behind her.

She stood for a moment, letting her eyes adjust to the dark. *This isn't McSwigg's.* The room barely had any light at all, probably because the owners wanted to hide their décor—or lack thereof. The tables were pocked and scarred. The wooden chairs looked stiff and punishing. She couldn't tell what color the walls were, maybe because of the dark, or the dirt. The crowd of about fifteen looked like a cross between a motorcycle gang and a street gang, although that was probably just her naive point of view. She had no idea if motorcycle gangs and street gangs would hang out at the same bar, or if it really mattered at this point when two of the largest biker dudes in the house were eyeing her like a side of fresh meat.

Stan put on her best "don't mess with me" face and strolled to the bar. Well, she hoped it was a stroll. Her legs were shaking, so it might've looked like she had a disorder. The bar wasn't in much better shape than the rest of the place, although it looked sturdier than anything else. The plastic covering on some of the empty stools was torn. Foam spilled out. The people residing on the rest of the stools looked as rough as the furniture.

And every person in the place—all male—stared at her.

Her jeans, long-sleeved T-shirt, and black ankle boots had seemed acceptable when she left the house. Now, she felt like she'd broken some kind of rule in here. Too many clothes? An uncomfortable realization. But thanks to the chew-'em-up-and-spit-'em-out atmosphere of corporate America, Stan had an edge. She knew how to keep a poker face, how to pretend nothing bothered her when in fact, she wanted to curl up in a corner and cry. She drew on every ounce of those tactics to look straight through the men leering at her as she walked. Finally she made it to the less-crowded end of the bar, AC/DC's "Hell's Bells" pounding through her brain.

The bartender, a greasy, foul-looking man with acne-pocked skin, ignored her for about five minutes. While she waited, she observed the other patrons. A guy with a shaved head sat closest to her, alternating between staring moodily into a beer mug and staring at her. Two seats away from him, two guys with black do-rags huddled together, talking in hushed tones. Their jeans hung way below their boxers, and Stan swore she saw a glint of black metal jammed into the elastic waistband of one of the guys.

What the heck was she doing here? Let Em come find

out what her husband was up to. Or better yet, Trooper
Pasquale. At least she got paid for this crap. And it was
really none of her business, after all. She'd just made up
her mind to leave when the bartender finally turned to her,
observing with flat eyes. "Yeah?" he said.

She'd lost her chance. She had to say something now.
Stan pasted on her best sexy smile and tossed her blond hair
over her shoulder. Her recent haircut had been a fabulous
one, and her hair felt extra bouncy and thick. She hoped it
would distract him. "I'm looking for someone who may
have been here last Thursday. Hal Hoffman? Do you by any
chance know if he had an appointment with someone here?
At eleven?"

The guy's eyes narrowed to mean slits, then he barked
out a laugh. Instead of answering her, he looked at his line
of customers. "Did he have an appointment, she wants to
know. Like this is some doc's office or sumthin'." He
looked back at Stan, the sneer returning. "Whadda I look
like, a secretary? How the hell should I know? You want a
drink or what?"

Stan's gaze fell on the dirty, smudged glass the guy dried
with a towel that looked like it hadn't seen a washing machine since 1978. "No, thank you," she said, backing away.
"I'll just, uh, ask around."

The bartender glared at her, then went back to his real
customers. Stan didn't care to have the same conversation
with any of the other patrons, so she headed for the door
and the safety of her dogs. But a body cut in front of her,
blocking her way. She found herself staring into the chest
of a leather vest, on top of a big beer belly. Tilting her head
back, she looked up into a face meaner than the bartender's,
racked with scars and half hidden by a huge, bushy mus-

tache that moved as he spoke. What she could see of his teeth under the mustache were yellow. He reeked of stale cigars and sweat. But by far, the most disturbing aspect of his appearance was the scarred-over hole in his neck, a perfect circle.

Like a bullet hole.

"'Scuse me, miss," he said with a leer. His voice sounded odd—slightly robotic. Probably something to do with said hole. "Couldn't help but overhear. You a friend of Hal Hoffman?"

"Yes," Stan said. Behind her, she heard chairs scraping, heavy boots hitting the floor as men stood.

"You taking care of his affairs? Since I heard he ain't with us anymore."

Stan glanced over her shoulder. Saw the bartender throw down his towel and disappear through a door behind the bar. "Yeah, I am." *She was?*

A couple of the men moved up behind her, circling. Blocking her way to the front door.

"We had an agreement. Beginning Saturday. I gotta know if we're keeping that on the books."

She swore she could feel someone's breath on the back of her neck. Possibly the click of a switchblade opening. Sweat trickled between her shoulder blades. An agreement? For what? Seemed dangerous to say no. But what would she be agreeing to? Could be any kind of criminal activity. Illegal gambling. A drug deal. A hit, for all she knew. Or she could stop acting like she was on an episode of *The Sopranos*.

But she'd honed her nonanswering skills well over the years. Maybe that would get her out of this. "Can you come by the farm Saturday?" she said. "We can finalize every-thing."

The guy was silent for the longest thirty seconds of her life, watching her. Finally he nodded, smoothing his mus-tache down with one hand. "I'll do that," he said.

"No problem," Stan said, pasting a smile on. Then she turned and headed for the door as fast as she could without breaking into a run. Now she just had to figure out what to do on Saturday.

Chapter 24

Stan got to Izzy's just as her friend was unlocking the doors Thursday morning. Enough was enough. Her friend had to talk to her sometime. And after last night's episode, both on the phone with Izzy and at Bruno's, Stan felt she deserved some answers.

After leaving Bruno's in a mad rush she'd called her mother, trying to sound normal, only for Patricia to tell her she was eating with Char and Ray. Just as well. Her conversation with Bullet Man had rattled her, and she wouldn't be good company anyway. Which would cause a whole slew of aggravation with her mother.

Stan had gone home after driving a few miles out of her way to make sure no one followed her. She'd locked her doors and sat in her den, in close proximity to a window, so she could see if he was coming to get her. Now she had to worry about what would happen on Saturday because she'd opened her big mouth. And Izzy was somewhere in the middle of all this.

No, Izzy would talk to her today if she had to tie her to the chair and pour espresso down her throat. Determined, she shoved the front door open just as Izzy opened it for her. Stan almost ended up on her face on the café floor.

Izzy raised an eyebrow. "Graceful entrance. You need coffee that bad?"

"No. I need to talk to you." Stan took a deep breath and regained her poise. "And don't tell me you're too busy, or too upset that I lied about pizza. I'm your friend and you can't avoid me forever."

Izzy listened to her dramatic speech without comment, then she shrugged. "Sure. Come on in. We'll talk."

Stan opened her mouth, then closed it again. That was easy. She followed Izzy into the shop. Coffee brewed, and Stan inhaled the scent of bold, bitter beans. Heaven.

"Want a cup?" Izzy asked, a hint of a smile on her lips. Clearly Stan needed to work on her poker face.

"Sure. Do you have someone to work the counter?"

"Oooh. This is going to be a *serious* conversation, then." Izzy winked at her friend, a hint of her usual spunk shining through. "I do have help today. Della?" she called, heading over to pour Stan a cup.

Della Leroy, one of Izzy's weekday staffers, appeared in the kitchen doorway and waved at Stan. "Good morning! You need me out here, Izzy?"

Della was Stan's favorite of Izzy's workers. She couldn't quite tell how old she was due to her youthful brown skin and her funky, purple-tinged hair (which may or may not have been hair extensions), but her best guess was early fifties. Della was as loud as she was round, and she had a knack for coaxing people to try something from the pastry case, or a new kind of chocolate-flavored something to accompany their intended purchase.

"Could you do the counter for me for a little while? Stan and I need to chat."

She figured Izzy would sit them down at a table in the back of the store, but instead she handed her the coffee and led her into the curtained-off area she reserved for small events, like poetry slams or exhibitions of local artists' work. They went through another curtain with a door behind it. Izzy unlocked it with a key from her key ring. It opened into a stairwell. They were halfway up when Stan realized Izzy was taking her to her apartment. And that she'd never been up there, in all the months she'd known Izzy. She hadn't really thought of it before. Maybe Izzy was just a very private person—something Stan could relate to—or maybe she didn't consider Stan a good friend after all. She pondered why that realization stung.

Izzy unlocked a door at the top of the stairs and led her into an adorable kitchen with sunny yellow walls, a cozy kitchen table, and three dogs jockeying for position to greet them.

"Hey, guys!" Stan got down on her knees to give all the dogs hugs. Baxter, Elvira, and Junior crowded around her, all looking for treats. Stan was happy to oblige. She had her usual treat bag she brought when visiting Izzy.

Once the dogs were happy, she got to her feet and brushed her jeans off. Izzy was pouring a glass of orange juice. "You all set with coffee? Want anything else?"

Stan declined.

"Let's go sit, then." Izzy walked into a living room that looked like a New York City penthouse featured in a photo shoot—black and white and modern with splashes of red. Stan wondered how she kept everything so pristine with the dogs there. She already felt like her house needed constant cleaning with two dogs and one cat.

She perched on the edge of the black sofa. Izzy sat across from her on the white chair with a red throw. She crossed her long legs, sipped her drink, and regarded Stan, looking more like a movie star than a café owner in a sleepy, rural town. "So, what's up?"

"We need to talk."

"You said that," Izzy said. "What are we talking about?"

"You know what. Hal Hoffman. And Bruno's."

"Bruno's? What about Bruno's? Did you go there last night?" She raised her eyebrows at Stan's nod. "How was your pizza?" Sarcasm tinged her voice.

Stan bared her teeth. "I didn't get pizza. After my experience in the pub I figured it wouldn't be that good after all."

"What happened?"

"Oh, come on, Izzy. I didn't come here to play games. I'm your friend and I care about you. You never told me the real story about the guy in your café, and now I hear you and Hal had some deal going. When I mentioned Bruno's you clearly knew what kind of place it was. Why don't you tell me what's going on?"

Izzy narrowed her eyes. "How did you hear about that deal?"

"Doesn't matter."

"Great. So the whole town knows about my bad judgment." She flopped back on her chair, put her head on the back, and stared at the ceiling.

"The whole town doesn't know anything unless you told them. Except maybe that you threw a chair at one of your customers," Stan said.

Izzy shook her head. "He wasn't a customer. You want to know why I threw a chair at that guy? Because he threatened me. Nobody threatens me and gets away with it."

"How did he threaten you? Did you tell Pasquale?"

"Yeah, right. You can't exactly tell the cops you borrowed

money from a scumbag like that and expect them to have any sympathy. So no, I didn't tell the cops anything. Fortunately, the scumbag was scared of being found out, too, so he dropped the charges. I figure he'll come looking for me eventually, some night when I'm near a dark alley alone."

"Izzy. Did you borrow money from a gangster? Does he operate at Bruno's?"

Izzy scooped Elvira, who had wandered into the room, onto her lap, nuzzling the dog's head against her chin. "I suppose I should start from the beginning."

"That'd be nice," Stan said.

Izzy ignored her sarcasm. "When I got to Frog Ledge and bought this place, I threw my entire life savings into it, between the mortgage and the repairs. This floor was perfect but I needed to redo downstairs. Expensive, but worth it. I wanted to own a business so bad." Her tone was wistful. "And I'm doing way better than I expected. I wish more of the locals would come around, but it's all good.

"Except that I don't have a cushion anymore. And I had a problem with some of the work in the kitchen, so it got a little out of hand, expense-wise. So I've been living on the edge a bit." She laughed self-consciously. "But who doesn't do that in America today, right?"

Stan stayed silent. She didn't usually live on the edge, financially or otherwise. Financially, she knew it was wise. In other aspects of her life, she figured she was shortchanging herself. Although this week alone she'd broken into someone's computer and made a possible deal with a gangster, both of which could qualify.

"I figured since the stock market was tanking, real estate might be the way to go to make some cash back," Izzy went on. "I bought a piece of commercial property and it was a disaster. Two businesses moved in, then moved out again in less than three months. I can't keep a tenant in there to save my life, and I can't sell it."

"Where is the property? Here in Frog Ledge?"

"Actually, no. It's in Willard."

Stan thought of her adventure last night. "Near where I was last night?"

Izzy was silent, but her facial expression said it all.

"Oh, God. It's not affiliated with Bruno's, is it?"

Izzy wrinkled her nose. "Not affiliated, but near enough that no one wants to be in that neighborhood. Between the bikers and the other . . . problems, it's not good for business. And I didn't do my homework well enough. Nothing new there, either. I can't unload it. So I'm even more strapped. And then, the perfect place came along for my second dream."

"Second dream? I'm assuming the café was your first?"

Izzy grinned. "Actually, marrying Brad Pitt was my first, but I gave that up a while back. I don't like his new scruffy look anyway. So yeah, the café. Next is a bookstore. Ideally, they would be in the same place, but my shop expanded more than I had planned, so it wouldn't work right now. Nope, there's a place a little ways down the street that's perfect for a bookstore. It was on sale a little over a year ago. It seemed like fate. And here's where the story goes wrong."

"Oh, God. What did you do?" Stan wanted to cover her ears. She hated hearing stories about bad financial decisions. She'd learned money at a young age, and her years in financial services gave her some great insights into investments and best practices. She'd been in such good shape being laid off hadn't even made her bank account blink. But it sounded like Izzy hadn't been as informed, or as thoughtful.

"I found a partner to buy the building with me."

"Hal Hoffman."

"Bingo! You get the prize behind door number three." Izzy rose abruptly and headed into the kitchen. She refilled her glass and returned. "Again, Impulsive Izzy. Not enough homework. My uncle knew Hal. They were both members of the regional Chamber of Commerce, years ago. I guess the fact that they were friends shoulda clued me in. My unc had some issues. Anyhow, he told me I needed to hook up with Hal—not literally, so don't wiggle your eyebrows at me—and get in on his real estate biz. Always had his eye on the prize, my uncle did."

"So where's your uncle now? Can he help?" Stan asked.

"In jail out west somewhere," Izzy said without missing a beat.

"Oh." Stan wasn't sure she wanted to know why.

"I listened to him. Came to Frog Ledge and started this business, and scoped out the opportunities with Hal. Hal came in the café a lot. Wanted to supply my dairy. Loved that I wanted to get in on the real estate stuff. I think he saw me as a good prospect to help him get rich quick. Hal's deals were pretty sketchy. But I wanted the store, so I got on board. And then I was on the hook. My fault, again. I didn't question where he was getting the dough. Plus, he was involved in a lawsuit. Supposed to be getting money off some countersuit, and he was going to dump a chunk of that settlement right into the building." She smiled wistfully. "I could smell my bookstore. But the lawsuit didn't get settled as fast as he thought. The payments stopped getting made. And he avoided me.

"When I finally confronted him, he confessed he didn't have his share of the money. So I tried to cover the payments—I really did. I didn't have staff for a while so I didn't have to pay salaries. He gave me the dairy supplies for free to try to help, but his wife caught wind of it and freaked out." She shook her head. "It all went to hell. The loan sharks started putting pressure on me when they realized he couldn't pay. Then they stopped coming around for a while, so I thought maybe he had gotten his act together. Turns out, he was gambling—don't ask me whose money. Turned a few profits, and then he lost big. The visits started up again. And then the son-of-a-gun got himself killed. And I have mortgages on three buildings that I can't keep paying." Her eyes watered and she turned away.

"So the guy in the chair incident. He was sent by the person Hal dealt with to get a loan?"

Izzy nodded, still facing away from Stan.

"Do you know his name?" Stan's mind immediately went to the guy with the hole in this throat at Bruno's. "What did he look like? Did he have a hole in this throat?"

"A *what?*"

Guess not. "Forget it. His name?"

"No idea. I let Hal handle it."

"Izzy." Stan got up from the couch and perched on the edge of Izzy's ottoman. "Do you think these people killed Hal?"

Tears dripped down Izzy's cheeks as she faced Stan. "I don't know. I wondered when . . . I saw the paper. But I don't know. And then I worry they might kill me. That's why I got freaked out that day. In the café."

"Understandable." Stan got up and paced, her brain working. "Have you been threatened in any other way?"

"Couple of phone calls, but can't prove who made them." Izzy waved a dismissive hand. "It doesn't matter. Nothing the cops can do. It's not like it was a legal loan or anything. I'm telling you, if I don't make one kind of stupid decision with a man, I make another. At least I didn't get involved with him, eh? Now everyone just thinks I was." She swiped angrily at her cheeks.

Stan rose and placed a hand on her friend's shoulder. "Izzy. Everyone makes decisions they wish they could do over. We just have to figure out how to get you out of it." She dropped her hand and paced the living room, her mind racing. "Have you talked to a corporate Realtor?"

Izzy nodded. "No one wants to touch the Willard neighborhood. And I don't want to sell the other building, just refinance."

Stan paced again. "Okay. We could also talk to a local bank. Sometimes they're better able to lend money, especially if it's to an established local person. We could try to get a better loan for all three. I'm sure the interest on whatever Hal did is insane, am I right?"

At Izzy's sheepish nod, Stan sighed. "Okay. That might lower your payment. Have you tried that?"

"No," Izzy admitted.

"Have you tried *anything?*"

"I've tried to stop crying. I've tried not to tell anyone." Izzy threw her hands up in exasperation. "Look, Stan, I'm not as business savvy as you. I messed up and I don't know how to fix it. And I'm terrified of losing my café."

"Okay, okay. Look. You won't lose the café. Let's put a plan together. Let's try the former owner's Realtor. Or maybe even ask the former owner if he knows anyone. If he's some developer, he might have a lead. Do you know who it is?"

"Oh yeah, I know him all right," Izzy said in a monotone.

"Well, who is it?" Stan demanded, impatient.

"Boy, you get bossy when it comes to money stuff." Izzy shook her head. "If you insist. It's Jake McGee."

For a moment, Stan was speechless. "Jake McGee?" she repeated. "Like, Jake McGee of McSwigg's?"

"Yep. The one and only. Ah, now your tune changes."

Jake was involved in real estate? So Jake knew about Hal's sketchy dealings. Had he been part of any of that, even unwillingly? Maybe Hal had ripped him off. Maybe he'd been angry with Hal about some deal. Angry enough to kill him? The thought left her cold. When had she turned so suspicious?

"Does he know what's going on?" she asked Izzy.

"Of course not. He sold the building and he was done. I didn't even know he was the owner until Hal made the offer," Izzy snapped.

Things were starting to click in Stan's brain, even through the fog of surprise and suspicion. Finally, the mystery of Jake and Izzy, solved. "So Jake found out— when? When his Realtor brought a cash offer to him?"

"I guess," Izzy said. "He wanted to know who the buyer was. Then he showed up at my door to lecture me. Before that, I'd only met him a couple of times. He owned this building, too."

"Really." And she'd thought he just owned a cool bar and mixed drinks.

"Yeah, really. I got mad. Couldn't figure out why he wanted to keep me from my dream. I had all these conspiracy theories." Izzy barked out a humorless laugh. "Like he didn't want me to succeed because I wasn't a local, or because I wasn't even from this country. You know, the usual self-doubt garbage. So I threw him out and told him to mind his own business. I guess I got even angrier at him when I found out he'd been right."

Stan reached for her coffee. It was empty. She had a blazing headache and wished she could inject some straight into her veins. "So you really don't know a guy with a hole in his throat?"

"Swear to God I have no idea who you're talking about."

"But you don't know who the actual investor is, so it could be him."

"I suppose, but . . . a hole in his throat?"

"Yeah. Looks like he got shot right through here." Stan pointed to the base of her neck. "Course, I'm no bullet hole expert, but it looked like it. He asked me about an agreement Hal had with him. Starting this weekend. Do you know what that's about?"

Izzy shook her head slowly. "Swear on my mother."

"Do you like your mother?"

"Love her," Izzy said. "She's a great lady."

"Okay. Because he asked if we were on. I had to answer."

"So what did you say?"

"I didn't say yes or no. I told him to come by the farm and we'd work it out."

"You did what?" Izzy gaped at her.

Stan shrugged. "I was hoping maybe it would flush out the killer. I'll probably have Pasquale at the farm that night. I should tell her."

"Girl, you're crazy."

"I know. Will you let me know if you hear anything?"

"About crazy men with bullet holes in their throats making arrangements for Saturday night?" Izzy laughed without mirth. "Sure, you got it."

Stan left Izzy's around lunchtime, after a grueling conversation during which she got Izzy to agree to talk to Jake—if Stan mediated. Stan wasn't thrilled about getting in the middle, but she wanted to help Izzy. And she got the sense that Jake wasn't as cold and uncaring as Izzy had initially insinuated. Stan was pretty sure Izzy's grudge had to do with her bad real estate choice rather than any real character flaw on Jake's part. Maybe she could help smooth things over between the two, if nothing else. That is, if Jake agreed.

At least they hadn't dated. For some reason, that made her feel lighter.

Her stomach was in knots as she headed to the farm. Halfway there, she realized she'd forgotten to check her e-mail in hopes Justin had cracked the code on those documents. She'd have to check later. In the meantime, she'd finish tidying up the office, check in with Roger, and call it a day. She had to get Benny's birthday party planned—it was Saturday and she hadn't prepared anything yet. She had a cake to bake, decorations to buy, and goodie bags to make up.

Lost in her own lists, she walked into the Hoffmans' driveway and didn't notice Em sitting on the porch steps until she called to her.

"Hi there, Stan." Despite the forced enthusiasm in her voice, Em looked exhausted and sad.

"Oh, hey, Em. Sorry, didn't see you." Stan changed direction and walked over. "How are you holding up?"

"I'm fine. So sweet of you to come to the funeral."

"Of course I would come! How could I not?"

Em nodded. "May I ask you a favor?"

Please, no cow pushing. "Sure."

"Can you come see Samson? He doesn't look like he's feeling well today. I wondered if you could tell me what to give him for food that might make him feel better."

Stan opened her mouth to say, *I'm not a vet, I have no idea what would make your dog feel better,* then closed it again. The poor lady had been through enough and probably didn't have money to go to the vet. "Sure," she said. "Where is he?"

Em looked relieved. "Oh, thank you. He's inside." She rose, slowly, like her bones ached, and motioned for Stan to follow her. "I'm sorry to keep sidetracking you, but the kids couldn't stand if it the dog was sick, too—"

She stopped midsentence as Jessie Pasquale's cruiser rolled to a stop in the driveway. Stan followed Em's gaze and watched Pasquale emerge from the driver's seat. She was alone. Of the times Stan had seen Pasquale in tense situations, she'd never seen her look so uncomfortable.

Pasquale adjusted her shirt. Fiddled with her big belt. Pushed the sunglasses from her eyes to the top of her head. Finally, she walked over.

Emmalee watched her. She must have sensed this visit was different, because her smile was shaky. "Hi, Jessie. You have news for me?"

Jessie paused in front of the steps, shifting her weight from one foot to the other until she realized she was doing it. She stilled her movements and put her cop face back on. She did not look at Stan.

"Emmalee, would you mind coming with me? I need to ask you a few questions about your husband's murder," she said.

Emmalee's mouth opened, then closed. "I . . . What do you mean?"

Jessie stood firm. "I need you to get in the car."

Em's hands went to her hips. "Jessie, what in the world are you talking about? I've got a farm to run!"

"Emmalee, please don't make this more difficult than it already is. I just need to ask you some questions about the day Hal died. Please."

In disgust Stan watched the scene unfolding in front of

her. How many blows could this family take? "Are you arresting her?" she asked.

Pasqale ignored her.

Em turned to Stan, her eyes pleading.

"What do you need?" Stan asked.

"The boys—" Em began, but just then Tyler came around the corner of the house. He took in the scene, then turned to his mother.

"Mom? What's going on?"

"Nothing, honey. I have to go with Jessie for a little while. Will you make sure your brothers all get home and start their homework? Call Ted. Ask him to send someone to help tonight." She nodded, smiled, and touched his cheek. "Go on, now." She turned to Stan and handed her a key ring. "Keys to the house. Hold on to them, okay?"

Stan reached out to accept them and squeezed Em's hand.

Tyler stared at his mother as she started walking toward the cruiser. "Mom?"

"Do as I say, Ty," Emmalee called without looking back.

Tyler raced forward and grabbed his mother's wrist. "Mom!"

"Tyler," Jessie said. She opened the cruiser's passenger door—at least she didn't make Em sit in the back like a criminal—and waited. Tyler didn't let go. Jessie stepped forward, as if to remove his hand. Emmalee pulled it away first.

"Don't touch him," she warned.

"Please get in, Emmalee."

Emmalee extracted her hand from her son's. "It's okay, Tyler," she said.

But Tyler didn't think so. He put himself between Jessie and his mother and said, "It's me you want."

"Tyler!" Emmalee exclaimed. "Go in the house right now."

"No, Mom. They're trying to arrest you for something you didn't do." He faced Jessie. "I did it. I killed my dad." He turned back to his mother. "I'm sorry."

Stan's mouth dropped open. What in the world was Tyler doing?

Emmalee's face had drained of color. "Tyler," she whispered. "What are you talking about?"

Her son ignored her. "Go ahead. Handcuff me if you want. I'm confessing. Leave my mother alone and I'll get in the car. Seriously. Ask anyone at school. I wasn't there that day."

"Tyler. Be absolutely certain this is what you want to do," Jessie warned.

Tyler shrugged. "I did it. So let's go."

"Do not take my son," Em hissed at Jessie. "He's lying! Neither of us killed Hal! My God, for all his faults, we loved him. He was our family." Her voice broke. "He was our family." She grabbed Jessie's arms, pleading with her. "You're like our family, too. You can't do this."

"Mom, just be quiet." Tyler's eyes remained on Jessie. "I'm ready. Let's go."

Jessie yanked the back door open, muttering something under her breath, and waited for Tyler to duck in. "You have the right to remain silent," she began.

Emmalee looked like she was about to pass out. Stan moved to her side and slid an arm around her. Em started to cry. "What is he doing?" she asked, but Stan knew she wasn't expecting an answer.

Jessie didn't look at them again. She shut the back door, got in the car, and drove away. Stan could see the back of Tyler's head through the rear window of the disappearing car. He didn't turn around.

Chapter 25

As quickly as the news had spread around Frog Ledge about Hal Hoffman's death, the news of his wife's would-be arrest and son's confession seemed to hit the wires even faster. Cyril Pierce must have been up at the crack of dawn the morning after the scene at the Hoffmans' to get his news printed and out the door. It was the only article in the edition. When Stan had first moved to town, she'd been told the *Frog Ledge Holler* came out twice per week. Now it seemed Cyril had thrown his schedule to the wind and was printing papers whenever he felt like it. Stan wondered who tipped him off to Tyler's arrest. According to the story, the arraignment was scheduled for ten this morning.

Stan had gone back to the farm after Tyler's arrest to bring dishes of seasoned turkey, rice, and butternut squash for the Hoffman animals. She'd been worried about Samson since Em told her he hadn't felt well. Samson and Petunia had both been grateful for the food, because Em and her children were gone. The house had been empty. Stan had wondered if she should take the dog home with her, but decided to see how he seemed the following day.

Now she and the dogs were up early, dressed for a walk

on the green. Nutty was sleeping in. Stan couldn't sleep. She wanted exercise. She also wanted to hear what people were saying. She was as bad as Char.

There was a crowd on the green already when she, Henry, and Scruffy crossed the street. They were doing yoga. When Stan got closer, she recognized Amara teaching the class, twisting herself into some kind of crazy pose. Most of the others struggled to follow her and keep their balance. She saw Stan from her upside-down pose and waved.

Stan was so surprised she almost forgot to wave back. Maybe Amara was ready to drop the grudge?

Frantic barking jolted Stan from her thoughts. Bracing herself for the inevitable, she turned in time to see Duncan racing down the green at top speed, tongue lagging, aimed straight for her. Scruffy and Henry saw him, too, and began their own barking and wagging celebration. Behind him, Stan could see Jake loping along, halfheartedly calling the dog. She really needed to make him understand how important a leash was.

But first, she needed to keep her balance as Duncan launched himself at her. She was better at preparing for it, though. When he jumped and threw his paws on her shoulders, she didn't even fall. Henry and Scruffy clamored around him, yelping for joy.

Stan grabbed Duncan's collar and coaxed him to the ground. Duncan had a tendency to get himself in trouble. He was slick, sneaky, and obsessed with Stan and her food, and went to great lengths to be with her—including busting out of his house and finding his way to hers, which he'd done on a number of occasions. She turned to look for Jake. Someone had stopped him to talk along the way, which was usually the case. Townspeople, young and old, loved him.

The elderly folks adored him because he helped them do things they couldn't do anymore. The younger folks liked him because he ran a cool bar. And most of the females in town liked him because, well, he was damn cute. She could see him in half-listening mode, one eye on their group, as he nodded in response to the little old man with the plaid sweater talking animatedly.

When Jake finally broke free and jogged over to them, Stan was handing out treats from her ever-present treat bag. Duncan sat at her feet, gazing at her adoringly, waiting for the next goodie to tantalize his tastebuds. Henry and Scruffy were following his example.

"Wow, you guys look like poster children for good dogs." Jake came up behind them and clipped Duncan's leash on.

"Why don't you do that *before* you go outside, instead of after you have to chase him?" Stan asked.

Jake sighed. "I know, I know. Bad doggie parent. I've heard it all before."

"Hmmph." Stan shook her head. "You're a slow learner."

"Jeez. We haven't even gone on a date yet and we're already fighting like an old married couple." He said it so matter-of-factly Stan was left gaping at him, her ability to form words completely vanished.

"Kristan!"

She groaned inwardly. Her mother. On the green. Was nothing sacred? She turned to greet her. The words died in her throat when she saw Patricia, wearing a pink velour jogging suit that looked like nothing she would ever wear, walking with Leigh-Anne Sutton, who was dressed in an equally ugly identical velour suit in teal. What on earth had come over her mother?

"Crap," she muttered, then pasted on a smile and waved back. "Morning!"

Jake followed her gaze with interest. "Isn't that other woman the one helping Em at the farm? Who's that with her?"

"That," Stan said, repressing a sigh, "is my mother."

"Your mother? I didn't know she lived around here."

"She doesn't. She showed up for an alleged visit the other day and decided she was afraid of my dogs. So she's staying with Char."

"Really." Jake's lips took on that hint of a smile, the one that meant he was trying not to laugh. "You sound thrilled."

"Terribly." Stan pasted on a smile as her mother and Leigh-Anne reached them and chirped greetings. She saw them both appraise Jake, from his backward Yankees hat to his unshaven chin. His typical morning look. "How are you, Mom, Leigh-Anne? You guys look like twins." She indicated their outfits.

"Oh, I had nothing to walk in. Leigh-Anne was sweet enough to offer me her extra suit." Now that she was closer, Stan could see her mother wasn't thrilled with the outfit either. That, at least, made her feel a little better. She had started to think her real mother had been stolen by zombies. As much as they disagreed on everything, it was still unsettling to see her acting so strangely.

"I needed a walking partner and thought your mom would love to see the green," Leigh-Anne said. "Isn't it beautiful? We don't have one like it where I live. This is the best one in the state." She turned a full-watt smile on Jake. "Hello, you sexy bartender, you!"

Stan didn't know whether to burst out laughing or

sputter in protest. Was Leigh-Anne old enough to be a cougar?

The look on Jake's face was priceless, too. He mumbled some kind of response that Stan couldn't even make out, and busied himself straightening Duncan's collar. It was the only time Stan had ever seen him at a loss for words.

Patricia squinted at Amara's group. "What are they doing?"

"Yoga," Stan said.

"Outside? Why would they do that?" Patricia wrinkled her nose. "It's so dirty. And so many allergens."

There she was. Despite herself, Stan smiled. "This is Jake McGee. Jake, my mother. Patricia Connor."

"Pleasure to meet you." Jake shook her hand. "Are you enjoying your stay at the B and B?"

"It's delightful," Patricia said. "The only damper is that murder." She shook her head, her gaze turning to the Hoffman farm. Stan turned to look, too, almost expecting to see the house with the empty, eerie look of other homes that had held murderous or murdered occupants. Of course, it didn't look that way at all. It looked like a run-down farmhouse that needed some TLC.

"Scary," Patricia went on. "To think your own child could do that to you. My goodness, I've had my challenges with my girls"—here she sent Stan a knowing look—"but I never once feared for my life. How terrible."

Such high praise.

"You know," Leigh-Anne confided, stepping closer and dropping her voice, "I'm not surprised, to be honest. After my experience with that boy."

Stan could feel Jake stiffen next to her. "What do you mean?" he asked. His tone was pleasant but his eyes were on fire. Whoa. Stan had never actually seen Jake mad, but he looked suspiciously like Jessie.

Leigh-Anne chewed on her bubblegum-pink lip. She looked genuinely worried. "I hate to say anything, but I'm afraid it will come out anyway. Especially during the trial. Oh, dear." She glanced around the green, saw no one close enough to pay attention, then spoke softly. "Tyler Hoffman came to my farm the weekend before Hal . . . died."

Silence. Stan spoke first. "What for?"

"He asked if he could tour the farm, see how we did certain things. I couldn't figure out what had prompted him, other than our cheese and ice-cream-making capabilities, which his family doesn't have. And that's the future of the farming industry, you know. Or, I thought perhaps he was taking a late interest in the business. I know that was one of the things that disappointed Hal—his oldest had no desire to go into the family business."

Patricia clucked sympathetically. "I felt the same way when Kristan fled the nest and chose her career."

"Mom, there was no family business," Stan said through gritted teeth.

Patricia looked offended. "Not a business, per se, but family *traditions,* Kristan. Fund-raising. Committees. Fulfilling a higher purpose."

Leigh-Anne watched them with interest. Stan opened her mouth to respond, then closed it again. *Let it go.* She certainly didn't need Jake and Leigh-Anne witnessing what would surely turn into a sparring match. But she didn't agree with Leigh-Anne about Hal and Tyler. Disappointed? Stan had gotten enough of a sense of Hal over the last week that she felt she understood him on a basic level. Being that farming wasn't his top priority, she doubted Hal would be disappointed over his son's choice to go to school and find a different career. Maybe he kept up the charade for his farming acquaintances. Or maybe she was giving herself too much credit for reading into a dead man's psyche.

Leigh-Anne, obviously realizing she wasn't going to witness this family drama play out, continued her story. "So when I brought Tyler to admire the new barn I'm building, he dropped a bombshell." She paused for dramatic effect. "He demanded I buy his parents out of their farm."

Stan's mouth dropped. "What?" She looked at Jake. "Did Hal put him up to that?"

Jake looked equally as surprised. He shook his head. "I doubt it."

Leigh-Anne shook her head. "Heavens, no. He looked very jumpy—almost like he was on something—and told me I needed to buy it. That his family needed cash, his mother needed health insurance, and he knew I could afford it. He got very belligerent. Had me pinned against the wall in my barn. I felt quite threatened. Luckily one of my staffers came in and broke it up."

"Then what?" Jake asked.

Leigh-Anne stared at him blankly. "Then he left."

"And did you call his parents? File a complaint with the police? Tell anyone?"

"Well, no. I felt terrible being the one to relay that message to Hal and Em." She cast her eyes to the ground. "I should have, I know. But I thought perhaps he was just acting out. Stressed. I know there were worries about tuition payments." She shook her head. "Being a farmer is so difficult these days. Believe me, I know. I can almost sympathize with the boy. But it was frightening."

Stan watched Leigh-Anne twirling her thick gold chain around her fingers and thought she probably didn't know.

At least not what it was like to be Emmalee Hoffman. Clearly Leigh-Anne's farm was a business venture above all else, run by other people until it came down to the dollars. And who knew, maybe that was the way to do it. She certainly didn't look like she struggled through life like the Hoffmans because of family tradition or loyalty. Or maybe Zen Garden Farm simply had more capital.

Jake wrapped Duncan's leash tighter around his hand as the dog started to stray behind Henry, who had lost interest in the conversation and was sniffing the base of a tree. Stan could see the stress in his knuckles. They were bone white.

Patricia shuddered. "How unnerving. Let's finish walking, Leigh-Anne. Kristan, will I see you for dinner?"

"Sure, Mom," Stan said, her mind on Tyler and Leigh-Anne's story. "I'll call you later. See you, Leigh-Anne."

"Yes, I'll see you at the farm, I'm sure." Leigh-Ann reached over and squeezed Stan's shoulder. "I'm sorry. I should probably tell that state trooper who's leading the investigation, shouldn't I?"

She didn't seem to realize that was Jake's sister, and Jake didn't offer the information, or even answer. Stan followed his lead. She waited until Leigh-Anne and her mother had gotten a quarter of the way around the loop, then looked at Jake.

"Wow," Stan said slowly. "Maybe Tyler confronted his dad about asking Leigh-Anne to buy them out and things got out of hand. Although I hate to believe it. He seems like such a smart kid with places to go." Another thought dawned on her. "I wonder if that's why I haven't been able to get anywhere with the financial work at the farm. Em put Tyler in charge of getting me the information. I don't have any history yet. I hate to say it, but maybe they do have the right guy."

Jake's face was grim. "I have a hard time seeing Tyler lashing out in a rage and killing his father, no matter how frustrated he was. I've known that kid forever, Stan. I just don't see it."

Fresh out of fresh vegetables, Stan walked to the Frog Ledge food co-op. She grabbed a basket, heading down the fresh produce aisle. She picked out some kale for her morning smoothies, along with organic pears and some raspberries. Rounding the corner into the local honey aisle, she almost crashed right into Amara Leonard.

Amara looked as startled as Stan. She still wore her yoga clothes. Her hair was scooped back with a hair band. Her glasses were perched on top of her head and she held a jar of brown rice syrup in her hand.

Well, here was her chance. "Sorry," Stan said. *Brilliant start.*

Amara shrugged. "No problem."

Stan sighed. She opened her mouth to apologize, but Amara started talking at the same time.

Stan motioned for her to continue. "You first."

"I just wanted to thank you. For speaking up at the town meeting. Your support is important," she said.

"It is?" Stan asked, surprised, then she recovered. "I mean, sure, yes, you're welcome. I think it's a great idea. The town needs a vet, and having both traditions available will promote good things. Glad I could help."

Amara nodded, clearly uncomfortable. She grabbed an avocado off the display and studied it intently.

Stan took a breath. It seemed to be the perfect time. If it didn't work, so be it, but at least she could say she'd tried. "I really am sorry about our misunderstanding," Stan said. "I . . . wish we could be friends. Or at least doctor and patient. Nutty needs you."

Amara hesitated, then sighed and dropped the avocado back into its bin. "I guess you're not Zen if you're holding a grudge," she admitted. "It's okay. I know you didn't mean to accuse me of murder. I was being overly sensitive. I'm sorry, too."

They both looked at each other for a minute, not really sure what to do next. *Ah, what the heck,* Stan thought, and gave Amara a hug, which thankfully she didn't resist.

"Thanks," Stan said. "It was a really rough time."

"I'm sure it was. What a terrible thing," Amara said. "So what's going on with Nutty? Is he sick?"

"No, but he really needs a checkup."

Amara pulled her phone out of her purse and opened the calendar. After perusing it for a minute, she said, "Can you bring him over Monday morning?"

Stan nodded. "I can. What time?"

"How about eleven?"

"That works. Thanks, Amara."

Amara keyed a reminder in and dropped her phone back in her purse. "You're welcome. Oh, hey, one quick thing."

"Sure, what?"

"You're not going to accuse me of murdering Hal Hoffman when you come over, are you?" Her eyes twinkled behind those glasses.

Stan grinned. "Touché. I'm trying to stay out of this one."

Amara snorted. "I see you walking over there every day. How is that staying out of it?"

"I'm just helping with some paperwork. Keeping my nose out of everything else."

Amara tucked the brown rice syrup into her cart. "If I know you, your nose may be out of it, but most other parts of you won't be."

She disappeared around the corner. Stan shook her head and selected some honey and spelt flour. *How does she think she knows me? She hasn't talked to me since the week after I moved in.*

Chapter 26

"They want *how* much to bail him out?" Stan stared at Brenna in disbelief. Her assistant had showed up soon after Stan returned from the co-op, desperate with the news of Tyler's proposed bail. Stan had just settled in with a personal-sized homemade feta cheese and black olive pizza and her favorite old-fashioned notebook to make a list of everything she needed for Benny's party.

She'd purposely avoided going to the Hoffmans' this afternoon. After the drama last night, she thought it best to stay away. Leigh-Anne and Roger could handle the work. Plus she needed to focus on her own business, for a day at least. Between funerals, cow pushing, and trying to keep her treats on track, her days were getting away from her.

"Fifty thousand dollars. I just left the arraignment. Em almost fainted." Brenna rubbed her forehead. Lines of concern were embedded into it. Stan was starting to worry about her. "A flight risk? How is this kid a flight risk?"

"Well, he's a young kid. He's mobile. And he confessed to a murder, Bren." She held up a hand at Brenna's withering stare. "I'm just saying. This is police business, not friend business."

"It's crap. Stan . . . they don't have any money. I don't think Em's family does either, and Hal's sure isn't going to help her out. At least not his mother or brother."

"So what are they going to do?"

Brenna didn't say anything. She kept her eyes trained on Stan. Sad eyes. Pleading eyes.

It took her a minute, then it dawned on her. "You want me to bail him out?"

Brenna nodded, her eyes pleading. "Those kids need the family together. Em's lost her mind. Danny's flipping out. And the little ones are with Em's sister, but she can't keep them long-term. If I had the money I'd do it, but I don't. And I don't know what to do." Tears filled her eyes.

Stan sighed. When had she gotten the reputation as a bail bondsman? Izzy was one thing. Stan had fully expected to help her friend, who hadn't needed it anyway. But was she going to be expected to bail out everyone in town?

"Bren. I can't just pull fifty grand out of my wallet," she began, but Brenna's shoulders drooped in disappointment.

"Okay," Brenna said, her voice almost a whisper. "I'll have to go pick the kids up and stay with Em at their house, I guess. I don't know how much she's going to be able to do in the state she's in. . . ." Her voice trailed off in choked tears and Stan felt like crap.

"Jeez, Bren. Where do I need to go?"

Brenna stared at her, then flung herself at Stan and hugged her. "Do you mean it? You really will? You'll get it back—Ty's obviously not going to flee the state or anything. I mean, where would he go, right? Em wouldn't let him anyway. Plus, I know he didn't do it."

Then why did he confess? She remembered her conversation with Tyler in the little office, where the evidence of Hal neglecting his duties—and his family—had been overwhelmingly present. Tyler's words rang in her head: *"I loved my dad, but he had other things going on. Things that didn't include us. And I think he hoped those things were his ticket out of here. But he never made it."*

Had he never made it because his own son had killed him?

"Stan, you're the best," Brenna was saying. "We should go. Now. I'll drive." She grabbed Stan's arm and pulled her out the door.

On the way to the barracks—a trip Stan was getting way too used to making—she sorted through her thoughts about this latest turn of events. In her old, corporate life, it helped her to pull out her trusty notebook and jot down the facts, then write up a SARS report: Situation, actions taken, results, and support needed. And then focus on a theme song until her mind solved the problem.

However, that worked best when she was alone. Brenna might think she was nuts if she burst out in song.

Instead, she ticked through what she knew: One, Emmalee and Hal had not been getting along. Two, Emmalee was nowhere to be found the afternoon of Hal's death and had even missed a parent-teacher conference—something those who knew her well said she would never do. Three, Hal hadn't been seen anywhere that day. Four, Tyler knew his father had other things on his mind besides his family and the farm. Five, Tyler confessed. What eighteen-year-old boy did that if he was innocent? But he was fiercely protective of his mother. Which could mean he had killed his father because he felt his mother was being wronged, or he lied about killing him to keep his mother out of jail.

Because he knew Pasquale was on the right track thinking of Em as a suspect?

If Emmalee had finally gotten fed up, who knew what could have happened? She and Hal could have been on the farm, engaged in a rapidly escalating discussion while Hal used his family heirloom sickle to trim corn. Maybe she lost her temper. Grabbed the sickle out of his hand and stabbed him with it, then took off when she realized what she'd done.

It was a great theory. But Stan wasn't feeling it.

Em was a serious, responsible woman who relied on her farm to provide a living for her and her kids. Stan could imagine her calling an angry truce with her husband. Making it clear she knew what he was about, but wouldn't rock the boat because they had work to do. Finding a way to get her revenge in some other way down the road. Plus, she had been with Em when Hal was found and her reaction didn't seem to be in line with that of a murderer, unless she was a phenomenal actor.

Tyler, she wasn't so sure about. The boy was intense. But kill his own father in cold blood, then drive back to school and wait for the call? And no one had heard or seen anything that day. No fighting, no screaming, no nothing. In fact, Roger had told Pasquale that he hadn't seen Hal on the farm since the day before his death. Had anyone seen Tyler there? And what about the mysterious, missing Enrico? Did his disappearance have something to do with Tyler's confession?

And then there were the unhappy business partners. Asher Fink's fight with Hal. Peter Michelli's dissatisfaction with the way Hal ran the business. Not to mention the real estate deals gone bad and people looking for their money. And Izzy's financial troubles. She had no one to blame but herself—and Hal.

"Stan?" Brenna stared at her. "We're here."

"Oh, yeah, sorry. Just thinking." Stan grabbed her purse. "Let's do this. Is your sister here?"

"I doubt it. She probably threw him in a cell and went home to eat dinner. I'm so mad at her right now." She swung her long legs out of the car and slammed the door.

Stan thought Brenna had probably been watching too much *Law & Order* or *CSI,* but she didn't say that. Instead, she said, "Let me talk."

They went in the front door. Luckily, it was a different dispatcher than the one who had witnessed Stan and Jake's attempt to bail Izzy out.

"Can you tell me how I would go about posting bail for Tyler Hoffman?" she asked, speaking into the microphone next to the bulletproof window.

The trooper picked up a book from his desk, skimmed it, then looked back up. "Actually, his bail's already been posted. 'Bout a half hour ago."

"By whom?" Brenna stepped over.

The guy sighed, like he wasn't sure why she cared, and looked back down. "Ted Brahm," he read.

Brenna looked at Stan. Stan raised her hands, palms up. Ted Brahm, the farmer? How in the world was he posting bail? At the tune of fifty grand?

"So they're gone?" Brenna asked.

"Yup."

"Well, that's good news," Stan tried.

Brenna nodded distractedly. "Can we go over there?"

"To their house? They might just want to be with the family right now. But sure, we can stop," she said, as Brenna opened her mouth to protest.

"Good." Brenna turned and slammed out of the barracks. The cop behind the glass raised his eyebrow at Stan, then went back to his computer.

Stan hurried out after Brenna and got in the car before she could take off without her.

"Why the heck would Ted bail Tyler out? And *how* would Ted bail him out? Where did he get that much money?" Brenna reiterated Stan's thoughts from a minute ago. She peeled out of the parking lot and hit the gas a lot harder than necessary.

Stan thought of her peaceful afternoon gone up in flames and shrugged. "They're friends, right? And business partners. He's been helping Em out since Hal died. I saw him over there that first morning, working on the farm with some of his staff."

Brenna shook her head. "It's weird. Em didn't have any use for any of the co-op partners. She just went along with it because Hal was passionate about it. And because it made them more money than just running their farm and selling milk." She went quiet until they pulled into Em's driveway. Em's truck with the NO FARMS, NO FOOD sticker was parked next to an unfamiliar Honda Civic.

"Ted must still be here," Stan said. "Should we bother her?"

"I'm going in." Brenna shoved the car into park and got out. With a sigh, Stan followed.

"Go to the side door," Brenna said, motioning Stan to the door near the garage.

Close on her heels, Stan almost tripped when Brenna stopped short. Stan regained her balance in time to see what had startled her: Em and Ted Brahm guiltily jumping apart from the embrace they'd been locked in on the stoop.

Brenna gaped at them, mouth open, until Stan nudged her with her elbow. She flushed and recovered. "Shoot, sorry. We, uh, just wanted to make sure you were okay. We went to get Tyler. At the barracks. Stan was going to post his bail."

Emmalee smoothed her flyaway hair back, red faced at being caught. "You did? Why, Stan, I just don't know what to say. How sweet of you. And yes, we're fine. Tyler is innocent. He did not kill his father. This will all get straightened out. The police are going to search his room at school. They got a warrant." She grimaced, but forced a smile back on. "But thankfully Ted . . . came to the rescue."

Ted tipped his baseball cap. "Afternoon, ladies. We'll all get through this."

"Well, that's wonderful," Stan said, her hand on Brenna's arm. "And we should go. Em, I'll bring Samson some food for his tummy later tonight."

"That's wonderful. We're actually leaving for a few days. To go stay with my sister," Em added, which told Stan she probably wasn't going to stay with her sister. "Would you mind checking on the dog and cat? I would be so grateful."

"Sure, no problem." *Why do I keep agreeing to these things?* "We're going to get going. Take care, Em."

With a nod to Ted, Stan turned Brenna firmly around and shoved her toward the car, her head spinning with this new revelation.

So Em had been getting her revenge on Hal after all.

Chapter 27

Sometimes, Stan regretted opening her mouth. Tonight, as she packed up bowls of food for Samson and Petunia, was one of those nights. She had no desire to go out again. She knew it was uncharitable, but with Halloween looming in the near future, all she wanted to do was curl up on her couch, watch scary movies, pour a glass of wine, sketch out her website, and catalogue the new recipes Brenna had come up with. But that poor dog and cat had been left behind while Em sorted out her life. Stan was a sucker for that sort of thing.

Nutty, as was customary when he heard the sound of certain bowls, arrived in the doorway and watched with a critical eye.

"It's just a little bit," Stan said. "Jeez, Nutty. We've talked about this selfish thing. It's much nicer to share."

Nutty fanned his tail in disapproval like an ornery peacock.

"You've gotten pretty snooty for a former street cat," Stan said, sliding the bowls into a recyclable shopping bag. She surveyed the dogs, both sitting at attention in front of her.

"You guys want to come for the walk?" Stan said. They both wagged in agreement. It was probably a good idea to have Henry with her, walking in the dark. Even though it was tiny little Frog Ledge and the police believed they had Hal's murderer, Stan still felt unsettled. Henry, despite being a big muffin, looked foreboding. The fact that he was a big mush, well, she didn't have to broadcast that.

She tucked her cell phone and keys in her pocket, clipped the dogs' leashes on, and headed out. The moon was well on its way to full, so it seemed as if someone had turned floodlights on. She pulled her jacket tighter around her. Definitely a chill in the air as they marched closer to winter. Stars blazed in the sky and the bare tree branches beckoned like skeletal fingers in the breeze. Very Halloween-like. In Amara's house next door, she could see jack-o'-lanterns flickering in the windows. The rest of the house was dark. Amara must be out. She made a mental note to stop by over the weekend, maybe bring some dog treats as a peace offering.

There was still activity around the green. A bunch of teenagers hanging in the library parking lot. A few people and dogs walking the loop. The company, though distant, comforted her as thoughts of Bullet Man danced in her head. When they turned into the Hoffmans' driveway she took out her cell phone and turned the flashlight app on to light their way. Scruffy pranced along happily. Henry was more cautious in his approach. Stan got to the front steps and paused, glancing at the dark house. She wished Em had left a light on. But she hadn't.

How did I get roped into this again?

Because you're helping animals, her conscience reminded her. Nikki would approve. Redeeming herself after the whole working-at-a-dairy-farm faux pas. With that as her catalyst, she headed to the front door, unlocked it, and hesitantly pushed it open. Samson immediately pushed his wet nose into her palm, thanking her for bringing dinner. Scruffy strained on her leash, trying to get to him, asking to play. He ignored her.

"You're welcome, boy," she said, patting his head. He sniffed Scruffy and Henry. They sniffed back.

All else was quiet. Stan flicked on a few lights as she made her way into the kitchen. The house looked the same, like everyone had left in a hurry and hadn't given much thought to what they would return to. Dirty dishes sat on a tray on the couch. Kids' toys were strewn about. Petunia streaked by, startling Stan and sending Scruffy into a barking frenzy.

"It's okay, Scruf. Hush," Stan said, though there was no one here to disturb. She heated the food so it wasn't cold and handed Samson his bowl. He politely devoured it. She set the cat's bowl on the counter for when she returned. She checked the back door to make sure it was closed and locked, flicked off the kitchen light, and turned to go. A light bounced around out in front of the building with the milking rooms and office area. Like a flashlight beam.

Stan paused. That seemed odd. At night, the one staffer would usually be in the cow areas, which had its own lighting. She mentally ran through the schedule Roger had given her. It was nine right now. There wouldn't be another milking until maybe eleven. Whoever was on staff should be checking feed and water and doing those chores. According to Roger, none of the cows was due to give birth any time soon, so that wasn't an issue tonight.

She caught herself and chuckled. When had she turned into dairy farmer of the year? How did she even know this stuff? Roger had clearly done a good job with his tour. She moved to the window. The light was still visible. Then she heard a clang. Beside her, Henry barked.

The light went out.

Stan frowned. That was odd. Or was it? The workers needed to see to get around, after all. She had no idea how one worked among the unlit areas of a dairy farm at night, so she wasn't about to jump to any conclusions.

Scruffy decided to bark in response to Henry, which set Henry off again. The two engaged in an absurd chorus of soprano and alto, ensuring the cat wouldn't come back to eat her dinner anytime soon. Samson, not being easily moved, raised his head to see what was going on before returning to his nap.

Well, if Samson wasn't concerned, she wouldn't be either. But she wanted to get out of the house, back to her safe, cozy home.

"Samson, you want to go outside before we head home?"

Samson raised one eyebrow. Stan swore he smiled at her.

"I'll take that as a yes. Okay, then, let's go." She led the way to the side door, which would let Samson right into the yard. Scruffy trotted along behind. Henry was already at the door, whining softly. Stan tried to ignore the hairs that stood up on the back of her neck. "Henry, it's okay. Come."

He ignored her. Very unlike him. She grabbed his collar and opened the door enough for Samson to squeeze through.

And jumped a foot at the sound of a crash in the kitchen. Scruffy immediately went into a frenzy of barking. Stan grabbed the nearest weapon—a half-burned Yankee candle jar—and crept back into the kitchen, Scruffy on her heels barking her head off. Her hand scraped the wall along the living room to flip on any and every light switch until she reached the kitchen. Brandishing her weapon, she scanned the room from corner to corner.

Petunia's bright green eyes stared at her in alarm from the counter, where an overturned vase leaked old water all over the counter. The cat once again streaked away. Scruffy's barks accelerated in volume until Stan raised her voice. "No, Scruffy!"

The dog quieted, but her tail vibrated with excitement as she turned in circles, looking for the cat.

"For crying out loud." Stan sighed, grabbed some paper towels off the roll, and mopped up the mess. She disposed of the towels, made sure the cat's food hadn't been soaked, flicked off the light.

And realized that Henry wasn't there.

"Oh, no!" She raced to the door, which stood open. She'd forgotten to shut it behind Samson. Samson had strolled back in, but there was no sign of Henry.

"Henry!" She left Scruffy inside and shut the door behind her, hurrying down the steps. "Henry, come!"

Nothing.

Then, from a distance, she heard him barking. Where was he? The sound echoed through the quiet farm. She paused, trying to pinpoint it. The cow area? She fished her iPhone out of her back pocket and turned on her flashlight app. Rounding the side of the building where she'd seen the light earlier, she paused. Maybe she should announce herself.

"Hello? It's Stan, just looking for my dog," she called.

No response. The worker was either out of earshot, or had no idea what she was saying. She pushed open the swinging half door leading into the cow area. A couple hundred sets of eyes landed on her. She raised her hand in a wave. "Sorry, ladies."

The cows seemed unimpressed. Stan supposed she would be, too. They didn't get excited about much. How could they when they spent their days in pens and being milked? She felt sad for them. Being a cow probably wasn't much fun. Stan scanned the room. It looked like an uneventful night in the barn. Some cows rested on their mats. Others stood, tails swinging in a lazy arc. She shined her flashlight in the empty pens. No Henry. She turned to go, then stopped. Turned back. Shined her light on the corner pens.

They were empty.

Where were the sick cows? They had been in here all week. Roger specifically said they'd have to stay quarantined for at least another week.

She illuminated the other small pens with her light to see if maybe they'd been moved to another empty pen, creeping closer to peer inside them. Maybe they were on the ground, resting.

Then something dull and hard cracked against the back of her knees. Her legs buckled under her. She pitched forward into an empty pen, slamming face first into a pile of straw and cow manure.

Chapter 28

Through the numbing pain in the back of her knees, Stan heard the clatter of something being thrown to the ground. Despite the aching pain in her legs, she pulled herself into a defensive ball and covered her head, anticipating another blow, and held her breath.

She prayed it wasn't Hal's killer back looking for the next victim. Or the guy from Bruno's with the hole in his throat, here about their "arrangement." That thought left her ice cold. Then she heard running feet, heading away. Still holding her breath, she waited. Straw poked her in the eyes and tickled her nose. The cows shuffled, unsettled, wondering what all the ruckus was about while they tried to sleep.

She had to get out. Now. And she had to find Henry. She lifted her head an inch or two and risked a glance around her immediate area. The dim lights afforded her a decent view, and she didn't see feet or anything else suspect. She should try to get up. But what if her knees were broken? Or messed up enough that she couldn't run? She stretched one leg out. It hurt, but it worked. She wiggled her foot. Did the same with the other. When she was convinced she'd be able to stand reasonably well, Stan braced her hands in the straw and shoved herself upright, wincing. Her phone was in the hay somewhere, but how long would it take to find it? The assailant might have a partner, and she didn't want to risk anyone coming back to look for her.

Throwing caution to the wind, hoping perhaps Amara or another neighbor might hear her, she shouted.

"Help! There's an intruder! Somebody call the police!"

Dead silence from outside. Then, suddenly, angry barking.

Henry. Had he cornered the intruder? Would the person try to hurt him? Stan's money was on the dog, but she couldn't take a chance. She dove back to the ground, scrabbling around in the straw until, mercifully, her hand closed around her phone. Grabbing it and the metal shovel strewn a few feet away—most likely the weapon used to take her down—she ran out of the barn, then stopped, not sure where to go next. Frantic, she punched 911 into her phone. "You need to send someone to the Happy Cow Dairy Farm in Frog Ledge," she blurted when a dispatcher answered. "I've been attacked!" Ignoring the calm voice asking her if she was injured, she yelled for Henry.

Nothing.

Then, in the distance, more barking. Frantic now.

Stan could still hear the dispatcher, now shouting for her, as she took off running, hoping she'd chosen the right direction. The night was so still and quiet that the sound echoed, leaving her with the unsettling feeling of being in a canyon and not knowing which way was out. She followed the sound farther onto the property, away from the cows, back toward the barn and corn maze. Had Henry chased the intruder out here?

The cops were probably ten or fifteen minutes away, depending on where they were when she called. If they were at the barracks, she had a long wait. On the other hand, if they were patrolling close by—or if they called Jessie— someone would show up any minute. Stan kept going. She needed to find Henry. She didn't want to call him away if he had a bead on the bad guy, but she needed to make sure he was okay, and that he didn't run off and get lost.

She slowed as she approached the corn maze, hesitant to enter it. There were so many hiding places in there, and after what had happened to Hal . . . She shivered.

Then she heard a voice behind her.

"Hey!"

Whirling around, clenching the shovel as if it were a baseball bat, she found Asher Fink standing a few feet behind her. Where had he come from?

Asher held his hands up. "What are you doing on this farm?"

"I'm helping Em out," she shot back, still wielding the shovel. "What are *you* doing here?"

Asher took a step closer to her, hands still in front of him. "I came to look at the feed truck. Emmalee was having trouble with it."

"At this time of night?" Stan shook her head, retreating back another step. "I don't believe you. I think you just tried to take me out in the cow pens. I called the police, FYI."

Fink did surprise really well. "Miss, are you hurt? What did you say your name was again?"

"Stay back," Stan warned, putting the shovel between her and Fink.

"Is someone else out here?" Fink asked. "There's only supposed to be one person on shift right now, and they should be milking. No one should be in the cow pens."

Stan hesitated. A little voice reminded her Fink had some

menace beneath that seemingly benign beard. Why would he be doing mechanical work at this time of night? He did have a lot of stains on his pants. Hopefully it was grease and not blood. Over her shoulder, she heard Henry barking urgently. It sounded like it was outside the maze, over in the direction of the field where the manure pit sat.

If Asher was the culprit, who was Henry chasing?

"Someone just clobbered me. With this." She thrust the shovel in his direction, causing him to step back. "I surprised someone in the cow pens. I think my dog is chasing the person."

"Are you hurt?"

She shook her head. "I'm fine. But I need to find Henry."

The night suddenly lit up with flashing strobe lights. The cops had arrived, albeit quietly.

Asher looked at her. "Are you going to meet them?"

Stan eyed him warily. "No," she said. "I'd rather wait here with you." *I won't be stupid and let you walk away.*

"Hey! We're over here!" Stan yelled, brandishing her shovel, eyes never leaving Asher. They didn't have long to wait before Jessie Pasquale appeared, one hand on her weapon, the other holding her radio as she spoke quietly into it. Didn't she ever take a day—or night—off?

Spotting Stan and Asher, taking in the shovel Stan held, Pasquale signed off the radio and stuck it back in its holder. She approached slowly, sizing up the situation.

"Ms. Connor. Put the shovel down," she called.

Stan obliged, tossing it behind her.

"Keep your hands where I can see them," she told Asher. "Who are you?"

"Asher Fink. I'm a partner farmer."

Pasquale moved to him and quickly patted him down. "What's going on here?"

"I was in the cow pen and someone knocked me down with the shovel. They took off. I think my dog is chasing them." Stan pointed to the field.

"Aren't you going to pat her down?" Asher asked.

"No," Pasquale said. "What kind of dog?"

Stan told her.

Pasquale pulled her radio back out and repeated the story in cop speak, and requested an ETA on her backup. The garbled voice on the other end spit something back that Stan couldn't quite catch, but seemed to satisfy Pasquale. "Call Roger Hardy, too," she said. "Tell him to get out here ASAP." She hung the radio on her belt. "Mr. Fink, come with me," she ordered. To Stan, "Stay here and wait for my backup."

What was wrong with this woman? "No way," Stan said, incensed. "It's my dog chasing the guy. And I was the one who ate manure when I got knocked down in the cow pens."

Finally, a change in expression. Stan seemed to be the only one who could make that happen, and it usually meant Pasquale was exasperated. Today was no different. She set her jaw, raised one eyebrow. Her brilliant red hair was, as usual, pulled back in a ponytail, leaving her face vulnerable to every expression.

But Pasquale was smart. Instead of wasting time arguing with Stan, she turned to Asher. "Let's go."

Stan shrugged, picked her shovel back up, and followed.

The barking got louder as they headed deeper into the farmland. She wanted to run ahead looking for Henry, but Pasquale would probably Taser her in the back if she tried it. Or even shoot her.

She followed them through the field to the long, dilapidated barn near the manure pit. The building had been the old barn, long before the farm expanded, and now it housed some of the machinery. And from the sounds of it, Henry was in there. With company.

Pasquale got to about one hundred feet from the door, then held up her hand. "Both of you wait here," she said, then noticed Stan holding the shovel. "I thought I told you to put that down."

Stan shrugged. "Added protection." She made no move to let it go.

Pasquale shook her head almost imperceptibly and approached the barn door.

"Wait," Stan said. "Let me go with you."

"Absolutely not."

"My dog is in there! I don't want you to hurt him. He sounds angrier than he is."

Pasquale hesitated.

"I'll stay behind you. I even have my own weapon."

The look Pasquale gave her could've downed one of the cows. "Come on," she said, and stalked to the barn door. Used her foot to nudge it open and peered inside. Henry's barking became more frantic.

"Police!" Pasquale yelled. "Get your hands up and move where I can see you!"

Nothing. Just barking. Then, from a few feet away, what sounded like sobbing and begging. It took Stan a minute to realize she wasn't hearing English. Pasquale entered the barn, gun drawn.

"I said get out where I can see you." Without turning, she said to Stan, "Call the dog."

Stan stepped in behind her to see Henry, hackles raised,

barking so hard he probably had a sore throat by now. Sure enough, he had someone cornered—a short, skinny Latino boy who looked like he was about to lose his dinner.

It was Enrico, the missing farmhand.

Chapter 29

They were all still in the barn when Roger arrived five minutes later.

"What's going on here?" he asked, barging in. His mouth dropped as he took in the scene. "Enrico?"

The boy, who looked like he was going to have a nervous breakdown, began babbling in Spanish. Pasquale frowned. "English, please."

"He doesn't know much," Roger said.

Pasquale turned to Roger. "When was the last time you saw him?"

"Saturday. He had Sunday off and never showed up Monday."

"So as far as you're concerned, he shouldn't be on the farm tonight."

Roger looked at Enrico. "Did you come back to work?"

Enrico hung his head, shook it slowly.

"What did you come here for, then?" Pasquale asked.

Enrico looked at her blankly.

Pasquale motioned for the kid to come forward. He did, hesitant, his hands still up, sweat beading on his forehead. Next to Stan, Henry growled. Pasquale pulled her radio out of her belt and gave her location, asked where her backup was.

"Arriving now. Just asking the cows for directions," the voice on the other end of the radio crackled back, and sure enough, a minute later two troopers strode in. Stan didn't recognize either. Trooper Lou must have had the night off.

"Either of you speak Spanish?" Pasquale asked.

They both shook their heads. She rolled her eyes. "Fantastic. He's gonna have to cool his heels until we get a translator." Pasquale stepped forward and fastened loose handcuffs on the kid. Stan almost felt bad for him, despite the throbbing pain in the back of her legs. He looked more scared than she'd felt when she hit the ground.

She tried to reach Emmalee on her cell, to no avail. Pasquale was tied up with the kid, so she and Asher went with Roger back to the cow pens.

"What happened, Stan? Why were you here?" Roger asked.

"I had to come back and feed Samson and Petunia. Em left for a few days."

"Yeah, she left me a message." Roger looked grim. Stan could barely keep up with them as they hurried across the dark grass.

"So I was leaving and heard a noise outside. Saw a flashlight. Then Henry took off. I checked the cow pens and got whacked."

Roger looked at Asher. "You didn't hear anything?"

"I was in the back barn with the door shut. I didn't want to disturb anyone while I worked on the engine." Asher, despite his monotone voice, looked troubled. "What was that boy doing, Roger?"

Roger didn't answer. He went into the barn and straight to the sick pens. Cursed.

"I noticed when I came in," Stan said. "That's when I got hit."

"Noticed what?" Asher asked.

"The two sick cows. They're not here," Roger said. He went into the main barn, moved slowly down the row of cows, looking at each of them. A few minutes later, Stan heard him call to Asher. They both hurried over.

Roger pointed at one of the cows. "That's one. She was in the sick pen."

Stan looked from one to the other. "So what does that mean?"

"If they're back in the general population, they'd get milked next shift," Roger said. "And then the whole supply would be tainted."

Chapter 30

Party day. Stan groaned and pulled her pillow over her head. Saturday. Over a week since Hal's murder, and things were crazier than ever, especially after the scene on the farm last night. After Roger's discovery, the cops had brought Enrico down to the barracks. No one had been able to reach Em. Stan hadn't heard a word since. Would charges against Tyler be dropped now? Had Enrico murdered Hal? First kill the farmer, then taint the milk supply?

Her legs ached. She hoped it wouldn't hamper her ability to throw this party. Her business's reputation depended on it. She had to finish icing the cake, which waited in the freezer. She hoped it was big enough. Benny was expecting five to seven friends, in addition to her own dogs. They were all, according to Benny's mom, looking forward to the party at one o'clock. She also had to bake a couple extra batches of treats.

Then she sat straight up, panic coursing through her veins. Costume party. She had no costume for Henry or Scruffy! She was a horrible pet parent. The other dogs would make fun of them, and they would be miserable in their own house. What was she going to do?

She grabbed her cell phone and dialed Char. "I need doggie costumes," she said when Char answered.

"Doggie costumes? For when?" Char asked.

"This afternoon. It's Benny's party, and it's here at my house. My own dogs don't have costumes and I haven't frosted the cake yet! This is going to be terrible. I'm going to get a bad review and no one will want me to do another party for them." She was on the verge of tears, but Char's rational, soothing voice of reason took over.

"Honey. This isn't like you, to be so worried. Your party is going to be lovely!"

"What about the costumes, though? And how's my mother? I didn't make dinner with her last night. There was . . . some excitement."

"Excitement? What kind?"

"I need to deal with costumes first," Stan said, not wanting to get sidetracked.

"I don't have any, but I bet Betty could help. She does costumes for the local theater company."

"Betty from the library?" Wow. The people of Frog Ledge led their share of double lives. "When does she find time to do that?"

Char chuckled. "Oh, Stan, honey, people find time to do what they love. You of all people know that, don't you? Anyway, call her. Maybe she can dig up something from one of the plays. They must have some doggie outfits in their repertoire. Then call me back and tell me the gossip."

Stan hung up and called Betty while she brought the dogs down to go outside. No answer on the cell. She checked the clock. Nearly nine on a Saturday. Betty was probably in her office at the library. Sure enough, she answered on the first ring. "Frog Ledge Library, Betty speaking," she chirped.

"Betty, it's Stan."

"Good morning, dear! How can I help you?" She lowered her voice. "Are you researching potential murderers? I'd love to help. What can I do?"

Betty had a thing for crime. Stan figured she'd been a detective in a previous life. "No, not researching murderers. I need your help for the dogs, actually."

"Oh, well, that's just as fun. What do those cutie-wooties need?"

"Costumes. Benny's party is this afternoon at my house and I have nothing for them to wear. Char said to call you. I'm desperate, Betty. I still have to finish the cake and I don't want my dogs to hate me for making them different."

"Oh, have no fear," Betty said. "Give me an hour."

True to her word, Stan's doorbell rang exactly an hour later. The treats were in the oven after one minor incident with Nutty diving into the batter for a taste—an incident that had set Stan back about fifteen minutes, the amount of time it took her to chase Nutty, wash his paws, and clean the batter trail. She was finishing the peanut butter cake with her special cream cheese frosting. The original cake she'd prepared for the party had vanished in the aftermath of Hal's murder, although Stan had a sneaking suspicion Benny had ended up with it. She'd seen him on the green the other day and he looked a little chunkier.

Betty followed up her ring with a rap on the screen, impatient as always. "Yoo hoo! Stan!" Stan had the front door open to let in the crisp, fall breeze. It felt delightful. Nutty thought so, too. He'd squished himself on the windowsill and had his fluffy face pressed against the screen. The breeze ruffled the hair in his ears.

Stan headed down the hall, the dogs trotting behind her.

"We're coming," she called out, then slowed as Betty proudly held up a glittery pink and green sequined vest with fringes. "What the . . ."

"It's for Henry!" Betty beamed, clearly proud.

Stan unlocked the screen and pushed it open. "That's for a dog?"

"Well, no," Betty admitted, stepping into the hall and shaking the vest out. Loose glitter and dust rained down on Stan's hardwood floor. Nutty sneezed and jumped off the sill. He stalked off, tail in the air. "It was for Len Crowley. His original play about a singing real estate agent. It wasn't one of our best, but we have to give people creative license." She shrugged. "Anyway, I thought this would fit Henry. And this"—she reached into her shopping bag and proudly thrust a black getup with whiskers at Stan—"is for Scruffy. From when we did an adaptation of *Cats*."

Stan tentatively took the outfit from her. "Um, thanks, Betty. This is lovely of you." She looked doubtfully at Scruffy, who was on her hind legs trying to sniff the clothing. Henry had taken one look at the sequined vest and dropped to his belly in the hall, covering his eyes with his paws.

"I'm glad you called. And I wanted to ask you a favor. How would you like to judge the pet costume parade tomorrow evening?"

"Me?"

"Yes, you, silly. You're a perfect choice. All the animals in town love you. There are two other judges. It's quick—forty-five minutes tops. It's right before we start showing the movies on the green for Halloween." Betty smiled. "Tomorrow's going to be a great day. So what do you say?"

"Sure," Stan said. "It sounds like fun."

"Excellent! I knew you would do it. Say, how's the cake

coming?" Betty marched into the kitchen to see for herself, and let out a squeal when she saw the perfect ghost shape. "It's gorgeous! Benny will love it."

"Thanks, I hope so." Stan glanced at her watch. "I still have to clean and get the decorations up."

"You should try on the outfits first. Want me to help?"

Stan cringed inwardly. "Oh, that's not necessary. They can be fresh about putting clothes on. I'll do it." *There's no way they'll be wearing these outfits.*

"Excellent," Betty declared. "And did I mention Nancy invited me to take pictures? I'll be able to see how adorable they look! I may even post them to the theater company's Facebook page." She squeezed Stan's arm. "I'll see you in a couple of hours, then."

Chapter 31

There was nothing like a doggie party to take your mind off murder. By the time Benny's party was in full swing, Stan realized she hadn't thought about Hal Hoffman or the farm in hours. The party had commenced in the backyard with tennis balls and Frisbees galore. Duncan and Jake were there. It was slightly unsettling to Stan to see Jake sitting so casually on her back deck, chatting with Ursula Schumacher, a local historian and mom to Tessa the beagle. Stan could feel Jake's eyes on her, though, as she ran around tending to the guests.

Duncan wasn't into the games. He followed Stan around hoping for extra treats. Benny wasn't into the games either, possibly due to his chunkiness. He preferred sitting in the grass, guarding his goods. Betty, who apparently had a third career as a photographer, snapped more photos than paparazzi. Henry, embarrassed in his sequined vest, had begged to go inside. Stan relented and took the vest off him before setting him free to go nap. Scruffy, however, was torn between wanting to play with the other dogs and ripping the cat suit off. Betty thought she looked adorable and wouldn't stop taking her picture.

After conferring with Benny's mom about bringing the cake out, Stan headed inside to get the cake. She was excited for the dogs to try it. She hoped they loved it.

"You should add party planner to your resume." Jake's voice appeared near her ear. He caught the door and held it for her as she stepped through.

Stan pushed back a lock of hair that kept falling into her eye and tried to smile. "I don't think I want to advertise this. It's much harder when you have to run the party instead of just catering. Need something?"

He held up his glass. "Just going to top off my water."

"I can get it for you."

"No need. I'm used to pouring drinks." He winked at her and moved into the kitchen.

"So you're off tonight?" Stan pulled the cake out of the fridge where it had been thawing.

"I may go in later and see what's going on. My people have everything under control, but if I have nothing else going on . . ." He shrugged.

Stan didn't know what to say to that, so she focused on the cake. She'd done the ghost in honor of Halloween, which happened to be Duncan's costume. Stan had a sneaking suspicion that was because Jake had found it easier to drape a sheet over the dog so he wouldn't have to hear Stan's criticism rather than because he had an affinity for ghosts, but she kept that opinion to herself.

Jake filled his water, then stood next to her, checking out the cake. "Looks like Dunc," he said, a smile pulling at the corners of his mouth.

Stan laughed. "I think he's the only one with a homemade costume. If you want to call that homemade."

"The abuse never ceases." Jake shook his head. "At least

I got him a costume this time." He started to walk back outside, then turned. "So. After you wrap up this shindig, any interest in having dinner?"

The knife dropped from her fingers and clattered to the floor. Luckily no animals were underneath it. Unruffled, Jake bent and picked it up, rinsed it, and placed it next to the cake on the counter. "You can let me know," he said, that same amused smile lurking on his lips. "You have your hands full right now." And he disappeared outside.

Ugh. Stan rapped her fist against her forehead. Why couldn't she get it together in front of him? She could hold a conversation just fine—until it got personal. Or until he asked her out. Which, admittedly, had not happened before today, so she had an excuse for reacting the way she did. Didn't she?

So, what to do? After missing each other last night, she and her mother were supposed to have dinner tonight. But she'd much rather have dinner with Jake. Which made her a terrible daughter. *Think about it later. The doggies are waiting for cake.* She put the cake and knife on a tray and headed outside. Duncan and Benny waited at the door, tails wagging, ears on alert. *Cake?* their hopeful expressions said. *We get cake, too?*

"Yes, you guys get cake. Come on over." She led the parade of dogs to the table and placed the cake on it. Nancy joined her.

"Oh, this is delightful!" she crowed. "I love it. However do you get so *creative?*"

Stan blinked. She didn't really think of herself as creative. She'd simply ordered a cake pan in the shape of a ghost from her new favorite supplier. But she didn't tell Nancy that. Instead, she winked. "I can't tell you all my secrets," she said. "Come on, Benny, let's get you the first piece."

At three o'clock, after only two doggie fights over cake, the party wrapped. Benny had finagled two pieces, Nyla the poodle had gotten a stint in time-out for stealing Toby the dachshund's piece, and every last crumb had been cleaned up. Goodie bags with cow trachea had been distributed. Nancy declared the day a success and promised to tell everyone she knew how great Stan's parties were, which had Stan floating on air. Henry had come back out now that he didn't have to wear his costume, and he contentedly sniffed around the fence with Scruffy in tow. Stan packed up the remaining treats and tried calling her mother to find out about dinner. She didn't answer. Again. And Jake was waiting.

He hadn't left yet. She saw him collecting paper plates the dogs had licked clean from the grass and other areas. Duncan followed, making sure each plate had no frosting left that was going to waste. Stan watched him for a minute, envying the ease in which he moved through life. Nothing much seemed to bother Jake, although Stan knew that despite his laid-back exterior, he wasn't lackadaisical. He knew everything he needed to know, and he cared a lot about the town and the people in it. Which is probably why he gave Izzy the advice he'd given her about her deal with Hal, and look what he'd gotten for it.

Crap. She needed to see if he could offer any suggestion for Izzy's situation. She'd promised.

He turned then, and caught her watching him. She flushed and busied herself pulling down the "Happy Birthday" banner she'd hung for Benny on the back porch.

"I think your yard is back to normal," he said. "Nice job, Stan. The dog lovers in town are impressed. Your business is going to do well here."

Sweet words to hear. Especially from him. Ah, screw it. "If you still want to go to dinner, I'm in," she blurted before she could change her mind. Could she be more socially awkward?

He looked almost as surprised as she felt, but recovered quickly. "Excellent," he said. "I'll pick you up at seven."

"Seven," she repeated stupidly.

He nodded, then clipped Duncan's leash on and exited through the gate to the driveway. Stan finished taking down her decorations. She had four hours to figure out what to wear.

Chapter 32

Stan couldn't remember the last time she'd been on a date. With a critical eye, she stood in front of the full-length mirror in her bedroom, finding a million things wrong with her hair and outfit. Nutty watched from the bed disdainfully.

"Why are you giving me that look?" she asked him. "Just because you have perfect hair." His orangey brown Maine coon coat was full and rich and thick. The neighborhood cats were jealous when they saw him sitting in his window.

Nutty flicked his tail at her and rolled over, bored with the human vanity routine. Stan grabbed a clip and twisted her hair up, smoothed her black dress and kicked off her red shoes in favor of blue ones. Refusing to second guess the outfit again, she marched downstairs and grabbed her purse. She had a voice mail on her phone. She dialed, then hit the End button when Jake pulled into the driveway. Fluffed her hair again. The dogs waited anxiously at the door.

"Nope, sorry, guys. You're not coming for this one." She took a deep breath. "Wish me luck. Hopefully I won't spill anything on him or otherwise completely embarrass myself."

* * *

The restaurant he'd chosen was just outside Frog Ledge—thankfully nowhere near Bruno's. It wasn't an Irish pub, either. It was a Thai restaurant. She'd mentioned once how much she loved Thai food, and he'd remembered. This place was awesome, beginning with the Asian pear martini she'd ordered in hopes of calming herself. Why on earth was she so nervous about this date?

Because he's adorable. And nice—definitely a trait that takes getting used to.

Jake had dressed up, too. Not fancy, but he wasn't wearing his usual bar uniform of jeans, a T-shirt, and a baseball cap. He wore a black dress shirt and a pair of gray slacks. His dirty blond hair was its usual shaggy self, which was a relief, but he had shaved, which Stan found unnerving. There were also no dogs to focus on. Usually Duncan was jumping all over the place begging for treats, or Scruffy was trying to get in someone's lap. Tonight it was just them. They'd managed to get through the vegetable spring roll appetizers by talking about Pawsitively Organic and Brenna's baking talents. Now they waited for the main course to arrive, and silence had settled.

And he kept watching her across the table, which wasn't helping, as he sipped his Sam Adams Harvest Pumpkin Ale. Stan took a big gulp of her drink and prayed for some aspect of her former social skills to return. They seemed to have been eliminated along with her former job.

"So did you hear what happened last night?" she asked.

He frowned. "With what?"

So Jessie and the rest of Troop E were keeping Enrico's arrest under wraps. She told him about the incident at the farm, glossing over the part about Enrico hitting her with the shovel, and focusing on the attempt to taint the milk with sick cows.

Jake listened intently, his eyes dark, twirling his beer bottle around on the table. When she finished he asked, "Did you get hurt?"

"Me? No." *Just bruised, nothing major.* "But I have no idea what happened with Enrico. Do you think this means he killed Hal and the charges against Tyler will be dropped?"

"I have no idea," Jake said. "I would presume right now they have him on trespassing and other criminal activity, maybe assault, and knowing my sister she'll look to tie him to the murder."

"Yeah." Stan sipped her drink. "I have to admit, I wondered if Hal's murder had anything to do with his real estate deals." She watched his face closely. It didn't change.

Wouldn't want to play poker with this family.

He topped off her glass of water with the pitcher on the table, then refilled his own glass. He replaced the pitcher deliberately, waiting for her to continue. Of course he couldn't make it easy. She wasn't very good at fishing, either. The waitress came and set down her plate of shrimp pad Thai and Jake's spicy chicken curry, giving her a minute to think through how to approach him.

"I think he was losing money all over the place," she said.

"How do you know that?" Jake added a dash of hot sauce to his already spicy food. Stan's tongue curdled, imagining the burn.

"Just stuff that I've heard," she said noncommittally, wrapping noodles around her fork. She took a deep breath. "And I had a strange encounter with a guy at Bruno's."

"Bruno's?" he repeated. "As in the bar?"

But her memory had finally gotten around to working. Her face drained. Bruno's. Bullet Man. He was supposed to show up at the farm tonight. And she'd completely forgotten to alert anyone because she'd been hosting a doggie party and worrying about going on this date.

She jumped up. "I have to call your sister."

"Brenna? Why?"

"No. Jessie. Shoot." She fumbled for her phone.

"Stan, what's going on? Sit and tell me."

She did, detailing her conversation with Bullet Man and her impulsive response to his question. "He's going to show up there tonight. I have to get your sister there."

But instead of agreeing with her, he laughed.

She stared at him. Had he lost his mind? "What's funny?" she demanded. "That guy was creepy. He could be the killer. That was completely irresponsible of me—"

"Stan," he interrupted. "Relax. That guy was Screech Monahan. I can see how you would think he's creepy, but he's harmless."

"You *know* him?" Apparently there was a lot about Jake she didn't know.

"I do. And you're right, that is a bullet hole. Screech had an altercation with someone a lot more dangerous than him a few years ago. That was the result. And they call him Screech because his voice is altered now. His idea," he said, holding up his hands.

Stan had no idea what to say to that.

"He and Hal had an arrangement, but it wasn't as sinister as you think. Screech drives an old hearse. Hal was renting the car for the corn maze, as a shuttle from the parking area down the street."

This was getting more and more bizarre. "A hearse? How do you know this guy again?"

Jake smiled. "He's a Frog Ledge legend."

"I see." Stan took a bite of her food. "Harmless, you say?"

"Completely," Jake assured her.

"Well, that's a relief, at least. But he's going to show up at the farm and no one's there."

"I'll take care of it." Jake pulled out his phone, scrolled through his contacts, and dialed. "Hey, it's Jake. Misunderstanding about the maze tonight. It's closed until further notice." He paused. "I know. Sorry about that, man. I'll let you know if things change." He hung up, pocketed the phone, and smiled at her. "All set."

Stan frowned. She'd learned a lot about Jake over the past couple of days. "Thanks," she said.

"No problem."

She turned her attention back to her food. "Oh, I finally talked to Izzy." She stuffed a forkful of food into her mouth, waiting for his reaction.

He kept eating. "So what was the story?"

Jeez, he was a tough customer. She swallowed and set her fork down. Beating around the bush never worked for her. "Izzy told me about partnering with Hal. To buy your building. And how Hal borrowed from bad people and dragged Izzy down with him."

Jake took another swig of his beer. Waited.

"That's why she threw the chair at that guy in her store. Because they're looking for the money now from her and she doesn't have it." Frustrated, Stan leaned forward. "Don't you want to say something?"

Jake finished chewing, wiped his mouth with his napkin. Picked up his water glass and drank. "What do you want me to say? People make choices, Stan. Izzy didn't want to hear it when I asked her to reconsider her deal with Hal. They offered the right price for the building. I'm sorry she's in over her head, but I honestly don't know what I can do to help."

"How come you never mentioned it? That you bought and sold properties?"

Jake did that half smile thing. "I didn't realize I was being interrogated."

Stan flushed. "You're not. But with you and Izzy . . . not getting along, I would've thought you'd want people to know why. If that's why."

"I don't need to justify anything to 'people.' If people like me, great. If they don't, I'm not gonna lose sleep over it. Most people," he amended. "But I have no control over what people think. That's a lesson I learned a long time ago. Believe me, life gets a lot easier when you figure that out."

How could she argue with that? She sighed and picked her fork up again.

"Izzy made a bad choice," he said. "Hal made a worse one. I didn't *make* them do it. Hell, I had no idea until the Realtor brought me an offer. Then I went to see her. I knew talking to him wouldn't get me anywhere. Remember, I've known the Hoffmans forever. But I found out she's pretty stubborn, too. And she wanted the building. Told me everything was under control. I had another building under agreement, so I closed the deal." He shrugged.

"Do you own a lot of properties?"

"A few," he said. "I started dabbling in rental properties when I moved back to Frog Ledge. Some, like Hal and Izzy, wanted to do their own rehab because they had specific ideas of what they wanted. Usually I buy, rehab, and sell. I'm picky about what I want and I stay in the immediate area. I'd like to see more opportunities for people to work in Frog Ledge. If we can get businesses in here, it'll be a good thing. Businesses need locations."

His dedication to his town was impressive. "When do you have time to do all that with the bar?" She'd never even seen him looking like he'd walked off a construction site.

"I have a crew who does the work." He smiled. "I don't want to do the work anymore."

"Makes sense." She ate more, thinking, absently looking around the room while she did so. He had connections, obviously. There had to be some solution for Izzy, even if it was simply getting a name of someone who might help her. "So what could we do to help—" She stopped. Stared across the room, at a corner booth half hidden by a human-sized bamboo tree.

Jake followed her gaze. "What?"

"That's my mother." Who was presently laughing, snuggled up with mayoral candidate Tony Falco in the middle of the booth. There was a bottle of wine on the table. Falco refilled her mother's glass as Stan watched. "Excuse me," she said to Jake, and rose, tossing her napkin on the table. She marched over to her mother and stopped in front of them, folding her arms across her chest.

"Hello, Mom. I'm glad I wasn't waiting to have dinner with you." As soon as she said the words, she realized how ridiculous they were. She was here eating dinner, too.

Her mother's eyes went wide behind the rim of her wineglass. She swallowed and set it down. Beside her, Tony Falco flashed a thousand-watt smile at her.

"Kristan. What are you doing here? Are you on a date?

With whom?" Patricia rose and scanned the room. Stan risked a glance over her shoulder in time to see Jake lifting a hand in a wave. Her mother squinted. "Is that the bartender?"

"He owns the place," Stan said through gritted teeth. "What are you doing?"

Patricia sat again, but she left space between her and Falco. "We're having dinner."

"A lovely dinner at that," Falco broke in, standing and extending a hand to her. "Lovely to see you again. I had no idea you were Patricia's daughter."

Now her mother was confused. "You know each other?"

"Yeah. I dumped a glass of water in his lap." Stan didn't elaborate. "Are *you* on a date?" *Great question, Sherlock.* "I didn't even know you liked Thai food." Not like that had anything to do with anything, but Stan was at a loss. Why was her mother here with this politician? And why was she acting like a jilted suitor? The irony of the situation almost made her laugh. The last time she'd seen her ex, Richard, she'd been in this very position at a different restaurant.

"As a matter of fact, I am on a date. And I do like Thai food. Does that suit you?" Her mother's tone had cooled considerably. She was in control again after being caught off guard.

"So this is what all the secrecy was about? Where did you meet him? Did Char set you guys up or something?"

Her mother looked uncomfortable, but Falco missed it. "Not at all. Patricia and I go way back," he said, with an adoring look at her mother.

Finally, it dawned on her. "So this is why you came to Frog Ledge. Not to visit me. You had arrangements to see him. Why didn't you just tell me that, Mom? Why go through all the pretense?" She shook her head. "I'll never learn when it comes to you. Enjoy your dinner."

She spun on her heel and walked back to Jake. He'd been far enough away that she doubted he'd heard, but he could tell the conversation had not been pleasant.

"Ready to go?" he asked. He already had his wallet out to pay. She wanted to kiss him for understanding.

"Let's go get a drink," she said.

Chapter 33

Sunday dawned sunny, crisp, and bright, not a cloud to be seen. If a stranger walked into Frog Ledge today, they would never guess the picturesque small town with its steepled white churches and rolling farmland had been the site of a recent murder.

The weather was perfect for the day of festivities—Char and Ray's annual open house at Alpaca Haven, followed by the pet costume parade Stan was judging and the outdoor movie night on the green, sponsored by the library. They were showing as many of the *Nightmare on Elm Street* movies as townsfolk could stomach, beginning at seven and lasting well into the night. A longtime Freddy Krueger fan, Stan had planned to catch at least the first one. Then Jake invited her to go with him to the movies when he dropped her off last night, which was even better.

As she walked to Char and Ray's with her dogs and a shopping bag full of animal goodies, she saw fellow residents out in full force taking advantage of the best of fall. Tag sales were happening all along Stan's road, on both sides of the green, part of a neighborhood effort in conjunction with St. Andrew's. The parish the Hoffmans belonged to was raising funds for the family, in light of not only Hal's death but Tyler's subsequent arrest.

Stan hoped they were successful. Normally she tried to get to the local tag sales, always looking for new cooking accessories or fun-shaped cookie cutters now that she was getting more creative with her treats. But she had to be at Char's early to help set up. Plus she wanted to see her mother. She felt bad about their confrontation in the restaurant. If her mother wanted to date some slimy local politician, that was up to her. Stan didn't have to be childish about it. As they rounded the corner to Char's already-full driveway, Scruffy realized where they were going and started yanking on her leash, *woo-woo-wooing* all the way. She loved visiting Char and Ray.

"Hang on, Scruf," Stan called, trying not to drop her bag full of food. Henry, always obedient, walked right next to her. Savannah saw them coming and ran out to the driveway, her tail wagging. She immediately ran to Scruffy and sniffed her from all sides. She did look great. Her coat was rich and full and she had no hot spots anymore. Stan felt a sense of pride that her food had contributed to the dog's health.

When she finished sniffing Scruffy and did the same to Henry, Savannah led them around the house to the yard. Guitar music played and the smell of coffee and pastries wafted across the lawn. Brenna had told her a number of times that the open house was one of Frog Ledge's biggest events of the year. But when she stepped through the gate, her mouth dropped open. Char knew how to plan a party, for sure. She had walked through a latticed archway decorated with purple, green, and gold bows, an entryway to the festivities. From here, she had a spectacular view of the entire backyard, which had been transformed into a Mardi

Gras fairyland. Shimmery streamers with all three colors decorated the sides of the house. Three tents were set up, one purple, one green, and one yellow-gold. They all had signs hanging from them—BEVERAGES, SNACKS, FOOD. The tables had festive tablecloths and the chairs were decorated with matching seat cushions.

A small stage was set up to the left of the tents. Stan could see a few people setting up equipment, others riffing on guitars. The rest of the property was the alpaca area. Stan could see a few of them out in their pens, watching the goings-on lazily as staff changed their water and cleaned the area. The enclosure had its own purple, green, and gold accents. Stan giggled. It was so perfect. So Char. No Mardi Gras in Connecticut, so Char brought her own.

"You like?" Her friend materialized behind her. She was dressed for the occasion, of course, in a bright green dress, with a purple scarf tied around her neck and gold shoes.

"I love." Stan hugged her and kissed her cheek. "This is amazing."

"It'll be a fun day." Char surveyed her kingdom, nodding in satisfaction. "I'm not thrilled about the color of my gold tent. It's not quite gold. But it was special order and kind of a pain to get, so I let it go."

"It's great," Stan said. "The whole setup is great. Who's the band?"

"Oh, the band!" Char clapped her hands. "You'll never guess. Leigh-Anne told me that Ted Brahm had a band. They do lots of fun music. He said they could do the bluesy stuff we like for Mardi Gras parties. They're called the Dairy Farmers. Isn't that adorable?"

It seemed rather predictable to Stan, but she didn't say so. Ted Brahm looked like more of a sixties hippie than a New Orleans expert, but she didn't say that either. She wondered if Char knew about Em and Ted. She had to. Char knew everything. But before she could ask, Izzy swept through the archway with a huge platter of petits fours and a bag presumably loaded with other goodies, her three dogs at her heels. "Hey, Stan! You brought doggie dessert and I brought people dessert. We're a good team."

"You girls are wonderful." Char kissed Izzy's cheek. "Go set up in the gold tent. Stan, Brenna's already here."

"Come on, then. You can pick your display spot." Izzy grinned and led the way. She appeared a lot more relaxed than the last time Stan had seen her. More like herself.

"So how's everything going?" Stan couldn't help but ask as they reached the tent and began unpacking goodies. Her conversation with Jake last night had been interrupted, and she'd never gotten to ask him about helping Izzy get out of her bad financial situation.

"Things are going much better," Izzy said, arranging her platter on the table. "I think I have a solution."

"You do? What—" She turned as deafening feedback screeched through the microphone. One of the men in Ted's band held up an apologetic hand as he went back to fiddling with his sound. By the time she'd turned around, Izzy was gone. Stan spotted her a few feet away, deep in conversation with someone Stan didn't recognize. Well, maybe she didn't feel like getting into it here. That was understandable.

Brenna came up behind her. "Isn't this sweet?"

Stan agreed. "Where should we set up?"

Brenna looked around. "Right here's a good spot."

Stan turned to her own bag to unpack and noticed she had six dogs—no, make that seven, a small Yorkie had crept up to the circle and was sitting behind Scruffy—all watching her intently. "Guys, you can't eat them all before the day even begins!" She smiled. "Good thing I brought extras."

She handed out treats to all her fans, most of whom plopped contentedly on the grass in front of her to eat them. The Yorkie took her stash and trotted away, the huge cookie clutched in her tiny mouth.

"Did you hear?" Brenna said. "Enrico was officially arrested and charged with trespass, endangerment, and something else—I can't remember what. But not murder."

"Really? Was this in the paper?"

"It happened yesterday. Cyril put it on the website."

"Wow. So they're back to square one with the murder, then."

"Yes. Back to Tyler." Brenna looked unhappy. "I know he didn't do it, Stan."

"If I know your sister, I'm sure she won't let it go if she has any doubt," Stan assured her. Brenna didn't look convinced.

"It's so odd, though. What did Enrico hope to gain by sabotaging the milk supply? Was he unhappy at work? Did the Hoffmans do something unfair to him?"

Brenna shrugged. "I have no idea."

"It's got to tie in somehow." Stan wished her brain would process all this information in a more organized fashion so she could examine it better. But it wasn't the time to try.

The day flew from there. It seemed the whole town had crowded into Char and Ray's backyard, and brought friends along. There were tours of the farm, visits with the alpacas, lots of eating and drinking, a number of doggie visitors, and to Stan's surprise, decent music from Ted Brahm and his band. As Stan paused at one point to watch the band perform, she wondered what the extent of Em and Ted's relationship was. How long it had been going on? Had Hal known? Suspected? Cared?

And what about Ted Brahm? In the few times Stan had

met him, the hippie-turned-farmer seemed gentle and laid back. If he really loved Em and knew Hal wasn't treating her right, would he still be laid back? Or could he turn murderous? *"Everybody's got a dark side,"* Kelly Clarkson reminded her. Had Ted killed Hal? Would he let his lover's son take the fall?

The whole thing made her head hurt. And she still hadn't seen her mother anywhere. Admittedly, it was hard to find anyone in the crowd of people in Char's backyard. She wondered if her mother had packed up and gone home, or maybe packed up and gone to Tony Falco's house. She hadn't had a chance to ask Char yet. Stan was too busy selling her treats and answering questions about her ingredients.

Jessie Pasquale walked in, in uniform. Immediately the crowd quieted. Stan saw her arrive and go straight to Char. They spoke quietly, then Char went to the stage and drew a line across her throat, signaling for the band to stop playing. Jessie motioned for Ted Brahm to get off stage.

"What's going on?" Brenna said.

"No idea." Stan slipped through the crowd until she reached Char, who looked upset. Em was nowhere in sight. "What's up?"

"Tyler skipped bail," Char said. "Jessie went looking for him at Em's sister's, where he was supposed to be staying. All his things and his car are gone."

Chapter 34

Stan had a hard time slipping away from Char's party to make her pet parade judging obligation. After Jessie showed up canvasing for Tyler Hoffman, the entire focus of the party turned to Tyler's possible whereabouts, whether anyone else was on his hit list, and what to do in the event of a sighting.

She finally got away and headed to the green. Her co-judges were already there, as well as what seemed like the town's entire animal population. She was delighted to see Amara in one of the chairs. The other judge was a fiftyish man who looked way too uptight to like dogs in costume. He introduced himself as the town manager.

The green buzzed with the news of Tyler Hoffman's escape. Stan heard bits and pieces of conversations: "Do you think he's dangerous?" "Would he go back to the scene of the crime?" "I wonder if they have police dogs hunting him."

"Sheesh," she said, taking the seat next to Amara at the judging table. "People are so quick to condemn."

Amara nodded, her face troubled. "I don't know what to think, honestly. I didn't know Tyler. But family problems can escalate so quickly. I hope they find him. And I *really* hope they figure out who did it—whether it's him or not."

"Agreed." Stan smiled as she looked around at the pets roaming the green with every kind of costume imaginable. "I've never done this before. I imagine it will be difficult."

Amara grinned. "The town hasn't had one before. Diane and I proposed it after last year's Halloween activities. It's a way to get more out-of-towners here, too. We're trying to raise the animal-lover status, especially with the new business." She sat back and smiled like the Cheshire cat.

It took Stan a moment to process what she'd said. "Oh! The council approved the clinic and shelter?"

"They did," Amara said. "So basically, none of us will have a life for a while, but we're so excited about what it will do for this town."

Stan agreed. "I can't wait. Please let me know what I can do to help."

"Funny you should ask," Amara said. "We thought we would explore selling a line of healthy organic meals. We should talk. Maybe it's something you'd be interested in."

Her own line of meals? Stan salivated at the thought. And if she prepared them under veterinary supervision, she'd have the nutrition issue covered. "I'd love to talk about that," she said.

Her spirits decidedly higher, she turned her attention to the town pets, who had begun their parade around the green. Some owners also wore matching costumes, a shameless plug for votes that had to be ignored. Only the animals could be judged.

There were three categories in addition to the typical Best, Most Original, and Scariest costumes: Best Inanimate Object, Most Likely to Be a Zombie Sidekick, and Most Likely to Hit It Big on Broadway. After seeing nearly fifty dogs, Stan conferred with her fellow judges and they announced the winners. Her favorite was the chocolate lab dressed as the rapper Eminem, who won for Most Original.

When Eminem and his owner approached the table for their bag of home-baked treats and gift certificate to the local pet supply shop, Stan realized it was Maddy, the McSwigg's waitress who had seen Emmalee ditch her car the day of Hal's murder. Stan handed her the goodie bag. Maddy murmured a thank you and turned to leave.

Stan rose. "Hey, Maddy?"

Maddy turned around, her gaze neither friendly nor unfriendly. "Yeah?"

"I'm Stan. A friend of Jake and Brenna's. Do you have a second?"

At Maddy's nod, Stan led her away from the crowd of winning dogs and their owners. Maddy was silent, waiting for Stan to speak.

"Congrats," Stan said. "Your dog is adorable."

"Thanks."

Okay. Not one for small talk. Stan dove right in. "Brenna told me you saw the Hoffmans the day Mr. Hoffman died. I know you saw Emmalee leave her car there. But I know Mr. Hoffman used to go to the bar a lot. Did you by any chance see him lately with an older guy, long hair, lots of earrings? Tall and kind of skinny?" Maybe Maddy would recognize Ted and place him near the scene.

Maddy shook her head slowly. "Who's that?"

"One of the farmers he works with." Stan didn't elaborate.

"I don't think so."

"What about a guy with a big beard? Sort of like ZZ Top?"

"Like what?" Maddy stared blankly at her. Stan felt old.

"Nothing. He just has a big, long, bushy beard."

Maddy shook her head again, picking at her cuticle. "He only came in there with the poker guys. Least that's all I saw him with."

"Poker guys?"

"Yeah. This group that got together twice a week to play poker. They came to the bar first. Tried to play at the bar a couple times, but Jake broke it up."

"Did Hal ever seem to not get along with them? Or was he stressed out about losing money, maybe? Did he look like he *had* to play? Like it wasn't fun?" She was grasping, but maybe there was a nugget here somewhere that would save Tyler.

"Nah. He was always laughing. And drinking." Maddy thought for a minute, then shrugged. "I never saw him mad in the bar."

Another dead end. "Thanks," Stan said. "I won't keep you." As she turned, Maddy spoke again.

"The only time I saw him mad was once outside the liquor store. He was having a fight with that blond lady with the curly hair. The sappy sweet one who was with that guy you spilled the water on that night. You know her, right?"

Leigh-Anne Sutton? Couldn't be. "You're sure it was the same woman?" Stan asked.

"Positive. She wears those ridiculous shoes."

"When was this?" Stan asked.

Maddy shrugged. "A few weeks ago. When they saw me coming they shut it down quick."

Stan watched her and the dog walk away, a shiver running up her spine. Her mind ricocheted back to Leigh-Anne's words that night at Jake's. "Such a delightful little town. I haven't been back since the co-op's annual meeting six months ago. I always forget how adorable it is."

Why had she lied?

* * *

The night carried the typical New England autumn chill, perfect for a scary movie on the green with plenty of popcorn on hand. Stan slipped on her bright orange Fila jacket, chosen in the spirit of Halloween, and went back to her small bag of popcorn. Next to her in the second row of the "movie seats"—rows of folding chairs volunteers had set up—Jake had his own bag. They weren't at the sharing popcorn stage yet. Both had acknowledged that silently.

The movie had drawn a good crowd. She expected it was more about the social aspect than the content, considering the *Elm Street* movies were pretty old. The *Halloween* series would've been a good choice, too, but the younger crowd seemed to enjoy Freddy. The audience would likely shift during the course of the viewings. It was early still, barely eight. The teenagers would come out later, probably around the third or fourth installment, if they could convince their parents to let them stay out that late. But for now, it was a good mix of Stan's age group and a little younger.

Stan couldn't concentrate on the movie. She'd been antsy since her conversation with Maddy earlier. Leigh-Anne Sutton had been in Frog Ledge, fighting with Hal, a couple of weeks before he died. Leigh-Anne had never given any indication she and Hal didn't get along. She'd even been the first one to offer to help. And she was also the only co-op farmer who had essentially abandoned her own business to move to Frog Ledge after Hal's death. Business partner goodwill? Or was there a more sinister reason behind it?

Stan thought back to the first time she'd met Leigh-Anne, in Em's kitchen the morning after Hal's murder. Even then, after offering her condolences, she'd taken right over. Acted like the farm was hers to run. Acted like the funeral was hers to run, for goodness' sake. All under the guise of being helpful. At the town meeting, it hadn't been Leigh-Anne who had made the motion to take control away from Em. But the group had voted for Leigh-Anne to have coleadership control. Stan remembered the folder she'd found in Hal's office, with the co-op agreement. She had to get back there and find it.

Her next thought stopped her cold. If Leigh-Anne and Em had joint control, what if something happened to Em? Then Leigh-Anne could take over the co-op. Maybe she'd even get her hands on Em's farm. Leigh-Anne might have seen Hal as her only obstacle to being in charge of the entire business. Now she'd taken care of him, but the path to the Happy Cow co-op still wasn't clear. Could Em be in danger?

To add to her jumpiness, Stan hadn't seen or heard from her mother all day. Patricia was good at holding a grudge, but she wouldn't vanish into the night without a word. After the fifth time Stan had craned her neck to look into the crowd behind them, Jake leaned over.

"Everything okay?"

"Fine. Why?" Stan settled back in her seat.

"You looking for someone?"

"Just wondering if my mother was still around. I haven't heard from her since last night."

"Why don't you call her?" Jake suggested.

Stan smiled sheepishly. "That's not a bad idea. It's been such a busy day, I just figured I'd see her at Char's." She patted her pockets. "Shoot. I don't have my phone. I must've left it at home when I dropped the dogs off earlier." Thinking about the dogs triggered her brain back into action and she jumped up. "Oh my goodness! The pets!"

"What's wrong with the pets?" Jake asked.

"Not my pets. Em's pets. I never went to feed Samson and Petunia tonight." Stan dropped her voice when the group in the next aisle turned to glare at her. "And Samson wasn't feeling well. I really need to run over there."

"Now? This is where it gets good. Freddy's on a rampage," Jake said. Johnny Depp was about to meet his demise in his bedroom.

"Yeah, before it gets too late. I already feel bad for being so forgetful."

"Want me to go with you?"

How sweet. She could tell he had no desire to take his eyes off the movie, yet he offered to be chivalrous. "No, stay and enjoy the movie. I already brought meals and left them in the fridge, so I don't even have to go home first. I'll just run across the street and heat them up. Honestly," she said when he protested. "I'm leaving my popcorn. Keep an eye on it for me."

"Okay," he said. "I'll be here."

She hoped so. Because while she did need to feed the pets, she also wanted to snoop around in Leigh-Anne's "office" at Happy Cow. Perhaps she would find something that would solve this mystery, once and for all.

Stan walked up the Hoffmans' long driveway and let herself in the front door as silently as possible. Samson lumbered over to see her. Stan flicked some lights on and patted his head. "Let's go get some food."

Samson followed her into the kitchen. She opened the fridge, grabbed the food, and spooned it into a dish. While it was heating in the microwave, she glanced out the window.

And saw Em's car parked on the side of the house. When had she returned? And where was she? Perhaps she'd been called back for some emergency. She should run out and check the barn. While she was out there she could slip into the office and look for incriminating evidence against Leigh-Anne. Like a note confessing to everything. That would make it much easier.

She put Samson's food in front of him and left Petunia's on the counter, and slipped out the back door. She knew her way around the farm as well as most of the staff by now. Dusk was settling, but she didn't even need a flashlight. The floodlights were on and she didn't want to draw any extra attention to herself.

She crossed the backyard and headed toward the barn. Then paused when she heard voices. Soft, as if they were some distance away. Maybe it was Em. She couldn't tell if they were male or female. Stan took a few steps in the direction they seemed to be coming from. Squinted. Was that Em over by the corn maze? She took a step forward, ready to call out, then gasped as Em's companion came into view. Holding Em's tied hands behind her back. Those blond curls were unmistakable.

It was Leigh-Anne Sutton.

Chapter 35

Stan froze. Then the voice in her head screamed *go go go* and she dashed back against the side of the office building for cover. She was certain Leigh-Anne hadn't seen her. She'd been intent on whatever she was doing to Em. She cursed herself for forgetting her phone. Now she had to get to one. The closest would be in the milking area offices. Where she was heading anyway.

She paused, listening. Other than the faint sounds of Heather Langenkamp screaming on the movie screen across the street, she heard nothing. Except her own blood pounding through her body. Praying the door wasn't locked, she slipped around the corner and tried it. It gave easily under her hand. Thank God.

She stepped into the milking parlor. It was empty. Not time for a shift yet. The door to the offices was around the back. She headed that way and stepped into the hall.

And almost collided with Roger.

"Oh, Roger, you scared me! Thank goodness you're here. We need to call the police. Em's in trouble. . . ." Her voice trailed off. Roger hadn't reacted at all to her appearance or her words. He simply stared at her.

"Roger?"

Roger slid his hand out from his pocket. The black metal of a small pistol glinted in the dim light. "Sorry, Stan. You're going to have to come with me."

The cornstalks shifted in the breeze, rattling against each other. Stan could smell the slightly musty odor of the stalks coupled with the sweet, smoky scent of someone's woodstove. It would've been a nice walk on a gorgeous fall night if her hands weren't tied and a gun wasn't poking her back. When they reached the crime scene tape blocking the maze entrance, Roger forced her under it. Her mind raced through escape options. Could she mule-kick him in the right place without him shooting her, then take off before Leigh-Anne realized what had happened?

Roger shoved her around the first corner. Shoot. The farther they went into the corn maze, the more problems. If she tried to run she could find herself in a dead end. But he stopped.

"Leigh-Anne?" he called out.

Silence. They both waited.

Leigh-Anne Sutton stepped out from around the first bend. She looked almost exactly as she had the last time Stan had seen her—blond curls falling out of a clip, jeans, the ever-present pink work boots. Except for a bloody cut on her cheek. And a gun in her right hand. Pointing right at Stan.

"Stan! So glad you could join us." Leigh-Anne's voice carried that lilt Stan had gotten used to over the past week working at the farm, but it had taken on a sinister edge. That could, of course, be attributed to the situation.

Stan processed the scene in front of her in a series of

aha! moments that felt like they'd taken a long time to reach, but in reality couldn't have been more than a few seconds. Leigh-Anne was guilty. She and Roger were in cahoots. Em was in trouble. Oh, God. Had they already killed her?

"Oh, don't worry about your friend." Leigh-Anne had read her mind. "Mrs. Hoffman is just fine. For the moment. We have a little business we need to take care of, so she isn't going anywhere. But you and I are going to take a little walk. Who knows you're here?"

"Jake does. He's on his way over right now. And his sister isn't far behind."

She chuckled. "Nice try. Trooper Pasquale has her man. Well, he's missing at the moment, but she'll find him. And then, as far as she's concerned, this case is closed. And if sexy bartender is on his way, well, it will be a shame but we'll have to get rid of him, too."

Stan paled. He wouldn't come over looking for her already, would he? She hadn't been gone that long. She sent him a telepathic message to stay away.

"Want me to take her?" Roger asked. He sounded tired. Like he was just trying to get a job done. And she could have sworn she caught a flash of guilt in his eyes earlier when he tied her hands. How had Leigh-Anne gotten Roger on board with this? Had he helped her kill Hal, or did he simply get in over his head and now he had no choice?

"Why are you doing this, Leigh-Anne?" Stan blurted out. "If you killed Hal, you should just confess. You're not going to get anywhere hurting other people. Do you think no one's going to put it together?"

"Of course they won't. Especially now that Tyler is on the run. They'll just think he's on a killing spree. He actually did me a favor. Let's go." To Roger, "Is Miguel handled?"

Her gaze was icy cold. Stan shivered. How had she not noticed the evil in this woman?

Roger nodded. "I left him in the barn."

Stan closed her eyes. Had they killed one of the workers? Some poor immigrant kid who could barely speak English and was just trying to make a living?

"Excellent," Leigh-Anne said. "Take her up to the barn." She motioned behind her. That must mean Em was still in the maze. Roger nodded and disappeared around a corner.

Now it was just the two of them. Stan gauged her escape options. It had been a long time since she'd taken a martial arts class, but she had been good at kicking. Maybe she could use her feet to kick the gun out of Leigh-Anne's hands.

But Leigh-Anne was on alert, with what looked like her brand new pistol pointed steadily at Stan. Fancy one, too. Stan didn't know much about guns, but this was clearly a high performer. At least it wasn't a sickle. If she could distract her, she could at least make a run for it.

Until the bullets caught up with her.

Leigh-Anne shoved Stan roughly forward, causing her to trip. "Walk. No funny stuff."

"So you did kill Hal." Stan forced herself to walk slowly despite Leigh-Anne pulling on her. Wherever they were going, she was sure it wasn't good. The longer it took to get there, the more chance she had of figuring something out to save herself.

"He left me no choice," Leigh-Anne said. "I didn't particularly want to, but I wasn't getting anywhere being nice, either. He's a hard man to be in business with. He cared more about those stupid cows than he did about making money. Always his problem, I swear. Too soft."

"Why? Because he didn't want you for a partner?" she pressed.

"Partner?" Leigh-Anne spat the word. "I didn't want to be his partner. He had too many *ethics* to be in this business. I should've been running this co-op. It would've been better for everyone. I even offered to take over his silly farm, and he shut me down." Her eyes blazed with the injustice of it. "Backstabbing fool got what he deserved. Threatening to report *me* to the Department of Agriculture for unethical farming? Me? I've made this operation more money in two years than he could ever *dream* of making."

So her story about Tyler approaching her to take over the farm had been a big lie. Stan should've seen it sooner. She mentally kicked herself for being so naive. Better to blame a sad, confused eighteen-year-old than a conniving, unethical farmer just because she was female? She had been so stupid.

The more agitated Leigh-Anne got, the faster she walked, dragging Stan across the field as she tried to keep up, both with the pace and the litany of words. That had to be what the documents on Hal's computer were about. He must've been gathering evidence for a complaint, and she found out.

"And he was snooping into my personal life," Leigh-Anne said. "Thought he could make the case that I got rid of my husband. I covered my tracks well, but I still couldn't chance it." She shook her head. "If he had spent half as much time trying to make the business money as he did trying to get me in trouble for the size of my cow enclosures, we would have been making a lot more money. He just had to go."

The words were chilling. Stan's eyes wildly searched the

property, empty on all sides, for some way out of this. They had moved away from the corn maze, the cow areas, and the offices, heading into the open field. Was Leigh-Anne going to take her into the woods and shoot her? Leave her body for compost?

"You really think no one is going to figure all this out, Leigh-Anne? Jessie Pasquale is smart," Stan said. "She doesn't buy for a minute that Tyler killed his father."

Leigh-Anne's grip on Stan's arm tightened, her nails cutting into Stan's flesh. "Shut up. You're lying. I have been living and breathing this hick town, making sure no one else knew about Hal's scheme to destroy me. That's why I had to come here. I needed to get rid of whatever evidence he had. But I had a little trouble finding it. You of all people understand my pain. Trying to dig through the mess in that place is like finding a needle in a haystack." She looked at Stan, waiting to see if they were going to share a moment. When Stan didn't respond, Leigh-Anne's voice turned nasty again.

"It would've gone faster if you weren't in the way. Stationing you in that office really threw a wrench in the works. But that's Em. She never did trust me." Leigh-Anne smiled at this.

Stan could make out the sinister curve of her lips in the shadows. She closed her eyes briefly, offered up a prayer to anyone who was listening. The farther away from civilization they went, the more dread settled in her bones. She couldn't even hear the movie across the street anymore.

"Good thing Roger was easily paid off. And Enrico, but that bumbling fool didn't do me any favors. At least he was too scared to talk when they caught him. But if he'd succeeded in damaging the milk supply, Em might have finally caved. Sold me the farm and got out of Dodge. But the best laid plans . . ." She sighed. "And too many people jumped in to help her. Even the rest of our business partners, who always professed their loyalty to my way of thinking. Except for Teddy, of course, but everyone knew he was biased since he was gaga over the boss's wife. This way." Leigh-Anne turned left, toward the vehicle storage area where all the big machinery lived. What else was back here? Stan racked her brain. A bunch of storage sheds for feed and hay. The manure pit. More woods.

"Where are we going?"

"For a swim," Leigh-Anne said matter-of-factly.

A swim? Stan's heart sank. The manure pit. She remembered Roger's chilling words on the tour, about the farmers who had died from the methane gas and the churning augers. With her hands tied, she didn't stand a chance if she went in.

No way. Stan wasn't about to sit back and let this happen. She had only been on one date with Jake. She had three animals who needed her and a new business that she loved. She was not dying at the hands of a lunatic dairy farmer. Sooner or later Jake had to realize she was in trouble. Or someone would show up at the farm. Wouldn't they?

But she couldn't count on that. She had to get herself out of this mess.

"Leigh-Anne!" They both turned. Roger headed across the field toward them.

"Everything all set?" Leigh-Anne asked when he was close.

He nodded, huffing slightly. "She's a wily one. Spitting mad, too. I had to subdue her. Moved her from the maze to the cow barn. She won't be trying to run again for a while. What's the plan for her?"

"We have to take care of this one first," Leigh-Anne said with a sidelong glance at Stan. "That won't take long, then

I'll deal with the rest." And then she calmly swung the gun, which until now had been trained on Stan, toward Roger. Stan watched in horror as she pulled the trigger. The shot cracked through the still night air like a firecracker. Roger went down.

"No!" she gasped.

Leigh-Anne raised her eyebrows. "Oh, hush. He just tied you up, sugar. Please tell me you have more self-respect than to feel bad for him. Let's go."

Stan stared at her, real fear creeping into her bones. This lady was nuts. They were the only two left standing on the farm. And Stan's hands were tied.

"I said, let's go!" Leigh-Anne jerked her arm. Stan started moving again.

She had to avoid going in, at all costs.

"What will you do once you've killed us all, Leigh-Anne?" she asked, forcing her voice to stay calm. "Someone will figure it out. You won't just be able to run the place like nothing ever happened."

"Such a doubter." Leigh-Anne chuckled. "You underestimate me, dear. I have been running my dear, dead husband's farms with no one the wiser. Everyone feels terribly sorry for me. And the farms are doing quite well, actually. Ever since I made some changes."

"Changes?"

"Of course. He was another one. Too much license to the cows. The tail was wagging the dog. The inmates were running the asylum. You know all the sayings. Once I tightened the ship, we started making money. Rather, I did. The same will happen with the Happy Cow name. We'll be the best and most profitable farm co-op in the state. Trust me."

They neared the manure tank. Stan was almost out of time. She started to sweat, imagining the last grains of sand falling through the hourglass, the remaining years of her life dwindling away faster and faster.

Leigh-Anne shoved her at the thin ladder leading to the narrow platform at the top of the pit. "Climb."

"How am I supposed to climb with no hands?"

"You're a smart girl. You'll figure it out. Or I'll shoot you." She jammed the gun into her back. "Climb."

Stan stepped on the first step, almost falling backward. She felt Leigh-Anne almost lift her from behind, forcing her to the next step. The woman was strong, but this might be Stan's only chance. She could pretend to fall and Leigh-Anne would have no choice but to fall with her. She could either buy some time to run, or the gun could go off. Which wouldn't be pretty.

She kept climbing. The five stairs felt like five hundred, but she finally made it onto the tiny square platform with Leigh-Anne's help. The crazy woman had shoved her over the last step, nearly face-planting her on the platform. There was barely enough room for the two of them. Stan felt dizzy looking down into the pit. Were the gases getting to her already? It could be her imagination. But maybe she could use it to save her own life. Either that or Leigh-Anne would just shoot her and throw her in, but that might be an easier death.

It would never work if she didn't try. If Stan could knock Leigh-Anne off balance long enough to dislodge the gun, she had a fighting chance of getting away. She slowed, let her body sag against Leigh-Anne.

"What are you doing? Stand up!" Leigh-Anne shoved at her—exactly what she wanted her to do.

Stan hip-checked Leigh-Anne with all her might, knocking her against the railing. As Leigh-Anne struggled to regain her balance, Stan used the advantage of the small space and the impact of her elbow to knock the gun loose. She heard the satisfying clatter of it hitting the platform. With a roar, Leigh-Anne went for it. Stan kicked it off the edge onto the grass below. She lost her balance in the process, falling against the flimsy railing. She closed her eyes, waiting for the rail to give and the free fall to begin. But it didn't. She ended up on her back on the platform. Opened one eye to see if Leigh-Anne was coming for her.

But her hip check had been effective. Leigh-Anne had lost her balance, too, and struggled to regain it and go for the gun at the same time. Stan kicked out with all her might, feeling her foot connect with Leigh-Anne's knee. Then watched in horror as the other woman fell, almost in slow motion, off the other side of the platform.

Into the manure pit.

Stan heard a scream, then a splash as Leigh-Anne tumbled into the waste below. Then silence. Stan rolled over to her knees and got to her feet, then screamed at the top of her lungs, "Help! Somebody help!"

She had to get Leigh-Anne out of there. No one should die that way. But her hands were still tied. Frantic, she searched for something sharp to slice through the wire as Leigh-Anne's cries grew louder, her hands waving as she tried to keep her head above the stench. Then she heard different shouts and turned.

Tyler Hoffman raced toward her. Stan was so relieved she almost cried.

"In the pit! She fell in the pit!" she yelled. "Hurry, help me get her out!" She had no idea how long someone survived in a manure pit, but Leigh-Anne wasn't screaming anymore. Tyler raced up the steps with a pocketknife and cut her hands free.

"Do you have a cell phone? We need to get her out!"

Tyler hesitated for a split second. "She killed my father," he said, his voice raw with emotion.

Stan grasped him by the shoulders. "Tyler. We can't let her die in there. Your dad wouldn't want that. And she needs to pay for what she did."

He thought about it for the longest few seconds Stan had ever lived through, then handed her his phone.

Stan punched in 911. Tyler grasped a long pole that was clipped to the side of the platform. It had a point on the end. He thrust it into the pit, trying to grab Leigh-Anne. Stan couldn't tell if she was even able to try swimming. She'd lost sight of her in the muck.

"Nine-one-one, what's your emergency?" the dispatcher's voice droned.

"There's a woman in a manure pit at the Happy Cow Dairy Farm! Hurry! Oh, and she's a murderer. But she needs an ambulance!" She hung up. Paused. That was quite possibly the most bizarre phone call she'd ever made.

Tyler still wrangled the pole, trying to find something to grab on to. Stan scanned the nasty, stinking brown liquid, hoping to see a hand, something. And then, a flash of blond hair that miraculously had not turned brown, just a split second before it disappeared again.

"Tyler, there!" She pointed. He balanced on the very edge of the platform, reaching, reaching. She grabbed his belt so he didn't fall in, too. And then she saw Leigh-Anne's lifeless body, pole hooked to her shirt, being pulled back to the edge of the pit. Tyler reached in and hauled her unconscious body out. Breathing hard, he dropped her on the platform.

"You're amazing. We should get her down on the grass," Stan said, her stomach turning at the thought of picking up the manure-covered woman. But she ponied up and grabbed her feet, trying to keep her balance as Tyler dragged Leigh-Anne down the ladder. Stan held her feet, inching her down as Tyler reached each step.

"Got her," he called. "Let go."

Stan did, jumping the rest of the way down. Tyler dropped Leigh-Anne on the grass. The stench was overpowering. Stan felt her stomach lurch.

"Is she breathing?" Stan asked, but her words were drowned out by sirens. Lots of them. Two police cars crashed right through the field, lights flashing, followed by an ambulance. Jessie Pasquale was out of the car running toward them before it had fully stopped, her weapon in her hand but by her side. When she saw Tyler she raised it. Stan raced toward her and planted herself in front of the boy. "It's her! She's the murderer!" she shouted, pointing at Leigh-Anne's still frame on the grass. "Not Tyler!"

The other cops swarmed out of the cars, followed by the EMTs. "Cuff the one on the ground," Stan heard her tell them. "And the boy, too, just until we know what happened here."

"He didn't do anything! He just saved her life," Stan yelled.

Pasquale sent her a warning glance, then nodded at the other cop, who followed her instructions. "Get a hose?" Pasquale shouted, wrinkling her nose as the stench of manure wafted toward her.

"How did you get here so fast?" Stan asked. "I just called."

"Your friend called us. Justin." At Stan's blank look, she said, "He sent me the documents from Hal's computer. I won't ask how you—or he—came across them. But there was enough evidence to send us looking for Leigh-Anne."

"Thank God." And thank God for Justin's computer

skills. "Em's tied up in the barn. With one of the workers," Stan said. "I don't know if she hurt them. And Roger . . ." She gulped. "I think he's dead. Leigh-Anne shot him." She took a breath, realized she wasn't making any sense.

Pasquale stared at her, then pulled out her radio and repeated everything. "We'll find them," she said. "Go wait with Tyler. Or maybe you want to go rinse off. Hang on." She went back to the cruiser, emerged with a towel. Stan accepted it gratefully and attempted to wipe her hands and sleeves.

"Stan!" She turned at the sound of her name. Jake raced across the field toward her. She'd never seen him move so fast. He didn't stop until he reached her, despite his sister yelling at him to stay out of her crime scene.

"What's going on? Are you okay?"

"Fine. Smelly. I—" She didn't get to finish her sentence before he yanked her into his arms, stench and all. And kissed her.

Chapter 36

Halloween, four days later

The line snaking around the Happy Cow Dairy Farm reached all the way into the street. The whole town had turned up for the grand reopening of the haunted corn maze. Em, Tyler, Stan, Jake, and Brenna, along with what seemed like half the town, had spent the last few days getting the maze ready. Em planned to let it remain open until Thanksgiving or until weather prohibited, whichever came first.

"This is great, isn't it?" Brenna clapped her hands in delight. "I'm so glad we got to do this, Em."

Em, Brenna, and Stan stood near the ticket booth, watching Jake oversee Tyler and Danny as they collected money. Jake also wrangled Duncan and Henry. Stan and Scruffy were in charge of the spooky music.

"Me, too," Em said. "And it wouldn't have happened without all of you. Especially you, Stan."

Stan shook her head. "I didn't do anything."

"Are you kidding?" Em exclaimed. "You figured out it was Leigh-Anne in time to save us! Lord knows what she would've done if you hadn't distracted her. They had already hurt Miguel, poor kid."

"Will he be okay?"

"He'll be fine. Nasty bump on the head. But he's already looking forward to coming back to work."

"Well, I hope she gets a million years in jail," Brenna said. "I'm glad you saved her sorry life, Stan. She should pay for what she did."

"Tyler saved her life," Stan said.

"Not without your coaching." Em wagged her finger at Stan. "I know my boy. He's a teenager, and he runs on emotion. He would've probably left her there. Regretted it later, sure, but then it would be too late."

Stan shrugged, uncomfortable with the praise. "Well, it will be one count of murder and one count of attempted murder, since Roger survived. Not to mention kidnapping and assault, I would think."

"How's Tyler doing?" Stan asked.

Em sighed. "Okay. He's still processing. He told me he's leaving school and moving to California."

"California!" Brenna and Stan said together.

"He wants a change of scenery. Can't say I blame him." Em looked around wistfully. "It's going to be difficult. Even with the changes I'm sure we'll be making."

"What changes?" Stan asked.

"Well, Teddy and I"—Em blushed a little just saying his name—"are going to consolidate our operations. We haven't quite figured out what that means yet, but I think it'll be for the best. Oh, look! Char's here."

Char came up behind Stan and laid a hand on her shoulder. "What a great turnout! So proud of y'all!" Char stood behind her, beaming, dressed in a bright orange dress and black scarf. "And, Stan! You deserve a medal of honor."

"Yes," Patricia Connor said, appearing behind Char. "You certainly do." And she reached over and hugged Stan.

Stan couldn't keep her mouth from dropping open. She finally remembered to hug her mother back. "Thanks, Mom. And I don't deserve a medal. I just did what I needed to do."

"Well, I'm proud of you," Patricia said.

Stan again was speechless. Especially since her mother didn't seem to have trouble saying the words.

"Thanks," she managed.

Patricia studied Stan's face. "You look happy."

"I am happy." Stan couldn't resist a glance over at the ticket booth. Jake happened to be looking in her direction at the same time. He winked at her.

Her near-death experience with the manure pit had been a good thing for them. They'd spent a lot of time together over the past few days. Stan hated to jinx anything, but there was a good chance they might be casually dating. When she turned back to her mother she was smiling. "I like it here."

"You like the bar owner. Perhaps more than the town. And I think that's great." She leaned over and kissed Stan's cheek.

Maybe her mother had actually thought about what it would be like to lose her daughter for good, and this was her attempt to tell her that. Maybe it was time for them to start fresh, too.

"About Tony," Patricia began, but Stan shook her head. "Mom, you don't need to explain. You have just as much right to be happy. Just make sure he's not a sketch. He was hanging out with Leigh-Anne when I met him."

"I know. He feels terrible about that. He's known her a long time and never suspected. It's so troubling, how people are able to hide their true selves. Oh, I think your friend is waiting for you." She pointed. Stan turned to see Izzy waiting behind her.

"I didn't want to interrupt," Izzy began, but Stan motioned for her to join them.

"Come over and meet my mother!" She made the introductions. "So how are you? You look great!"

Izzy did. Dressed to the nines in pink jeans, a white jacket, and a green scarf, her long braids gathered together in a high ponytail, she looked better than she had in weeks. The twinkle was even back in her eye.

"So what's the story? Any good news to report?" Stan walked her a little way from the crowd, leaving Scruffy with Brenna, so they could talk.

"Actually, yeah. Really great news." Izzy took a breath. "I think I have a solution for the real estate stuff. And I'm going to be able to have my bookstore after all."

"Really? That's great!" Stan hugged her friend. She deserved to be happy. "So what's the solution?"

"Well, it's all because of you, girl. Really. You had the idea. I just had to get the guts to follow through."

"Aww, Izzy. You have plenty of guts. You just needed to hear the options. So what'd you do? Contact a local bank?"

"Nope. I went to see Jake. We talked for a long time."

"Wow. Really?" Jake hadn't mentioned it. "Fantastic. Did he have a lead for you?"

"Not exactly." Izzy took a deep breath. "We're going into business together."

RECIPES

Dog Bone Cake Recipe

Ingredients:

Bowl One:
   1 cup peanut butter
   3 eggs
   1.5 cups water

In a separate bowl combine:
   2 cups wheat flour
   .5 cup oat flour
   3 Tbsp baking powder
   3 Tsp baking soda

Grease and flour the bottom of a 9-x-11-inch cake pan. Combine all cake ingredients. Do not overmix. Pour into pan and bake immediately at 350° F for 40 minutes. Let cool completely before turning out. Cut out bone shape. Wrap and freeze.

Ingredients—Frosting
   16 oz cream cheese

Frosting is best to work with at room temperature. Only frost a frozen cake. Frost by adding small amounts of frosting by hand to the cake and spreading, creating a smooth bone shape.

Ingredients—Decorating
   Cream cheese
   Food coloring

Trim as desired.

Pumpkin Cookie Recipe

Batch: This recipe will produce approximately 24 large cookies.

Ingredients:

      4 cups whole wheat flour
      2 cups canned natural pumpkin
      2 cups water
      2 Tbsp baking powder

   Mix all ingredients in stand mixer and knead for 4 minutes. Ensure dough is pliable and not fracturing. If dough fractures, add small quantities of water and mix. Bake at 350° F for 25 minutes, then check. Dehydrate for minimum 10 hours.

Recipes courtesy of the Big Biscuit.